ANTLER PLAN

A KONRAD LOKI THRILLER

JOONAS HUHTA

RANDOM REVOLVER

ANTLER PLAN: A KONRAD LOKI THRILLER

Copyright © 2017 Joonas Huhta

ISBN 13 digit: 978-9-529-392-766

ISBN 10 digit: 952-939-2761

Published by Random Revolver

Edited by Lizzie Harwood, lizzieharwood.com

Cover design by Anna Cowie, The Pixel Pusher

Cover image "Time Traveler" by Alessio Lin, Unsplash

Printed in the United States of America and Europe

www.joonashuhta.com

For my family

CONTENTS

Note to Reader   ix

Chapter 1   1
Chapter 2   6
Chapter 3   13
Chapter 4   22
Chapter 5   30
Chapter 6   40
Chapter 7   44
Chapter 8   46
Chapter 9   54
Chapter 10   57
Chapter 11   67
Chapter 12   73
Chapter 13   77
Chapter 14   84
Chapter 15   89
Chapter 16   94
Chapter 17   100
Chapter 18   102
Chapter 19   106
Chapter 20   115
Chapter 21   120
Chapter 22   124
Chapter 23   131
Chapter 24   137
Chapter 25   141
Chapter 26   145
Chapter 27   149
Chapter 28   154
Chapter 29   160
Chapter 30   163

Chapter 31	168
Chapter 32	172
Chapter 33	177
Chapter 34	182
Chapter 35	185
Chapter 36	188
Chapter 37	191
Chapter 38	195
Chapter 39	198
Chapter 40	200
Chapter 41	203
Chapter 42	208
Chapter 43	211
Chapter 44	214
Chapter 45	217
Chapter 46	220
Chapter 47	225
Chapter 48	230
Chapter 49	235
Chapter 50	236
Chapter 51	238
Chapter 52	241
Chapter 53	244
Chapter 54	247
Chapter 55	252
Chapter 56	259
Chapter 57	262
Chapter 58	264
Chapter 59	267
Chapter 60	269
Chapter 61	272
Chapter 62	276
Chapter 63	279
Chapter 64	282
Chapter 65	284
Chapter 66	289
Chapter 67	293
Chapter 68	297

Chapter 69   301
Chapter 70   303
Chapter 71   305
Chapter 72   309
Chapter 73   312
Chapter 74   318
Chapter 75   322
Chapter 76   324
Chapter 77   325

Acknowledgments   329
About the Author   331

NOTE TO READER

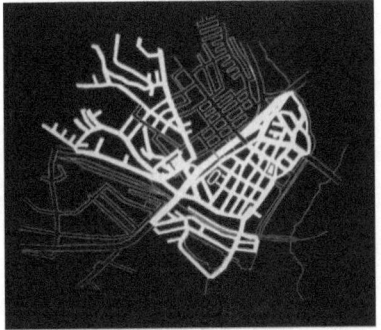

*Map of Rovaniemi, Finland, showing how the town was
planned in the shape of a reindeer's antlers... the "Antler Plan."*

THE SNOWFALL BURIED Konrad Loki alive.

Raw cold stung his face and made his eyes spider with frost; he felt his blood freeze white. The snow weighed next to nothing, but it made certain his head wouldn't budge. With each second the thick snow became more packed with fat, lazy flakes, the nagging truth sank deeper into his mind.

His mistress was a suicide bomber.

Accompanied by tinnitus, Konrad reasoned that no algebra of the mind could have predicted her stunt. But failing to assess reality with both hemispheres of the brain was something that happened to other people, not him. Flying saucer zealots, priests, and fairytale men—whoever miracles happened to— would have been watchful for premonitions: whispers in the wind, a deep chill in the bone, or sudden darkness, with grasshoppers going biblical and obscuring the Sun. Unfortunately, reality was under no obligation to conform to human fantasies.

Konrad tried to blink snow out of his eyes. He focused on the hush around him. Dead silent. Finnish Lapland—a place where birds didn't sing. Where only the snapping fibers of the ice-stiff-ened branches, exploding into muted gunshots, broke the deaf-ening silence. Where death was most alive.

Could a man cycling to work in the blood-freezing weather be blamed for failing to read the suicidal signs behind a flirting woman's smile?

His mind-altering stupor made him see his wife Julia's expressionless face. A sudden swell of relief erupted in his chest. No more unpredictable melancholy streaks, no random cold shoulders, no deep funks with short-fused answers to simple questions. One less mystery in the universe. Besides, if he were going to find a way out of this mess, he would have to come out as clean as Gandhi and as elevated as the Father of the Nation.

If I live through this, I'll be a better father.

After Konrad had swallowed past the cactus of guilt, some-thing moved. A snow-crackling cacophony underfoot.

"Oh my God." A woman's voice trailed off in disbelief. "Is she dead?"

Konrad heard whispers. Hands digging into the snow around him.

"...an explosion..."

"...never seen so much snow falling in my life..."

"...is it safe to be in here?"

Konrad registered being logrolled, this way, then that. The dark-haired woman came into view. Frosty lashes, beautifully curving lips, brutally butchered body. No snow angels tonight. A ghost of a smile seemed to touch upon her face.

Sitting amid the papers flung from his briefcase, exposing his life to the world, was the biggest piece of his exploded helmet. It looked like a cracked egg.

A banshee wail of sirens crept up the valley below him. A flash. Someone took a photo. More smartphones were firing away.

Something stirred the crowd.

A voice yelled in a pursuit, "Stop! Thief! That's his bike!"

I don't mind. I stole it in the first place.

A man dashed through the crowd with a hero's confidence in his voice. "Make space. I know CPR." Upon placing his big hands on the woman's chest, his confidence deflated. "She's... *dead.*"

A few people's hands shot to their mouths, the obvious confirmed.

"What's taking the ambulance so long?" came an old woman's voice.

The big-handed man shifted over to Konrad. Unable to hide nervousness in his voice, he said, "H-hang in there, buddy! You'll be just fine."

I'm already doing mental cartwheels...

Nearby, a car's ABS clattered, controlling the wheels as they locked up on the slippery surface. With a devil's whisper, the black ice under the fresh powder snow carried the car much farther than the driver intended.

"Look at this," a woman's startled voice said. She picked up a gun.

"Neat-o! A Parabellum!" A hooded teen squeezed through the crowd and shoved, sending a granny to the ground. A prison mug shot waiting to happen—the outcome when parents saddle their child with the lifelong curse of neglect or suicide. Or worse —too much control. He snatched the weapon from the woman's hand.

Take it, and I will hunt you down.

"Gideon put down the weapon!" A woman's voice cracked the air like a whip. "Move back! All of you!"

Two black-clad men entered Konrad's peripheral vision and assumed control with ramrod exactness. A woman dressed in urban camo patterns that screamed 'military' came straight to him. She was small, sinewy of arm and springy of leg, which carried her through leaps on the balls of her feet with ease. A cat-woman oozing sex appeal and sending off not-to-be-messed-with vibes at the same time.

"Blink your eyes if you can hear me," she said in rasping, sore-throat voice.

Konrad did, gleefully.

"Doing graceless somersaults, Konrad?"

"Who... the hell... are you...?" he managed.

"Amnesia, your old friend." A wink revealed her inward smile. "It's me, Ruut Stark. You were my teacher in junior high. You have a severe head injury. Stay completely still. I'll supervise your care."

"Captain," one of the black-clad men said, "you'd better take a look at this."

Ruut took a paper handed to her and checked it with one cursory glance. She spoke to Konrad with a grave cast to her tone. "Blink to confirm, do you know the woman you collided with?"

Konrad put the pieces together. A suicide note? He kept his stare stable.

She stared back in a freeze frame of confusion.

Allahu akbar! She declared that God is great, and since I didn't...

"Medical team and police are here, Captain."

"Assist the police. Then head back to the base and wait for further instructions."

"Affirmative."

A medical team closed in with a clanging stretcher.

Ruut kept him company, refreshing his memory. "I'm the girl who always shot her hand up, unasked, salivating with my questions. You must have hated me."

Konrad's mind was blank. His world teetered.

Should I remember you?

The metallic rattle stopped next to Konrad. Paramedics prepared him to be lifted. Ruut mentioned to a paramedic something about frostbite, then turned to him. "Something doesn't add up."

An oxygen mask appeared on Konrad's face. With last reserves of strength, he forced his eyes to stay open.

A paramedic screamed, "Pressures dropping, we're losing him!"

"The woman carried something personal on her," Ruut said. After stealing a glance at the dead woman for one strangely static second, her gunmetal eyes bored into his. "A will."

Konrad slipped into oblivion with an echo as his only company.

...it bequeaths everything to you...

2

L IGHT PLAYED BACK and forth across the floor from the cracks around the door. Konrad stepped inside—into brightness.

A slicing pain spread through his head, as if his skull had been torn to shreds, ripped like fabric, then sewn all the wrong way round.

A big man dressed in white pointed at him with a penlight. The doctor's great, gray side-whiskers framed a face blessed with unnaturally white teeth. He was big-bellied and plump-cheeked, a self-congratulatory smile planted on his face. Like a hundred-meter bronze Buddha statue with the satisfied face of a man post sex.

"Open Sesame, Mr. Loki," the doctor said. "My name is Doctor Olaf. You are high on pain medication, so go easy. I know that you don't believe in miracles, but your recovery has been remarkable. You must have a guardian angel. But since keeping up with the world affairs in a coma can be challenging—here's someone who'll bring you up to speed."

Having assessed Konrad's status, Olaf nodded over the bed at another man in the room who was dressed in black. The man evaluated Konrad from under a pronounced brow with onyx eyes and colorless lips thinned into cynical lines. The nametag on his chest declared authority.

"Excuse us, Doctor," the man said.

Olaf made his exit.

"My name is Kaspar Nyman. Police. A few routine questions. Your name, age and birthplace?"

For a moment Konrad's tongue was stuck as if on cold metal. "Konrad Loki, 38. Born in Helsinki."

"Your occupation?"

"I'm a professor at the University of Lapland. Teacher Education. I bet you have figured that out already."

Kaspar's eyes glowed with animal pleasure. "Oona Louhi—does the name ring the bell?"

In a burst of memory, Konrad saw the dark-haired, suicidal woman smiling at him.

"Never heard of her."

"Did you know she's dead and buried? That she is being mourned by a husband and two children?"

Konrad remained quiet and fought against the penetrating gaze under which he could feel his defenses melting away.

"I'm sorry to hear that."

Kaspar took a magazine under his armpit and threw it on Konrad's chest. The awkward headline leapt out:

LOVE PROFESSOR'S EXTRA-CURRICULAR ACTIVITIES.

"You've been harassing women students at work."

An invisible fist hit Konrad in the chest. "What? That's bull—"

"Shit has hit the fan," Kaspar said, mid-flow. "Deal with it."

Konrad pursed his lips. Kaspar wouldn't hear that this misconception could have come from the way he always spoke about sexual education and pedagogical love frankly. In

Finland, the majority received a silent sexual and emotional upbringing, as parents were oblivious to how to deal with children's questions. People didn't even touch each other. He was never touched, only when someone bumped into him by accident. Or when he found himself cramped in an overpopulated sauna of 100°C, being hit by birch bath whisks with lukewarm beer spilled upon him. Finnish men didn't talk to strangers but saw no problem in spanking each other. What can you expect when you've sauna-ed out emotional problems for centuries?

"Theories about your relationship with Oona keep popping up like mushrooms in the rain," Kaspar said. "Especially now that everybody knows about the will."

"Excuse me?"

Kaspar shot a glance at Konrad. "The will found at the crash site by Captain Ruut Stark, who probably saved your life."

"Has she also accused me of sexual harassment?"

"Does she have a reason to do so?"

"Mother of Thor! I've managed to insult everybody. Ruut promised to take care of me, and since she's not here—"

A monitor beeped.

"You are not supposed to get angry," Kaspar said, indifference in his voice.

The door opened. Olaf said, "I'm sorry, but Konrad's blood pressure—"

"We're fine!" Kaspar boomed with all the grace of a cannon.

Olaf withdrew his head, and the door clicked shut.

Kaspar continued while searching for a cigarette in his pocket, "Anyway, the sexual harassment complaints are the least of your problems..." He lit a Camel.

Breath bottled up in Konrad's chest.

"Wait a minute. The woman blew herself up, and *I'm* the suspect?"

Kaspar opened a window. Cold air streamed in. "Tell me about your weapon."

Konrad recalled the teen. "I had the Parabellum P08 disabled. It can't be fired. I kept it in my briefcase."

"Why were you carrying a Nazi weapon with you? We also found an old compass and knife, both with marks like they'd been hit by a bullet."

"I collect anything authentic that might motivate and intrigue my students. They're my mementos. Once a Soviet sharpshooter shot at my father in the Winter War when he attended a wounded comrade. The bullet tore through his clothes by his heart but stopped when it hit a metal-framed compass he kept in his breast pocket. Currently, a student of mine is doing a master's thesis about the upbringing of the Veterans. The Parabellum is purely a source of inspiration."

"And the knife?"

Konrad looked at the man's inscrutable face. "It could be a lesson in history, philosophy, or psychology. If the close-hit wasn't traumatizing enough for my father, another close-call was when another bullet struck his thigh, near the artery. Fortunately, the bullet hit a sheathed knife, penetrating only the deer-leather and the wooden handle, coming to a halt in the thinnest piece of metal of the tool. Fooling death twice, he collapsed. He became unhealthily interested in collecting wrist-watches from dead Soviets. Looting wasn't an uncommon practice—everybody is interested in the background of the dead."

Kaspar blew smoke out one side of his nose. There was a silence loaded with unsaid thoughts. "So, Love Professor. Are you a religious man?"

"Irrelevant question. Religion is just a miserable creation the human species tries to impose on itself so it behaves better."

Kaspar's forehead wrinkled. "It strikes me as odd that Oona named you as the receiver..."

"Of?"

"How well do you know the Ten Commandments?"

"I like to break the first four commandments as much as I can."

"In her will, Oona left you a message," Kaspar said. "'*Not in the seventh commandment.*'"

Konrad recapped, "The seventh commandment says, 'Thou shall not commit adultery.' Is she saying that something is missing?"

Kaspar tilted his head. "What does adultery mean to you?"

"Men cheat to get laid, women for another life. But the manifestations are the same: feeling you are sinking to the lowest degree of existence and sorting it all out in a sea of tears and beer. From a historical perspective, adultery has always existed. Some adulterers still get tarred and feathered and driven out of town, others are stoned to death."

"Intriguing," Kaspar said. "What about the year 1631. Does it mean something to you?"

"The Age of Reason—many supernatural matters became natural. How come?"

"Are you familiar with a book called *The Wicked Bible*?"

"Now I get it. Oona speaks about reversed scriptural meaning: 'Thou shalt commit adultery.' Surprise. God doesn't write perfect books, after all. After the printing error, the Church wanted to destroy every book to prevent moral and mass panic from spreading. We're talking about a collector's item."

"You have done your homework." Kaspar's eyebrows hunched low. "Speaking of which, now it's your task to figure out why Oona Louhi bequeathed *The Wicked Bible* to you, an anti-Christ."

Konrad arched his eyebrows. "She left me the Unholy Scripture? Why? How did she own such a precious book?"

"Don't ask me," Kaspar said. "You killed the priest."

"S-she was a priest?"

"Recently graduated."

Konrad huddled in his hospital gown. The cold air flowing in from the window gave him the feeling he was back in full control of his body. "But... Where is the Bible?"

"Heaven alone knows." Kaspar threw the cigarette out of the window, looked at his watch, and offered Konrad a handshake. "Time is of the essence. It's Independence Day tomorrow. I'm going to Helsinki to the castle to meet the president. If I'm lucky, I'll get to dance with his lady."

Konrad gave a quick grip and release.

Kaspar exited the room and gave instructions to a guard behind the door.

Konrad kept his hand in a tight fist until Kaspar was gone. Then he opened his hand and looked down at Kaspar's watch he had stolen. On the back was an engraving:

TRUE LOVE WAITS. —JULIA

The message made Konrad wonder where his wife was. By coincidence, Kaspar was married to a woman with the same name.

The watch face also displayed the date.

The fifth of December? It's our wedding anniversary already? Have I been unconscious for two weeks?

The length of Konrad's body trembled. He weighed the watch flat on his palm. In the new light, a carving of another familiar word hit his eyes.

Abracadabra?

Konrad considered the most universally adopted phrase, pronounced in all languages without translation. The ultimate meaning was a conundrum. Stage magicians and conjurers and fantasy characters used it to summon mysterious powers to perform their magic, but the ancients ward off sickness and keep away evil spirits. A combination of the Hebrew words *ab*—father

—*ben*—son—and *ruach acadosch*—Holy Spirit—as in Trinity. A Gnostic word for God, *Abraxas*, meaning His dead body. Attributed to God's might, it meant *What I speak is what I create*. The meanings varied between creation and destruction, between love and hate, upsetting virtually all linguists around the globe.

Konrad sneered. He knew another nonsense magical incantation as well.

"Hocus pocus."

He threw the watch out the window, which Kaspar had deliberately left open, and went on reading the garbage news. The interrogation was weird. But whatever Kaspar truly had in mind for him, one thing was sure.

Gone was all love.

Abra-goddamn-cadabra...

3

RUUT STORMED TO her workroom, and slammed the door behind her. She had once again vented her frustrations at her husband and daughter and already regretted it.

Netta had only spilled milk on the floor. And before that, the TV remote control was not even where it used to be, where she preferred, between the sofa pillows.

Ruut stood still under a lamp with her thumbnail jammed against her teeth, stopping her hand from slipping to her throat, which was on fire.

Jake and Netta were preparing themselves for a sauna, and she felt left alone.

There was a formless twist in his head that cracked her strength. Her marriage with Jake was good. Not that everything was all roses on the home front, he was an open and a loving husband, scatterbrained as they come, but he mostly understood her neurotic tendencies and childish outbursts. The reality behind today's temper tantrum was still the fact she wasn't allowed to help Konrad. The orders were unbelievable and unforgivable: General Eric Pantzar—an ill-tempered, barking walrus—had strictly prohibited her from intervening in the case, without explanation, or further apology.

Why?

Ruut occupied her mind in her private chamber and slumped in front of her MacBook Pro. In the screen's reflection, her eyes looked like holes poked in clay. Her cheeks pinked, like a serial worker about to kill herself.

She began her aimless drifting by reading the headlines of the day, speculating what women were going to wear in the castle for Finland's Independence Day. Utterly uninterested in the fashion, she shifted to Lapland University's site, pondering where best to invest her time. Probably finding an occupation where pulling back her shoulders was not a requirement.

A teacher? PTSD day and night?

She switched to Facebook. Konrad popped up in a shared link, the picture taken in the hospital bed. A woman commented why Konrad was famous for disfiguring the face of the Church and fostering equality between genders: "His hard crotch-kick of truth castrates all converters' and priests' weapons of dominance—AKA dicks—and sends them back to Genesis to wonder *who* created a woman out of man's rib."

"Preach it, sister!" another woman commented. "Men have portrayed us crooked and sly as the rib bone, curving away from virtues. Two-millennia-long second-class citizenship because of total BS! No wonder why no women have written a book in the New Testament, as Konrad pointed out."

Many saw Konrad as a spiritual teacher, but conspiracy theorists warned of him being a closet racist and misogynist in disguise.

Ruut found her hand on her throat once more, and a memory of a bar incident crept in. While having fun with her friends for the first time in five years, some jerk had hit her in her throat and tore her left vocal cord. Apparently, an offered drink was supposed to be accepted.

Giving up on the shameful headlines, she found herself quickly moving back to explore the snowflake logo of the university. She bit her lower lip as she read the motto beneath the logo: *Learn to live, live to learn.* She scrolled down the page of the staff of the faculty of education. Academic minds always seemed satisfied. Why didn't she try to be a researcher? She could have stayed in her office, just reading and contemplating the world from the lofty places of intelligence.

Unlimited privacy.

What a privilege.

She went to Google and entered *Konrad Loki.* She clicked the first YouTube link, a video from 2012, entitled "Are We Better Off Without Religion?"

A handsome and hawk-like host, yet as boring as a shop-window dummy, welcomed the audience in the University of Notre Dame and listed Konrad's contributions to science.

Through the wall, Ruut heard Netta coughing hard. She froze, finding herself at the edge of screaming and asking what was going on. Burdening herself with the thought that he didn't care about her enough made heat flush through her body. She buried her head into her hands. She would soon suspect Jake of doing things he'd never do if she continued being paranoid.

Netta coughed again. Ruut contemplated the poor little girl and her current status: a mold refugee. She was being bullied in school, and all because she just couldn't breathe and reddened easily because of it, despite coloring being partly genetic. The day had been unbearable for Netta. Two idiot boys had captured her. They had drawn her away from the school path and spread her books and notebooks into a ditch. Instead of going ice-fishing, they had organized fly larva's Paralympic games in her mouth.

Ruut sighed. Finland's suicide rates were one of the highest in the world, and she had long seen the problem. Boys and men didn't talk; they dressed their nonverbal communication skills as fists in schoolyard, streets, and bars. In school, kids learned to humiliate and degrade the weak, and later, they refined this skill into leadership. Generations of leaders stared at the lines of zeroes in profit, and in case sales dropped, all it took was to kick out the weakest and grow the breadline to keep the Big Caravan on the road.

Bullies were terrific at getting rich on the backs of the broken.

In all her doom-and-gloom, a limping man with wooden crutches walked across the stage toward a podium. The clothes Konrad wore were gray and dull as dishwater, but he owned the stage with his latent intensity and retro-design glasses; the spherical lenses gave way into his mischievous spark in his mismatched eyes, making gooseflesh whisper across her arms.

"*Good news—I've gained new followers,*" Konrad announced, emphasizing the word so that it meant stalkers. "*I fell down the stairs in my home a few days ago and broke my leg. I'm crippled and slow, which makes believers ferociously think that I'm now an easier target for converting. Everybody wants a piece of me. I'm like a big feather in the cap of sky-point bonuses.*"

Konrad grinned like he knew something no one else could.

"*As you probably know, I'm here to debunk the most romanticized story ever told. My opponent will defend that story, the miraculous work of an imaginary friend, who gives useless advice like 'open your inner eyes and keep your spiritual ears attuned.' I like more practical advice that comes from my fans: 'Remember to calibrate your bullshit detector,' and, 'Don't forget to crowd surf!' Of course, the hate mail from the guardians of faith can be useful sometimes: 'You don't own enough fire insurance to avoid the flames of perdition!' I guess I should consider changing my insurance company.*"

The audience laughed.

"*A threat to Faith. An enemy of God. A Bastard Son of Satan. An Evil man. If you only knew how busy these titles keep me, updating my CV and dating profiles...*" Konrad placed the crutches against the stand. His face hardened. "*Now, let me ruin the story of your life. First, what do we mean by the word 'evil'? Frankly, there is fundamentally only one good reason to denounce someone as evil. If you plan to hurt or injure someone, naming or thinking one is evil makes it psychologically easier to do so. Evil is the strongest word we have to prepare ourselves for personal relationships, conflicts, tragedies, and war zones, especially when we prepare to kill each other with ease. And why is it so effective?*"

Konrad gave the audience a few seconds to think.

"*Because it is the word that prevents us from thinking.*" Konrad straightened himself. "*But when we mix our animal attributes with scriptures, we push human capacity to hate beyond healing...*"

Ruut skipped forward.

"*In my latest book, 'His War, Her Pain,' I discuss an interesting taboo against women. Women are considered softer, dove-like, and slower to resort to physical violence. Men have socialized and brainwashed women into this gender role, especially with the aid of The Bible. Women have always been the symbol of why wars are fought —the ultimate justification. In the battlefield men dream about women, because it reminds them of home, family, warmth, balance and love—things the both sides of the ideological fence are trying to preserve. There's a saying in Hindi that all causes of war are due to 'jar, joru aur jameen,' which translates as 'land, gold, women.' The bodies of women will continue to be the biggest battlefield as long as testosterone continues to fight with gunpowder...*"

Men—so easily seduced by power, explosions, and dreams of whore houses made out of solid gold bars. She clicked ten minutes forward.

"*...Men's conception of sacrificial heroism is deeply flawed. Call of*

*duty, honor and glory, faith that the cause is just—all cherished to
ensure seeing evil around us. When we think of war heroes and idols
we salute Alexander the Great who did conquer the world, or we
might pick up Napoleon, or Caesar who was the example of boldness
and braveness, a real tactical genius. Then we cherish the names of
mythical legends and demigods like Achilles, Hercules, Beowulf, and
even Xena, who is a fictional character with male attributes derived
from the Demigods of Greek mythology. Our role models in history
—his story—are all bloodthirsty killing machines."*

"True," Ruut said to herself. "Where are all the unsung
heroes, thanks to whom no battle had to be fought?"

A click. Konrad was again effortlessly eloquent in
unleashing his venom.

*"...'He's almighty and above evil'—that's my opponent's argument
about Creator. But when a catastrophe happens, why isn't your All-
knowing, All-loving, All-powerful and the most active force in the
Universe motivated enough to overcome misery and death by
preventing disasters and diseases?"*

What was feeding the rebellion in him? She clicked forward
again.

A bearded man in the audience stood up, yelling, "Blasphemy!" He lobbed an egg toward at Konrad and seemed to hit him
right in the chest, but Konrad spun around while receiving the
oncoming force, and pitched the egg back with full force. The
standing man received a slimy blast to his forehead. A few other
activists hid their eggs in their clothes as guards came to escort
the humiliated man away.

Konrad adjusted his suit. *"Some call my words blasphemy—I
call it honesty."*

Ruut got bored. The show went on so smoothly that she
suspected that the whole egg-episode was planned. She skipped
to near the end for final statements. Konrad was at the top of the
game. Suddenly, he smashed the crutch over his knee and

finished it by hitting it against the floor, like a guitar hero destroying his instrument at the end of the gig. He showed one piece of wood to the stunned audience, and it looked like a snake.

"*Let's step back a few millenniums to the dawn of primitive superstitions. Which one do you think is a safer bet from the stand of human evolution, that our ability to believe the stick is a snake and fear it, or believe that the snake is a stick?*"

Konrad's eyes scanned his captivated throng.

"*You want to know what religion is all about? Just like us, snakes constantly grow new skin cells and shed the old ones. We shed ours continuously in small quantities, but snakes shed their skin in a continuous sheet. Religion is the snake reversed: the snake sheds its skin and becomes smaller, smaller, and smaller until a handful of scale is all that's left. There was no snake in the first place, no original sin. Nothing. Only an empty shell filled with fear and false hope in disavowed, deep existential dread.*"

The hall remained still long after he had stopped talking.

"*By the way,*" Konrad said. "*You don't need a crutch to get through life. I ceased to feign—now it's your turn.*"

Ruut heard a knock. Jake was naked by the door, wreathed in ghosts of steam. He was smiling, and Ruut answered it with a soft laughter. "I'll join you in a minute."

A knot of counter-arguments racing in her mind, Ruut went back to the site of the University of Lapland and located Konrad's phone number. There was nothing ground-shaking in Konrad's militant atheistic views. His arguments drew on popular psychology and were convincingly disapproving many established beliefs with inviting logic. But being brain-centric and biologizing all human problems was not a solution, but part of the symptom.

An odd connection between Oona and Konrad rose from the rubble like a smoke sign. Once during mass, Oona had said that the world needed the era of atheists' rise because they were the only one able to purify religion from its idiocy and lunatic aspects. She had described this period as a spiritual adultery. Man was getting closer to an animal. Carnal desires dominated, and primitive pleasures were wellbeing. The world had exchanged love for lust.

'It is better to marry than to burn with passion,' Ruut recapped the last quote from the Bible Oona had made.

But why did Oona will *The Wicked Bible* to Konrad? Something unsettling urged her to speak to Konrad as soon as he was out of the hospital.

Even though injured, his eyes had been bizarrely lewd.

A HUNDRED METERS away from the house where Ruut closed the screen of her computer, a black Mercedes van sat buried in snow in the shadows between two street lamps. Inside, over the shoulder of one of his comrades, Colonel Patrick Praytor evaluated what he had seen on screen. He had hoped the woman would forget the incident.

The tech agent cast his eyes away from the screen. "We have a problem."

Patrick clenched his teeth.

A phone rang in his hand.

"Is it the Veteran?" another agent asked, maintaining a sniper rifle. "The boss won't be delighted."

Patrick answered the phone.

"Status?" a toneless voice said.

"A minor nuisance, sir," Patrick said. "She's gathering Intel."

Silence fell.

Patrick waited.

The voice spoke again. "The level of threat?"

"Zero, sir. She's on our leash."

"Keep it short. And our man?"

"Recovering." Patrick shared a glance with the agent, now attaching a suppressor to the muzzle of the rifle. "His employer has urged him to come to the university ASAP. Everything is going as expected."

"I expect better. Contact me should the book appear."

The call ended.

Patrick grabbed the rifle and aimed through the scope at the house. A girl was in the window, trying to catch a snowflake on her tongue. Her innocence gave him a glimpse of his son. His heart filled with instant love. It took only the experience of carrying one's child against one's chest to know one carried the innocence of all children of the world. Every good parent knew the truth.

Fortunately, the new frontier offered the promise of a new beginning. Soon he would cease to hear the cries of the children with his son's face in his mind. Children would grow up without the torment of the inevitable and consuming paradox that comes with the truth about Santa Claus.

Man's inhumanity to man.

4

KONRAD STOOD IN the doorway of his office with his fist clenching around the handle. His papers sat in neat piles, each book on his shelf lined up. Only one black-spined master's thesis was nudged out of line in the platoon of his graduate students' works. The room was the same as hospitals: cold, clean and clinical, as devoid of life as humans could make it.

Revulsion crept up inside his chest. Had his first dust-allergic girlfriend visited the room?

Konrad stepped in and placed his compass and knife on the shelf, next to an empty leather holster. The police had returned the items but were shrugging about the missing gun.

The teen assaulted his memories. He clenched his jaw.

I'll find you...

He undressed his black parka, slung it on his chair and sat.

A tall, thin woman materialized in the doorway.

Dean Eliza Mathlin.

Konrad raised his gaze to meet her glacial blue eyes. She stood with her arms crossed over her black velvet jacket (as always) but with her arms an inch higher than normal.

"What have you done?"

The finality in her tone was not lost on Konrad. "Nice to see you too, Eliza. How's your husband and the kids? Would Marcus be up for ice swimming and grabbing a beer tonight?"

Eliza's fingertips now massaged her hands that creeped you out with their unnatural skinniness. "I don't see that happening."

"Come on. You of all the people know gossip when you hear it. I've done nothing wrong."

Eliza took a step into his office, almost wincing at sharing his space. "As a friend, I believe you. As a colleague and your supervisor, I can't—"

"Yes. You can."

"Konrad," she cut him dead. "The credibility of this faculty is at stake. I can't ignore the students' allegations on you. You know our policy."

"But—"

She raised her hand. "Zero tolerance."

"Meaning?"

"You're fired."

Konrad's jaw dropped.

Eliza raised her chin. "Clear the office by the end of the day."

Konrad offered an open palm, "Please, hear me out."

She took a step back. "I strongly advise you to keep your mouth shut."

"Or you will accuse me of sexual harassment, is that it?"

By the end of a long second, he realized the question was too much.

Two workers brought large carton boxes to the doorway. Their sides bore the name of a moving company.

"They're here to help you," Eliza said.

"I'm not leaving."

Eliza sent the workers away with a jerk of her head. "I feared you might not cooperate."

"At least you got that right." Konrad stood up.

She backed to the corridor.

"The guards are instructed to remove you from the premises by six. They have the right to use force. Any personal items you leave will be treated as waste."

Konrad reached for the door handle. "I had better get busy then."

He closed the door, placed his head against it and gripped his temples. Something primitive in him wanted to choke someone with his bare hands, to see blood.

What's happening to me?

Konrad slumped before his computer. He turned it on. Its slowness competed with a snail crawling up a brick wall.

A knock landed at the door.

Konrad jolted up, steaming. He opened the door and yelled, "I'm busy!"

The teen, with earphones a tangled death around his neck, stared at Konrad with contempt. Dressed in an AC/DC tee shirt and open, battered leather jacket, he held a big carton package under his armpit.

"Son of a bitch," Konrad squeezed through his teeth. "Where's my weapon?"

In a heartbeat, the teen dropped the package onto Konrad's toes and rushed away. Konrad shrieked in pain and tried to launch a pursuit, but pain shot nails to his brain. "Run, you shit-head. But you know what? I live with a woman! In my own house! A woman who isn't my mother!"

A dozen colleagues peeked into the corridor. A few dodged Konrad's gaze and curses. Others stayed to look at him.

"Why are you pretending?" Konrad mocked. "We all hate teens. Admit it!"

Using his leg, Konrad nudged the package into his room, closing the door. He hit the keyboard with his fist and kicked the chair, flipping it over. He pulled it back up, sat and took a spin, eyes closed. As the motion stopped, he faced the only decoration he'd nailed to his office wall. Black text on white:

That which does not kill us makes us stronger.

Discovering this thought in his youth had guided him through the worst. People, in general, liked the idea, but not the man who wrote it. The most misunderstood and disrespected philosopher.

Friedrich Nietzsche.

The man was a legend, his work marked by a puzzling combination of optimism and pessimism. The more Konrad contemplated him, the more assured he was that Nietzsche had delved further into the dark, inaccessible tunnels of the human psyche than neuroscientists and psychiatrists combined. Despite how troubled Nietzsche was, Konrad regarded him as the only man who knew his mind. Drawing energy from the thought gave him focus.

He had accidentally crashed the pictures of his two kids flat on the table. As he put them back up, he cracked a smile back at their adorable and prankish faces, the pictures taken in their childhood. He took Nicholas' photograph on his lap, held its silver frames. Seeing his face always pulled him out of his why-bother pessimism to the heart drilling self-questioning: why breathe?

"Alright, I'll give your brother a call," Konrad sympathized. "Who knows, maybe he'll put me on hold this time instead of rejecting it."

A shadow moved in the small crack under the door. Someone stood behind it.

A knock.

Konrad placed the photograph on the table. In the glass reflection, he was in need of a serious resurrection.

Calm down. No one has any business in my office, not until six.

The knock repeated in two quick hits.

Three impatient knocks.

Konrad bolted to the door and tore it open, seething in rage. "What!?"

It took a few moments to place the face of the woman, who wore a streamlined, asphalt gray running jacket with tight thumbholes.

Ruut Stark stared at Konrad, completely under control. She tilted her head. "You look just like my mom when she died."

"What are you talking about?"

"My mom," Ruut repeated in her husky voice, "she was a devoted Christian suffering from Alzheimer, and you know what she said to me on her deathbed after I'd taken care of her and dealt with her sudden aggressions for a year?"

Konrad considered his words. "Thank you?"

"Want to try again?"

Konrad shrugged.

"She told me to 'Go to hell.'"

"I see," Konrad said. "And you're telling me this because...?"

"I just told you."

"No, you didn't."

"I did," Ruut said and walked past Konrad into his office, leaving him astounded, taking a glance at the package on the floor. "I mistook you for my mother for a second."

"I'm sorry to disappoint you," Konrad said, scratching the back of his head. "Look. I'm having the worst day of my life, and I could do with some privacy..."

"I thought this was luckiest the day of your life." Ruut picked up the package.

Konrad looked at it and Ruut in turns. "Is it a bomb? The

teenager from the day of the incident... dressed in AC/DC shirt... Twice he has appeared and twice he has made my life miserable. He probably broke my toes."

"We all love teens," Ruut said with a hint of a smile. "The young man has a name, Gideon. And you mistook the logo on his tee shirt. It had the familiar lightning in the middle, but read something that anyone could be diagnosed with these days: AD/HD."

"I see," Konrad said, not remembering seeing the difference at all. "Are you family with him by any chance?"

"I see you've got the attention deficit disorder."

He admired her boldness with mild irritation. The similarity in their face bone structure was indisputable. "Could I ask your son a few questions?"

Ruut raised the package higher on her chest. "Sure. Gideon is also my student. I teach teens in my free time. We discuss God and everything. But you should thank him."

Konrad snorted. "Now why I would do that?"

Ruut pushed Konrad's chest with the package. "It seems he's your private messenger."

He caught the package in mid-air. "Is this what I think it is? Where did he get it?"

Ruut shrugged, sat and crossed her hands and legs. "*The Wicked Bible*. I bet I know the content of the Scriptures better than you. Shall we deepen our understanding?"

"I don't like taking money from a lady."

"I think you do," Ruut replied.

Konrad considered the offer. She spotted the artifacts.

"Now look at these old weapons on the shelf. You have polished all your weaponry to mirror sheen. I can smell gun oil, well taken care of. An expertly customized piece this one here. Custom fit slide. The interlock with the frame is tighter than the original. The change adds precision. And this one has a tactical grip. Tuned for total reliability..."

Konrad rubbed the back of his head. He glanced at the clock that read 9.11 a.m. Clearing his throat, "Discussing the Bible would only deepen disagreements. And I hardly know you."

"Nobody seems to know you, either. You are not nearly as evil as they say. 'A broken-hearted man set on revenge.'"

Konrad weighed her direct quotation from the garbage news. She managed to get under his skin. He wanted to keep his mouth shut, for he was getting paranoid at the image that media was conjuring. She could become a target as well.

"This is not a good idea. I would only offend you. When it comes to religion, I have the gift of spoiling others' party. Leave me. Take the Bible. Leave your phone number if you want, but go."

"Don't you want to study it?"

Konrad shoved the package into her arms and pointed at the door.

"That's your crusade."

RUUT'S LUNGS DIDN'T FILL. Unable to gather her thoughts, being once again turned down, she rose and spotted a white bathrobe hanging behind the door. Was this office a Playboy Mansion?

She walked past Konrad without sharing eye contact. He murmured something and closed the door behind her.

She held the package close to her chest, and walked away, feeling her cheeks pinking because she didn't protest at the unexpected gift. Her bravery always made the impact she wanted, but not this time. She wandered the corridor feeling herself a ghost in a wrong building. She was air for all the students flowing by. Outside, she took deep breaths and started walking toward her car. She had a day off, and decided to go to Netta's school. In her mood, she was ready to kill should she see her daughter being bullied.

In the parking lot, she walked past a poorly brushed black van and side-glanced inside the cab. The side view mirror on the other side of the van showed a man holding a tablet, and in the screen, a woman was lying on a hood of a sports car.

Pervert.

Ruut circled the van, opened the door and yelled at the man who wore a white winter jacket.

"The best way to get people talking about cars is by selling a woman's body. But, you know what? The woman isn't included!"

The man's stare was rock solid. Their gazes met and cut.

Slowly, the man hid the tablet inside his jacket and said, "Beat it."

Ruut's blood froze. The depth of his tone resembled an army command.

His eyes, like sharp daggers, drilled into hers. He started the engine and sped away.

Ruut confirmed her theory with his erect pose. An involuntary shiver ran down her spine. She hoped she hadn't pissed off someone outranking her.

A shadow loomed over her. A hand landed on her shoulder. The intention was gentle.

"I'm sorry," Konrad said. "My life is a disaster zone, and I..." He paused. "I didn't even thank you for saving my life."

Ruut faced him.

Konrad smiled. "Can I offer you a cup of coffee?"

5

T

HE UNIVERSITY CAFETERIA was quiet. Konrad crumbled a swastika-shaped Christmas tart over the pages of *The Wicked Bible*.

"Sorry," Konrad said with another bite. "These are my weak spot."

Ruut wiped the crumbs away and pretended she didn't notice, as she stroked her throat, which she had been doing for quite some time. She concentrated on the black, leather-bound covers of The Bible. Konrad looked around him: the staff of the cafeteria huffed and puffed behind the counter, the smell of salmon wafting from the kitchen. A cook glanced at Konrad but went quickly back to his work.

A woman teacher student with bare cleavage walked past them. He had once arrived late to supervise her electrified class where she wore the same peek-a-boo dress. All the girls took hits on their self-esteem as hormone-driven boys asked the teacher's help in turns to see her bend over their desks. He had immediately guided the children outside to play football and asked her to dress more decently.

The woman's upper lip raised on one side as she spotted

him. She walked away. Her face reminded him how much such toxic dumping he had practiced in his failed marriage.

Ruut's eyes were matte with rapt concentration. She hadn't touched her coffee. "Look at these marks."

He frowned.

"Get me a knife," she demanded.

Questions unasked, Konrad went to pick up a knife. As he returned, Ruut grabbed it and aggressively scratched at the leather surface. The yellowish pages were ravaged by time but exhumed the enigmatic aroma of ancient wisdom.

"These pores aren't from an animal," she said.

"What is it made of then?"

"Human skin."

Konrad rubbed his brow. "You sure?"

"Positive. Why would anyone bind a book with human skin?"

"Do you have the stomach to hear?"

Ruut laughed. "Cinderella-Boy, I'm a doctor and a professional killer..."

Konrad smiled. "Anthropodermic bibliology. The books of human flesh are unusual bindings only because the books we know about them are relatively rare. It's not that grisly if you forget today's standards, where unique is frowned upon. In the past, the skins used were mostly taken from murderers, mental patients, and John Does." He laid his hand on *The Wicked Bible.* "What kind of books would you bind in human skin?"

Ruut shrugged. "Perhaps something with deep personal meaning."

"Yes, the books that deserve to have a human covering deal with death or praise soul. Anatomy books, testaments, poems and prayers, judicial proceedings, erotica volumes, the list goes on. There are far more books like these kept in private, for also lovers and families have left behind a memory in the form of a book. The art dates back to the 17th century, but some Bibles were wrapped with human skin hundreds of years earlier."

Ruut face was expressionless.

"Not convinced? Shall I go into the details? Erotica books take their skins from—"

"Breathtakingly unerotic. But why this book?"

Konrad pulled back slightly in his chair.

"Oona was a priest, did you know?" Ruut said.

"Yes, as a matter of fact."

"You knew her?"

"A police officer revealed it."

"Did you love her?"

Konrad took salt and pepper shakers close to him and toyed with a few chopsticks. He knew the question would arise. He managed to let down his guard. "I admire your courage. It was a crush. For two months, she would smile at me on my way to work. I came to like her smile more as each day passed. But I didn't even greet her until the day I did. I had divorced a day before. I was free, and I said hello to her just to say good-bye. Consider the irony."

He continued shifting the place of the objects on the table as if it were a chessboard.

"When my mother died," Ruut said, "I thought I needed space. I fell into depression and was angry with my husband for reasons I didn't understand. He remained close to me. But I blamed him for not being compassionate enough, although he gave everything he had left after his work and taking care of our daughter. I didn't know how to mourn. I was reliving the moment when my mother told me to go to hell. I had misled myself into thinking I was tough like my father who was a farmer, who knew endurance. That sheer memory had become my prison, and I had to realize that freedom is not a place but a condition. Oona taught me that."

"Easing grief through spirituality is normal, although there is grief beyond belief," Konrad said. "Your husband did the right thing. It's an illusion to think that people need space in crises. You were hurt, but you didn't have to say that no cared about you."

"I knew there's a spiritual side inside of you. Did your life pass before your eyes when you lost consciousness?"

"No. But Hugh Hefner's life did."

"Don't dodge," Ruut exasperated. "You're famous for thorny opinions that raise the gastric acid into people's mouths. You're not a threat to my faith. The tests of faith are never-ending. It's easy to become a believer, but staying in the faith isn't. You see religion as irrational, useless, and dangerous. I see it as a source of inspiration and love. Science doesn't inspire the average human being the way religion does. Because of your standpoint —that God is unnamed, unidentified, undetected, and unneeded—you can quickly come up with a counter-argument. Humor me, what comes to your mind first. Oona once said, '*Religion is an apple tree, and God its roots.*'"

Konrad blinked.

"Your initial impression?" Ruut asked.

"The venomous roots of a dead standing tree."

"See?"

Konrad smiled. "Your point?"

"Zero critical thinking. Zero reasoning. Zero credibility. Your believer profile. Sometimes you hit the target, but you are no better when going berserk with science."

"I'm just a man who casts a skeptical eye over the stories that are either lies or unreasonably interpreted. Religious people should thank me for showing them their rotten condition."

Ruut riffled through the pages. "You're right. People should appreciate every atheist, skeptic, pessimist, and dark mind out there because if correctly understood, you serve the Cause.

You're not anti-God—you're anti-religion. Every religion is bound to become blind to its actions and routines: corruption, idiocy, anti-science, anti-unity and abuse of the children, young, and women. But you are ready to throw the beautiful baby out with the bathwater because the water is so dirty that you don't see the baby in it."

"I'm sorry. Some things don't deserve to get legs. And most deserve to be cut at the knees."

Ruut swallowed a laugh. "God's porch light is always on for you."

"God's infinite cabinet of unearthly delights awaits me then."

She leaned forward. "You honestly think that faith is sugar-coating reality?"

"Like cotton candy," Konrad replied, "sweet and easy to consume, but less than nutritious."

Ruut spat some angry clichés, and he feigned interest. He focused on rubbing his jaw, surer than ever that as long as there was religion, mankind was unfit to build a civilization with shared values.

Ruut tapped a page of The Bible rhythmically with her index finger.

Konrad read the line. "You shall commit adultery. What about it?"

"Why did Oona want to share this information with you?"

"Beats the hell out of me."

Ruut craned her neck to meet Konrad's eyes.

Konrad raised an eyebrow. "*The Wicked Bible* is worth a great penny. Perhaps she wanted me to sell it. But how did Gideon come to possess it?"

Ruut's phone rang. "Maybe Oona had paid him to deliver the package." Locating her cell, she swung her jacket and melted snow fell on the page. "Shit."

Konrad stopped Ruut from drying the paper with her hand

and signaled her to take the call. She started talking to her phone while Konrad swept the crumbles off a napkin and pressed the paper gently.

His eyes flew wide open.

The water scratched off a letter A. Underneath came forth a corresponding red letter.

Konrad looked at Ruut who noticed it too and was letting the phone do the talking. She laid her phone on the table and sat, her gaze never leaving the letter. She then came to the other side of the table, stood so close to him that their shoulders touched.

Konrad swiped the pages with the napkin. Another colorful letter revealed itself.

Ruut wet her napkin in Konrad's glass and went after him.

More letters.

Then a few more.

All scaled in different colors.

"A rainbow?" Konrad marveled. "Is this a gay bible?"

Ruut was writing something down to her napkin. "Wait, they form a sentence."

Her handwriting was scrawling at best. Konrad asked, "What's it say?"

She wrote the line in big letters below the first. Together they studied the message and each other's faces.

A SIN IN TWO RACES.

"I still get gay vibes," Konrad said.

"Haven't you read *The Da Vinci Code*? Where every intellect, detective and cryptographer is brain-dead compared to Robert Langdon? Let's try a different word-order."

Konrad shrugged.

Ruut sat on the opposite side of the table. She started writing, and Konrad contemplated for a while how close to him she had edged into his personal space. They both started writing letters to napkins. Ruut went to pick up more. Konrad played with words and came to the conclusion he should start doing crosswords. For an extended period he was relaxed, something that usually only his research could offer.

They spent fifteen minutes in silence, reorganizing the letters, eliminating the absurd and the inconsistent.

"Anything?" Ruut asked.

"Some words. Shall we compare?"

"Show yours first."

Konrad showed his list in two napkins.

Ruut whisper-read through the words and landed to an underlined three-word. "*Wore satanic sin*?"

"How about you?"

"I underlined one as well: *Satanic ire sown*."

Konrad planted a devilish grin on his face. "My kind of book."

Ruut squinted and poked out her tongue.

"So, we've got Satan and Rainbow and a lustful commandment," Konrad said. "We only need to invite God, and the party will go on forever. Who called you by the way?"

Ruut shot a hand on her forehead. "Damn. It was my daughter's principal. I need to go and pick her up. She reacts with her stomach when being bullied or feeling the threat of it. A simple mean word penetrates her skin and works like acid inside." She rose, donning her outerwear. "If she only knew that even many adults bully each other in work, she might give up."

A stream of students entered the cafeteria. Konrad pressed The Bible against his chest, and Ruut was once again close to him, her perfume dancing the rumba in his head. "Shall we continue our demonology at a better time?"

She blinked as if sharing a conspiratorial high five. "I wouldn't miss the chance."

"If your husband doesn't mind, of course."

"My husband is a domestic god. Not a jealous type, although

sometimes I secretly wish he were." Ruut rolled the ring between thumb and index finger and stared at the table, and through it. "I was a difficult companion to live with in the past. I got offended even on such innocent occasions when he happened to stare at an actress too long during a movie."

Konrad nodded. "We all must go through our uncertainties."

Ruut pulled a pink-white knit cap from her pocket and put it on. "That's true. I didn't trust my attractiveness, and I didn't trust my husband. Now, thank God, mixed-up feelings are not the end of the world."

"Why do you thank God?"

"For the same reasons as you do."

Konrad gave his head a shake, amused. "That's a focus illusion. There's a difference between talking to oneself and talking to *oneself*, believing that it's God. Talking to ourselves relieves the feeling of loneliness and makes us smarter, like psychological self-programming."

"You don't grasp faith."

"What else could it be than reinforcing the message we believe in? Faith is nothing more than tuning out distractions and controlling mixed emotions, focusing on our goal, being a good believer for example."

Ruut brought forth an inspective eye. "Obviously, we all strive for optimal performance. But faith is not schizophrenia. You don't ask God for answers. He doesn't give any. You don't thank God for gratitude. He doesn't care."

Konrad was flabbergasted. "If it's not for answers and attention, why do people pray then?"

"Simple," Ruut said, smiling a good-bye. "God gives *Himself*."

"I see," Konrad said.

"No, you don't. Now excuse me for I'm going to commit a *sin*."

"Are you planning to end the bullying?"

Ruut mimed a baseball bat in her hands. She stage-whispered, "I'm going to whack these boys with a bat so hard that for a week they'll spin and on Sunday they'll fall."

"Yeah," Konrad whispered back. "Play God Hardcore."

Ruut closed her one eye and raised a finger to her slightly curved-up lips. Then she left.

Konrad plunged into loneliness. Darkness surrounded him on all sides. He exited the cafeteria, started walking toward his office. Halfway along a long corridor, a tall man with stern set jaw and relaxed shoulders walked past him with perfectly erect posture. He seemed boringly immune to any whims of destiny or cataclysmic events. But did the man rub his forehead or was it an army salute?

A fresh flood of anxiety took hold of his body. Unpacking the office already build new mazes and dead ends to his mind: the division of property at home that awaited him later was another Minotaur in the dark labyrinth of his brain. With *The Wicked Bible* in his hands, he felt punished, and buried by shame.

Moments later at his office, he stared at nothing for half an hour. Then he took an old, battered medical bag from the shelf and put *The Wicked Bible* inside. The bag still smelled of the sweat of previous bearers. There were no last words, nor silent moments for the office, he just left the door open and exited the building in no rush.

It was cold outside. He had forgotten to plug his Trabant's block heater into an electrical outlet. Not without a campfire under the car would he be able to drive home.

A bus parked behind him to pick up students. Shrugging, he walked in and edged all the way to the back of the bus. Before the bus jerked, a beautiful French-looking woman student with coyote brown eyes sat next to him. Konrad closed his eyes and leaned back. After a few minutes, the woman was leaning closer to him. Seconds later, she was sleeping against his shoulder.

Konrad contemplated the woman.

He gave a gentle push; the woman leaned against the window for a second, then she came back.

With another shove, the woman swayed away.

But this time, when she returned like a kitten searching for warmth, Konrad had the medical bag between them.

6

KONRAD ENTERED HIS home in the cloak of nightfall. A permanent twist in his chest was wrenching his heart out. In the kitchen, he dropped the medical bag on the table. Then he took a bottle of Renault Carte Noire Extra, filled a glass and emptied it while looking through it at the note Julia had left on the table.

PACK AND LEAVE.

Konrad contemplated their first meeting at the University in a copy room. It was the day he became a doctor. He walked into the room dressed in his best and only tuxedo and saw a pony-tailed woman struggling with a copy machine. Paper was stuck inside, so he helped her, and saved her. But then his cuffs got stuck in the machine, and she tried to help him in turn. They stayed in the small room for an hour, waiting for back up. They laughed and chatted, shared the stories of their lives, eventually waded into deep waters. The best day of his life. Half a year later they got married, happily confused about the sensation of love and bonding. A few years later they were only confused.

Konrad poured another glass. He frowned. Their huskies

weren't in their cage outside. She had probably taken them to her father's, who owned the biggest Safari company in Lapland.

Konrad let the alcohol burn at the end of his tongue, tried to beat the pain before swallowing.

Did they grow apart or were they ever truly together? He had been an answering machine, always reassuring his love to her. He grabbed the bottle and started carrying items he considered his own into the trailer in front of the garage. The snowfall was rain now, strong winds howling in the darkness of the woods and around the house. Snow was melting away.

During the next hour, he emptied the bottle and filled the trailer. He slammed the cover closed. An unexpected scene unfolded before his blurred vision.

The trailer slid down the hill. It struck a metal mailbox, booming like a shotgun blast, bending it like a backward cracked spine. Konrad rubbed his head, staggered to a carton box he'd forgotten to load and took out something heavy. Then he stumbled to the trailer and put it under the tire. "Don't move!" He smiled. "Atta boy."

Suddenly a hollow sound of bells started ringing. Deep in the woods, reindeer were running, the bells ringing around their necks, the sea of antlers looking like birch branches moving in the wind. One of them had reflective paint sprayed onto the antlers, and it reflected light from a car's headlights with weird, devilish effect. The idea must have come from Julia's reindeer herder father.

Something foul spilled into Konrad's stomach. There was painfully much of his past life drawing away with the disappearing reindeer that he fell to his knees, and threw up.

Next moment of some sort of clarity, he was lying in a snow bank. His body was numbed. Crawling back inside in the slush and dirt of the lawn was the weirdest trip since his birth, as though if he had crawled out of a cozy womb. In the hall, he caught a breath for a few minutes, stood up to his shaky legs and walked into the living room from a wall to another, and switched on the television.

In the retrospect news, Kaspar Nyman was meeting the president. He took the lady's hand to his and planted on it a bold, lingering kiss.

Konrad fell on the sofa. He managed to switch channel before submitting himself to the spin of sleep. The voice of a newsreader spoke:

...The many Russian airspace insults are still being left unanswered by the Kremlin despite Finland's growing demands. Furthermore, Russia holds massive military exercises near the Finnish border, involving more than five hundred aircrafts, including new models in the Sukhoi jet fighter family. Fighter jets and bombers are also being practiced mid-air refueling from a tanker plane above the Arctic Circle. The planes are prepared with improved friend-or-foe system, super-maneuverability at low airspeeds, and destructive weaponry...

Konrad opened his left eye and saw a familiar mustached face that even a child could draw from memory.

Monopoly man.

Viktor Vodyanoy—the president of Russia.

Anxiety wrapped itself tightly around his chest. But his academic mind caught like grease-fire, wondering the quality and the gap between the global military toolbox and education toolbox. Less than 1 percent paid for the world's weapons was enough to put every child to school, but the world leaders made sure that the world remained an altar of materialism by sacrificing education and care.

No wonder why there was more instability, more war, and a greater likelihood of war in entire human history.

∾

A DARK MAN picked the lock of the professor's back door lock of the house. Standing on a small hill, the house's front windows looked over the sleeping, misty outline of Rovaniemi. An electrical failure had dimmed the city center. Patrick turned and took a glance into the woods.

In the distance in a curvy forest road, a van's headlights flashed twice.

The way was clear.

As clear as the Veteran's orders:

Seize the Bible.

He removed his wet shoes, turned the door handle and slipped inside.

Night vision on.

Patrick noted dirt tracks on the lobby floor and black hand marks in the walls. A voice spoke somewhere in the back of the house. The voice was a woman's, gentle and soft as falling snow. Slowly, it became more intense. He flashed a grin to a mirror he passed by. The television was left open.

The pungent smell of alcohol wafted to his nose.

Like stealing candy from a baby...

He walked to the living room, feeling the sensation of being home after many years.

He passed the television where the woman was starting to moan.

The man was snoring on the sofa, uninterrupted.

Sweet dreams, professor, he thought and went on with his search.

7

RUUT WAS DREAMING. Konrad's forehead bore a horseshoe-shaped fold between his brow, sadness or grief written all over his face. But the skin in his neck mottled. There was something in the ground at his feet.

An apple broken in half with a small object in the center of the halves.

A prism.

Konrad planted his feet wide apart, his hands clenching slowly at his sides.

Ruut stared at him, tried to ask what he was doing, but her voice carried no sound.

Behind Konrad and a great apple tree, a staggering sight materialized in the sky.

A rainbow.

Doing full circle.

Konrad had closed the gap between them in a blink of an eye, his hands reaching around her neck.

Ruut opened her eyes, dodged, fell from the bed. Adrenaline rushing through her body, her lips quirked up in half a smile as she realized she was in Netta's room and saw red digits in a clock on the night stand.

3:34 a.m.

The fog began to lift.

An apple, she thought. *Could it be...?*

She listened and confirmed Netta was breathing. Gently, she smoothed strands of hair off the girl's face. In Netta's art class in school, they had just been talking about the father who invented the original color wheel. The rainbow was the primary element of her drawings hanged on the wall.

She stood up, readily dressed for she had fallen asleep while putting Netta to sleep. She went to her work room, opened her Mac and wrote the publishing year of *The Wicked Bible*. Then she wrote a name in the Google picture search and checked the timeline.

Building on the momentum, she took a pencil and wrote a note on paper:

A SIN IN TWO RACES.

Then she reorganized the words, drumming her feet against the floor.

She stared at the result and compared it with the picture on the screen, and swallowed laughter with a hand over her mouth.

She believed she had just discovered the original owner of *The Wicked Bible*.

8

KONRAD WOKE UP to a shadow falling across his face. A throbbing headache blurred his vision, and everything in his instincts told him someone had been staring at him.

The red dot on the television sprang to life. Probably a short power failure had shut down the television and disturbed his sleep.

He massaged his temples, rubbed his arms and thighs in a vain attempt to generate heat. Every position made the hangover worse. The sofa was ruined. Judging by the dirt and moisture it was like a wild pig had made love on it.

A sneeze.

A flu. Way to go, Konrad.

He waddled to the kitchen and took a can of Fanta from the refrigerator. It collided with Finlandia Vodka, but as much as he wanted to continue his streak, even the sight of the bottle put him on the verge of vomiting.

He opened the can and took a sip, counting the costs of his night-time packing adventure. The trailer rested against his neighbor's mailbox stand. He turned away from the window, sat on the floor and leaned back against the wall.

A bang sounded through the ceiling.

Probably a squirrel dropped a cone on the plate roof.

Outside, the motion sensor lighting sprang to life.

Konrad looked at the time on his phone display.

6.20 A.M.

Someone was either early, or rabbits and reindeer had found food under the snow in the yard.

A hailstorm started drumming the roof. Rapidly changing weather conditions were something everybody would have to get used to. Extreme weather was soon to be a new norm.

A shadowy figure materialized at the window.

Ruut Stark.

Standing on the terrace, she had her hand raised for an apologetic greeting. Konrad lifted an eyebrow at what she was holding in her other hand.

"Sorry for the ungodly hour," Ruut said.

"I'm glad you came. Coffee?"

"Please." Ruut sat at the table, scanning the house. "An addict needs her daily dose."

Konrad walked to the kitchen, sneezed loudly and studied the coffee machine and tried to fit the filter paper into the machine. His hands shook, so Ruut came and took the filter.

"Rough night?"

Konrad rubbed the back of his head and searched a tissue into his hand for his running nose. "I've never prepared coffee."

"That's why woman was created." She quickly evaluated his clothes. "Your coffee machine is older than antique. You might want to take a cold shower while waiting."

Konrad's eyes went wide in search for an answer. "How do you know I like cold showers?"

"I have a crystal ball." Ruut switched on the coffee machine. "Go clear your head. I need to pick your brains."

Konrad tilted his head with the slow smile that builds and was about to say something but withdrew to the bathroom. Meanwhile, Ruut's attention was caught a strange painting on the wall, representing the city of Rovaniemi from the bird's perspective.

Reindeer Antler Plan.

She sat, leaned forward, sliding the chair closer. She had seen pictures about this in local history books, but this was a personal painting. The city center was wrapped inside the reindeer's head, with the sports stadium as the eye. Roads branching north, west, and south made up the antlers. Because of the grand architecture by Alvar Aalto one couldn't go anywhere straight. But he had laid the foundation for a tourist hub in the frozen north, and a national goldmine. With tourist flocking by the thousands from all corners of the world, it was easy to claim Rovaniemi to be the resident home of Santa Claus.

Ruut spotted the signature of the painter, and as she leaned closer to decipherer it something rolled in her stomach.

Julia Loki.

She clasped her knees tightly together. The overall feeling of the painting was now a catalyst for murky thoughts. She contemplated the antlers.

After WWII, the demolished capital of Finnish Lapland was laid out as a head of the reindeer to symbolize regeneration and strength.

But in the painting, the antler-roads were partly menacing in red.

Like the Devil's horns.

~

"SEXY WHITE BATHROBE," Ruut said. "Doesn't even reveal all your leg hair."

"This is my ex-wife's. I forgot mine at the university." Konrad sat and placed a hand on *The Wicked Bible* on the table. The heat of his hand left a hand mark on the frosty cover. "I still can't believe I used it as a block."

Ruut made no comment.

Konrad sneezed. "I don't even recall the last time I indulged. My tolerance has lapsed."

She flashed a hurried smile at him, drumming her fingers together.

"Konrad."

"My wife once stood there at the exact place twenty years ago, the same intonation in her tone, telling me she was pregnant."

Ruut raised her eyebrows.

"The only time she wasn't on we-need-to-talk mode. What did you want to say?"

"I broke the code."

"That's... wonderful."

"You don't sound very excited."

Konrad sneezed into the tissue. "Elaborate."

The coffee machine struggled to produce the hot steaming liquid Konrad sincerely hated.

Ruut was once again so close to him that she could take a bite at his earlobe. "You helped me to solve the code in my dream."

"Really? I thought only God specializes in the impossible."

"In my dream," Ruut continued, uninterrupted, "I saw a smashed apple on the ground, a prism inside, and a sky streaked by a beautiful, round rainbow. You were somehow angry, but that helped me to be alarmed and watchful. As you probably know, The Bible doesn't say that the fruit eaten in the Garden of Eden was an apple."

"True," Konrad said, "Where the Tree of the Knowledge of Good and Evil was located, an apple is never mentioned."

"Then I came up with somebody who unwove the rainbow in the 17th century."

Konrad took a sip from the can. "Who?"

Ruut wrote three letters in her hand.

S.I.N.

"You're killing me. Tell me."

"Konrad, we are talking about a man who plowed the deepest track in the history of science, and the one who knew the seeds of religion."

"Now I know why God holds off answering questions: Tantric storytelling, delaying satisfaction."

"Last clue. The man knew that an apple didn't fall far from a tree."

Konrad's eyes widened. "You mean the original owner of *The Wicked Bible* was...?"

"Yes, sir," Ruut said. "Sir Isaac Newton."

Konrad mentally sorted out the letters: A SIN IN TWO RACES. He crossed his arms and frowned. "You may be right."

"I found it hard to believe at first. *The Wicked Bible* saw daylight in 1631 and Newton made his first cry only—"

"A decade later. December 25. On Christ's birthday."

Ruut gave a nudge on Konrad's shoulder. "Thanks for spoiling my chance to shine, Alexandria."

Konrad smiled proudly at the comparison to an ancient library once considered the center source of knowledge in the ancient world. "Newton owned a personal library, and he had tens of bibles in store. The vast majority of his books were on the subject of theology. The world remembers him from his tremendous scientific achievements, but he wrote more studies on religion and biblical interpretation and his dark addiction, alchemy. He was a formidable biblical scholar."

"He was?"

"His interpretation of the Bible differed from that of the Church. For instance, he didn't believe in the doctrine of Trinity, which defines God as three consubstantial persons: The Father, the Son, and the Holy Spirit."

"Simply one of the essence, like the three forms of water: solid, liquid, and gas." Ruut shrugged. "Or in modern terms: me, myself, and I."

"Science and religion weren't at odds for Newton as it was for the Church. He used his scientific works as a means to reinforce belief in the biblical truth. The Bible was true in every respect for him. He had extreme religious views, and knew how religion affected people's minds." Konrad went to the kitchen and poured a cup for her. "Consider his famous law of gravity, which is said to have been inspired by the fall of an apple."

"You don't believe it happened?"

"Irrelevant question. It's not important what gave Newton his epiphany on gravity. He deliberately honed the story; over time it got better with the telling. Newton knew the symbolic power of an apple, how it resonated with the Biblical account of the tree of knowledge, to the downfall of man. Not to mention the shape of the apple in relation to the law of gravity; the Earth-shaped object being attracted to the Earth. Newton liked giving thorny lessons to the Church, to reveal its wrong interpretation of the Scriptures."

"You two have something in common," Ruut said. "By the way, you attacked me in my dream, but I think you were trying to make me understand something."

"Distorted memories resurfacing from your subconscious, perhaps?"

"There are so many coincidences. Newton invented the color wheel. There was a prism inside the broken apple..."

"Do you want to know what Newton did to his eyes when he came to the conclusion that light included all the colors?"

"Shoot."

"He shoved a needle into his eye and looked at the sun as long as he could stand it. He needed information for his new theory of optics to eyesight."

Ruut squinted her eyes. "No one can escape such acts without permanent ocular damage. But miracles happen."

"One sees a miracle, the other a coincidence," Konrad said, sneezing with a cough. "Newton nearly went blind while operating on himself. After staring into the sun, he needed to be in darkened room for quite some time." Konrad pulled the skin down below his eye with his finger. "Of course, he didn't shove the needle into his eyeball, but as near the back side between the eye and the bone as he could to stimulate the retina manually. The eye socket was the end of the rainbow, the treasure. Newton was the first to understand the rainbow, a phenomenon that had and has preoccupied human mind throughout its existence. From Aristotle to Descartes, sunlight was considered pure, but Newton proved them wrong."

"White light is a combination of all the colors of the rainbow," Ruut said.

"Yes," Konrad said, "but the rainbow has, unfortunately, a long history of corroding the wheels of rational thinking. It's the greatest subject of myth and mystery of and a cause of superstitions. Some cultures still like to see the rainbow as an attribute of goddesses and their garments, belts and headbands, and some believe it is a bridge where messengers can bring messages from the gods. In Greek mythology, it was a footpath between Heaven and Earth."

"God's rainbow covenant," Ruut murmured. She moisturized

her finger and started turning the pages. "Rainbows are the only sign God has placed in the sky for us. It was originally for Noah and his family, a simultaneous reminder of the destruction of the Flood and that it will never happen again. The rainbow reminds us of His protection. Let me see, Genesis 9... 'And God blessed Noah and his sons, and said to them, Bring forth fruit, and multiply, and replenish the earth... I have set my bow in the cloud, and it shall be for a sign of the covenant between me and the earth. And when I shall cover the earth with a cloud, and the bow shall be seen in the cloud, then will I remember my covenant which is between me and you'... Ouch!" Ruut stopped, her brows furrowed. "Holy fuck."

Konrad nearly choked on his Fanta. "Did you get a paper cut?"

"The text is melting." Ruut raised up her glance. "The letters... I can pull them off like scabs..."

She stroked the paper, spread the blood upon the text.

Konrad's heart pumped in his chest.

"Interesting," Ruut said with the calmness of a surgeon in her voice. "Something is coming up..."

Konrad tried to get up to his feet, but his knees were jelly, his legs failed him.

"Another hidden message!" Ruut raised her bloody hands at the delight. She looked up. "You look pale."

She stretched out her hand, but was too late.

Konrad collapsed head first onto the floor.

9

T HE VETERAN'S STEADY hands focused the image under a high-powered microscope. A sapphire blue sphere, all alone in the little frame of cold microcosmos. It was not only the future of man but a cure for inhumanity, casting off the bonds of flesh and blood.

A little tightening of moral screws...

The Veteran's hands unfocused the image. Time was short. The field of moral enhancement was currently unregulated and unsupervised, but once its potential was discovered, humanity would tie its hands into a Gordian's knot with bureaucracy and ethical thinking. The Ascension to a new and infinitely richer existence was a window of opportunity soon closed.

The Veteran turned away from the microscope, walked through and out his private fluorescent-lit laboratory to his workshop, to his passion. On a workbench, he lit a candle. The hands opened a blueprint scroll and unwrapped it on a table surrounded with drawing tools for finishing his minor craft. The plan was titled *Going Clear*. The hands laid a Koran on the side of the scroll for a weight and palm-pressed the other end against the table. Then the Veteran opened the Koran to a marked page and read a passage about the 'Three Dark Stages of a Child':

"...*fee thulumatin thalathin*..."

Empowered, the Veteran grabbed tools to carve and polish a puppet, which was but a wooden block eight months ago, while recapping the passage. Threefold darkness—fee thulumatin thalathin—was the origin of every human being, an expression of the three dark regions involved during the development of the embryo:

The darkness of the abdomen.

The darkness of the womb.

The darkness of the placenta.

Modern medicine spoke about the embryological development of the baby in the same manner as revealed over a thousand years ago, when no one had access to such profound knowledge. Muslims considered this as proof that the Word was from Allah, especially because each of the regions consists of three layers, and because a human being is created in the mother's womb in three distinct stages. Science had verified the ancient knowledge, but the Veteran knew the Divine Messengers, the teachers of the dominant religion, had more in store than was uttered about human potential.

And potential was not about determinism. It was about what *can* be achieved.

The Creator works in counter-intuitive ways, always acting in the gaps of knowledge...

It was time to bring the Creator on the stage. The hands of the Veteran carefully found its place behind the puppet's back and neck and raised it gently in the air.

A flawless design. The Veteran needed only to write a message along with the gift before sending the puppet into the morally darkest corner of the world, Rovaniemi. After all, necessity was not only the mother of invention; it was what fulfilled the image of the Creator as the parental figure.

The Veteran relied on the soldiers on the ground, their oath-sworn ability to tie off any loose ends. The plan, once executed, would spin the world into the final confrontation with destiny—the redefinition of humanity.

The Veteran took in control of the puppet and tested its mouth mechanism:

"*Si vis pacem, para bellum,*" the Veteran ventriloquized. "If you want peace, prepare for war..."

10

S EEK THE MENSTRUAL BLOOD
    OF THE SORDID WHORE
    WHERE
THE SUN AND THE MOON SHINE ACROSS,
AND KNOCK ON WOOD
TO OPEN THE CREAKY DOORS
OF PERCEPTION.

RUUT'S EYEBROWS WERE heavy with suspicion. The new enigma was as visible as a watermark on a dollar bill. The text was written inside a big but narrow corridor of a thumbprint spiraling like a labyrinth. It sounded nothing like Newton.

How did my blood react to the text like that?

Konrad had fainted at the sight of her blood. She had dragged Konrad on the sofa, checked his pulse and vital signs. The chest of a sleeper was enough proof that he was now resting off the toll of his wee hours.

Ruut's toes kept curling up on the carpet, a paranoid part of her anticipating Mrs. Loki's coming home. She pulled her knees together, evaluated the catalog-perfect living room. The books on the bookshelf were not alphabetized but neatly color coded into the colors of the rainbow. She gazed at the family-framed wall. One black-and-white photo portrayed a smooth-cheeked major with a woman, both looking grim. A picture of a NCO— her grandfather she never knew—materialized in her mind, haunting with the same kind of stare as Konrad's father in the picture. Her grandfather's medal of honor, acquired by masquerading and sabotaging an enemy air strike plan on civilian targets in the Winter War, was something she always kept with her in her breast pocket. It was a badge on her chest; it made her proud and gave her determination in the work and world dominated by men.

She saw Konrad back in the days when he had just been promoted to Principal. Her Swedish teacher had asked her to throw a book on the teacher's desk, and she had thrown the book, yelling "Catch!"... straight at the teacher's eye. The teacher rushed away from the classroom, crying like a baby. Konrad came a minute later. He stormed the classroom with the ramrod exactness of a soldier, located her and lifted her desk above his head. He yelled back, "Ruut! Catch!"

The sound of the desk smashing on the floor echoed in her ears. Konrad dragged her through wood splinters and books among shell-shocked friends to the longest detention she could remember.

Principal Konrad Loki.

Pure intensity.

Although she had never approved of his actions, she deserved it. That single act communicated to her that Konrad actually cared.

She connected her thumb and forefinger in a circle and filliped him on the forehead.

Konrad's eyes enlarged.

"You would make a terrible vampire," she said.

He blinked five times.

"Forgive me my Freudian slip—Drama Queen—but let's get back to work." Ruut showed him the Bible. "Feast your eyes..."

Konrad swung her hand away.

Quickly, red color rose high on her face.

"I don't want to see any blood," Konrad said.

"Fainting at the sight of blood isn't—"

"Uncommon, I know," Konrad said, deadpan.

She tilted her head. "How are you, Konrad?"

Konrad was bemused at the sudden compassionate question. In Finland, the question was not to be presented lightly. One often got the whole truth. "I'm OK. What does your husband think of you being here?"

She leaned closer, made focused strokes on his forehead with her fingertip.

"What are you doing?" Konrad said.

"Just smoothing up the worry lines."

Konrad blinked. He grabbed her wrist gently and guided it to rest on the back of the sofa. Giving a spin on her delicate skin around her wrist in his mind, he took The Bible to his lap. She shifted closer to Konrad's ear and amplified the lines with a serious, disembodied voice.

"Menstrual blood..." Konrad said after her, stabbed by the bizarre yet familiar words.

"Menstruation is what all men have always shied away from confronting," Ruut said.

"Mainly because in religious perspective a menstruating woman is an impure creature," Konrad added. "Female blood is an age-old taboo. For example, in Islam, a woman on a period still can't touch the Koran." Konrad scrambled up, went to the bookshelf and pulled a thin book. "Ovulation was a mystery to science till the verge of Second World War because in human females the ovulation is hidden. Women were thought to be able to conceive at any point of their cycle." Konrad returned to the sofa with the little book. "It's good that women don't experience animal heat, you know why?"

"I'm all ears."

"The key word is *choice*. Although we cherry-pick, the freedom of choice omits the compulsion, which keeps men close and the tray of selection wide. That one difference to animals makes us somewhat capable of complex relationships, being friends, and having work colleagues and companions. Women are the privileged gender: they can have sex whenever they want, men only when they can."

"You think it's easy to be a woman?"

"I'm aware of women's historical burden, down to the last sad detail," Konrad clarified. "But men do most of the physical hard work—and the greater the hazards of a job, the surer the men do it. You don't see women up building skyscrapers or down in coal mines. Death professions for males, safe jobs for women."

"What? It's an art being a woman these days," Ruut started her frosty response.

"'All art is quite useless,' said Oscar Wilde." Konrad stroked his chin. "Meaning art creates mood; it doesn't cause action. Women conform to the stereotyped roles too easily. Care is in their instinct, but it's invisible in global affairs. Women shouldn't maintain their silence at times of crisis."

Ruut opened her mouth, but turned away, looking into the distance, finding a reference point. Then she turned to *The Wicked Bible* on the table. "Either you push a woman upwards or downwards, the aim is the same: dehumanization. How would you live your life when you would be shouldering thousands of years of oppression and prejudice? There's much more structural violence against women than you can or want to see, and you just need to look up to see the proof: all the highest government, corporate and clergy positions of power are men's."

Konrad rubbed his temple. Her gray eyes enraptured; they blinked excessively while listening and opened wide while talking, making his eyes involuntarily water on her behalf. He was confusingly happy he had discovered a new friend to argue with. "Good points."

"Good points, my ass. What difference does it make if you don't smell the shit you're shoveling?" Ruut flashed a wry smile. "What did you want to show me?"

"My favorite book: Paulo Coelho's *The Alchemist.*"

"Fascinating," Ruut said. "An overrated piece of fiction is all we need. Turning lead into gold, never succeeding in it."

"There are stories we should listen and learn from, in the past."

"From who?"

"Isaac Newton of course."

Ruut's brow furrowed. "That boringly unsurprising book has nothing to do with Isaac Newton."

"The Alchemist, the most prominent figure of the story, is as mysterious a character and as incredibly powerful a practitioner of alchemy as Newton was. They both speak through riddles and cherish personal experience over direct instructions as the most efficient way of learning. The metaphors inside the labyrinth are beyond the shadow of doubt Newton's words."

Ruut stuck out her tongue, concentrating. "Wasn't alchemy considered to be black magic? Why would Newton risk his reputation for such nonsense? If someone actually would have discovered the fabled philosopher's stone, it would have ruined the gold standard."

Konrad nodded. "Which is why alchemy was illegalized."

Ruut crossed her hands. "Fill me in with the metaphors. You can't wait for talking about your morbid curiosities."

"The alchemists," Konrad began, "had no access to the periodic chart. They knew only how basic elements combined and created their terminology, often projecting either human or animal characteristics onto their cocktails. The realm of alchemy is filled with hidden and double meanings. It combines philosophy and poetry. The coded language composed of old metaphors and the best way to look at the metaphors is in the light of riddles." Konrad guided Ruut's stare on the first lines of the riddle. "The 'menstrual blood' and 'sordid whore' are a code riddle. The first means a metallic form of antimony, which is extracted from the latter, the antimony's ore."

"Antimony, huh?" Ruut bit her lip. "I know it from my work with bullets. It's used to harden lead—which is fairly soft—to any level of hardness a shooter wants. But why did antimony interest Newton?"

"In the alchemical school of thought, antimony was the essence of femininity. Think of the standard gender symbols, Mars for a man, Venus for a woman. The arrow pointing upright in man's symbol is an iron-tipped spear, a manly weapon to wield, and the woman's symbol has a bronze mirror."

"Go on."

"The presence of alchemy is in the symbols," Konrad stressed. "One of the alchemical symbols for antimony still stands for female today. Speaking of which, the rainbow of the previous riddle included an interesting detail. Some ancient people have believed that if you passed beneath a rainbow and you were a man, you would immediately become a woman. And if you were a woman, you would instantly become a man."

Ruut took the Bible on her lap. She returned to the page of the commandments. "*A sin in two races*. Why does he refer to gender so much?"

"You would have to be Newton to answer that question. His mind was like a Rubik's cube. He seemed to know everything and succeed in everything, but on his deathbed, he confessed he had never once known a woman. He never married or had sex. Died a virgin. The 'sin in two races' might have something to do with the fact that especially as a teenager, Newton saw himself a big-time sinner. He kept listing the sins he had committed."

"Does the labyrinth fit Newton?" Ruut asked.

"I suppose. Symbolic meanings were his specialty. Labyrinths tend to have one possible path, the rest leading into a dead end or back to the starting point. Repeatedly losing the track of direction is a strong comparison to human life and the difficulty of transforming ourselves. We keep trying and reaching, but return into square one. In the Middle Ages, the labyrinths symbolized a path to God, and the journey to salvation was like a pilgrimage."

"Just a wild card," Ruut said, "but what if Sir Isaac Newton was a woman?"

Konrad chuckled. "That's a stretch."

"You said Newton succeeded in everything. If he were a woman, then against our intuition that every great philosopher or scientist or spiritual teacher is a man, he would have known the hell of womanhood. That would leave only one question open, whether he succeeded discovering the philosopher's stone."

"Hold your horses. There is no way Newton was a—"

Ruut took a phone to her hand. "Google... Picture search... Isaac Newton..."

"What are you doing?"

"Verifying my theory."

"Ridiculous. No one of the scientific community would have taken him seriously."

Ruut's eyes were glued to the screen of the phone. "If the master of secrecy can't keep a secret, he's no master at all."

"You don't understand. In England women legally had no

rights at all." Konrad tried to meet her gaze. "The husband had absolute control over his wife's personal property."

"And men also debated whether women had souls," Ruut replied. "Like it is today, men thought they owned their wives and their bodies. Men have shamed our sexuality as a guilty pleasure. If a woman believes she's filthy during periods or a whore, men can control women. Control is most effective when a woman is put to guard herself. Make woman an evil seductress, a closet succubus, and men are free from guilt, remaining morally stronger. So, if I were Newton and a woman, I might have chosen freedom instead of accepting a list of predestinated humiliation. Here are the pictures. See anything unusual?"

Konrad looked at one particular painting made of Newton. The poet William Blake's stunning painting, *Newton*, was a much deeper painting than met the eye. Blake portrayed a muscular scientist oblivious to God's creation by making his wrapped-up thoughts stuck in the circle he draws with his compass. Found at the bottom of the ocean bending over naked to draw a circle on a scroll growing from his head, Newton is quietly downgraded to an alone man living in a bubble, unable to step outside of his circle. The compass is a scientific instrument that clips the wings of imagination, leaving Newton blinded to the beauty of the surrounding world.

Art is the tree of life. Science is the tree of death, Konrad contemplated Blake's bizarre poem he had related to the painting. He shrugged. Blake was convinced his paintings were divine art instructed and encouraged by Archangels.

You don't want to debate on angels' genders...

"Look at the Adam's apples," Ruut said, touching her throat.

In the many portraits of Newton, painted by all the leading artists of his time, he wore a fashionable full-bottomed wig of the 17th century. Konrad stroked his own prominent Adam's apple. "The neck area is covered... and his head's angled badly in all of them."

"Coincidence? What if the most famous scientist known through an apple had no Adam's apple? What if Newton is revealing his greatest secret to us?"

"Impossible."

"Don't shoot the messenger yet. The riddle is layered like an onion. Apparently, the pattern is taken from Matthew 7:7, where Jesus says: 'Ask, and it shall be given you; seek, and ye shall find; knock, and it shall be opened unto you.'"

"You think that if we break the code, Newton will reveal his true gender? Even if the historians see him as a misogynist?" Ruut continued.

"Not being interested in chasing girls and wanting desperately to get laid, wouldn't be a symptom of misogyny, now would it?"

Konrad gave a tight smile. He leaned deeper into the sofa, put his hands on the top his head and let out a deep, weighted sigh. "Nothing is 100 percent accurate in history, not even if the evidence points in one direction..."

Ruut's phone vibrated in her pocket. She looked at the screen and said, "Jake. Excuse me a sec."

As she took distance and privacy, Konrad reluctantly pondered the plausibility of her idea, scrunching up his nose in distaste. As an avowed atheist, he had dedicated his life to promoting science and skepticism; he had an eye for superstition and pseudoscience, and he knew the weight of the gauntlet of criticism. The critique made him work even harder, but the meaning of their pursuit got lost at his wrecked reputation. Even though it seemed they were moving in the direction of a grand reveal of Newton's personal life, it would only hit entertainment news. There was no career springboard.

"Where do the moon and sun shine across?" Ruut said to the

phone. "Uh-hum... Right..."—a giggle—"Thank you, dear."

Konrad cleared his throat.

A slow flush spread across Ruut's face. "Sorry, I forgot this was our thing. But Jake guessed that the moon and sun shine *to* a cross, not across."

Konrad contemplated her repeating blushes. Why did a woman with high self-confidence hesitate like that?

"Unless it's hidden in plain view. I used to hide candy from Jake and Netta in a coffee machine or vegetable box, and they couldn't find it even though they'd sweep through the kitchen closets." Ruut inspected the cover of The Bible. "The cross... Jesus's cross was made of wood. Knock on wood..." Ruut tapped the cross with her forefinger. Something flashed in her eyes as if she'd seen the future in a clairvoyant's flawless quartz sphere. "Holy cow!"

In a heartbeat, Ruut grabbed The Bible and rushed into the kitchen, Konrad tagging along.

"What are you doing?"

Ruut opened and slammed the door of the freezer.

"You put it inside?"

She breathed from the top of her lungs. "I found her."

Konrad probed her enraptured eyes. "Whom?"

"The whore!"

A heavy knock landed on the door.

"Are you expecting somebody?" Ruut asked.

Konrad glanced outside of the window. He ducked.

"My neighbor. Pretty pissed off. I'm not home."

"What have you done now?"

"Nothing." Konrad sighed. "I think I just killed his mailbox."

"Are you a drunk?"

Konrad shook his head. "I don't drink. I only take a few beers now and then, and then I become someone else. He's the drinker."

RUUT LEANED BACK against the freezer, protecting it like a guard except for the permanent smile.

"Your neighbor saw me." Ruut took gum from her pocket, started chewing, waved. "His jaw dropped. Eyes wide. Now he's leaving."

Konrad stood, chewed the inside of his cheek, unable to string a single sane sentence. He had walked this path to its end, and the boots of logic were stuck in sucking mud.

I need a cold shower. A vacation. A reboot.

"Konrad," she said, her voice unable to mask her enthusiasm. "I'm glad you used *The Wicked Bible* as a tire block last night."

"Why?"

"Because Newton's sordid whore has one rare specialty with water—antimony expands on cooling."

"How do you exactly know all this? I thought lead is all you need in ammunition. Mass is one of the variables in determining kinetic energy. The heavier the bullet, the more energy it has and the more damage it does, right?"

"Lead is dense. It gives it good flight characteristics and good penetration. It's fairly soft, so it's easy on the barrels. But depending on the level of hardness the shooter needs, it can be easily hardened with simple alloys. Antimony makes the adjustments possible."

"There's antimony in the cross," Konrad hypothesized.

"There she is," Ruut said. "There's a higher purpose for all the puns and riddles. I believe Newton's imitating the essential feature of God's design for the world."

You managed to pick up my curiosity. Damn woman.

Konrad folded his arms. "What are you expecting to find? A new tantric manual?"

She slightly lowered her head. "If so, can I keep it?"

"Sure." Konrad uttered a laugh. But without warning a sharp memory bombarded his psyche: Oona slowly licking her lips in a sign of lust. Coldness seeped into his bones. He turned toward the window, willed his trembling hands still, stared off into the woods. The memory of her smile whipped past him like a breeze of wind, but that was all. Even the incident was still a black hole if he tried to probe his memory.

"My ex-wife repeatedly warned me about my crusades against religions: 'Without spirituality, you build rooms that run out of oxygen.'"

Ruut snapped her gum in her mouth. "She sounds smarter than you. Is she an architect?" Before he managed to answer, she offered her phone and asked, "Can I borrow your charger?"

He took the phone and plugged it to a free cord. The screen sprang to life.

"The house," Ruut said, "it feels healthy. Did your wife build it?"

"I peeled the logs, broke the ground, poured the foundation, raised the frame, and—"

"Liar."

"Well, I did paint the rooms. Julia did everything when I was at work. She even ran the wires. There's nothing she can't fix."

Ruut buried her smiling face into her palm, her expression stating the obvious: "Men's hazardous work..."

Her phone rang on the table, only once, but Konrad managed to see the caller's Facebook picture on the screen. The abnormal eye contact of the boy's cheerless gray eyes. The punch-worthy face.

Gideon.

"My big man," Ruut said. "Old enough to think he's independent, but money is always welcome."

"Where is he?"

"Long story. He lives with his dad, who's not into discipline as I am. Gideon probably asks for a youth gathering. I'll tell you about it later."

"Why do you care about teens so much?"

"Remember my mom? She once reversed her car from a garage to the road and over it to the ditch. As I went to save her, looking at the front of the car aimed at the sky, I thought she probably died of a heart attack. She survived, but she was mad at me."

"She accused you?"

"No. She swore and blamed teenagers for sabotaging the rear mirrors of her car. That's why she couldn't see the road."

Konrad chuckled.

"Although her eyesight was weakening, no doctor canceled her driving license. She managed to drive off the road into a snow bank twice before I realized that she couldn't see where the road stopped and snow banks began. She always blamed someone else. I had to steal her keys."

"You did the right thing."

"I guess," Ruut said. "But my mother's bad behavior forced me to follow her prejudice to its roots. I found fear. And I realized that the only human tragedy in life is unrealized potential. It's the greatest enemy of the younger generations and to anyone who thinks being right is more important than unity."

Konrad crossed his arms, contemplated her words. They spent one minute with the freezer humming over silence.

He took a step closer. "Open Sesame?"

Ruut's eyes crinkled at the corners. "Cross your fingers."

She took the Bible out of the freezer and set it on the table. She instinctively turned the cross like a door handle.

They stared at the cover.

Then at each other.

Flabbergasted.

Ruut spat her gum into the trash bin. She had been right with the antimony; the cross did expand and solidify. But it also crumpled like a King's wax seal, revealing a Latin carving.

"*Coitus more ferarum*?" Ruut said.

"I'm no Weird Sex Buddha," Konrad said, scratching his head, "but I guess Newton dreamed of thoughtless and careless sex without consequences just before a major disaster."

"Apocalypse sex? Is that what it means?"

Konrad was pulling at his ear. "For the ancient Romans, it meant sex in the manner of wild beasts."

"Doggy style," Ruut said with loaded puzzlement as if to gain more insight. "What does that have to do with the end times?"

"Everything and nothing," Konrad replied. "All pronouncements of doom are tragicomic. Every generation has believed it was near the end. See the symbols underlining the text?"

"Seven symbols. Trumpets? As in the Revelations, in the visions of the Apostle John?"

"The seven Trumpet Judgments," Konrad concurred. "The first six are wake-up calls to the sinners, each subsequent trumpet's blast bringing more death and destruction. The seventh trumpet's blast, however, marks the end of human government and the establishment of the Kingdom of God."

Ruut examined the trumpets closer. "The seventh is broken."

"Maybe you broke it."

"Or it could mean that the final warning can't be heard. Do you like porn by the way?" she suddenly asked. "I happen to know that in the army men don't only have itchy trigger fingers..."

"What does that have to do with anything?"

"According to Oona, porn works as a substitute for the deeper need of intimacy. You said Newton lacked a close relationship. Even you can't look nor appreciate a woman's beauty anymore without making it erotic. That corrupts the chance for the real intimacy. And that damages the fruit of sexuality—the children."

"We can argue the effects of porn later," Konrad said. "Do you still honestly think this has anything to do with Newton? That he somehow kept his sexuality in control through this book?"

"Yes."

"So, for Newton even wet dreams were forbidden? No nocturnal adventures?"

"Actually, God provides men the release of extra sexual power during the night..."

Ruut's phone rang.

"You have to take the next leap of faith on your own," Ruut started for the door. "Jake is expecting me."

"What about our crusade?"

"Your crusade," Ruut said with a blink of an eye and seductive swing of her hips at the closing door.

How to seduce an army.

Konrad went to pack the medical bag with *The Wicked Bible*. There was something strange in the trumpet symbols and font that just now met his eyes. Runic writing. Scratched letters that bore no curving forms but direct, sharp lines that were easier to carve into a tree or hit in stone. He guessed it was typical to Nordic shamanism.

There was one expert specialized in Nordic mythology at the university.

Out of the cauldron into the fire...

12

A CANON DIGITAL REBEL EOS 300D bobbed against Gideon's chest as he made his way deeper into woods of Ounasvaara. Past the burn of strained tendons in his back, he coughed and grimaced, considering quitting snowboarding after all his torturing accidents. He didn't even remember where he had hurt his back.

He had always been good with snow. His snowboarding videos on YouTube with a hundred thousand subscribers proved it. But success in social media was filling a void. He wanted to focus on photography, to turn a new leaf. Either it was the deathly dull lull in front of a computer—like most of his friends —or interacting with the real world.

The trees stood naked barely without any snow covering their limbs, which made him rethink the month and the days left till the Christmas holidays. Only a fortnight until freedom when he could do this all day and with better equipment. Pictures told not only a thousand words; they were much safer than other people anyway.

Photography keeps me rooted; it's my family.

The winter woods fed and kept its secrets in a tight fist, but here the animals that usually survived by fighting the cold for food seemed to end up being the skeletons of its closet. He planned to immortalize a bit of that mystery. That despairing silence. He wanted to become a freelance photographer just like Kaspar, his father.

I'll make you proud.

A raw instinct told him to stop. He checked the ISO setting, and raised the camera on the bony hollow of his cheek. Eye pressed against the rubber eyepiece cup, he looked through the viewfinder, steadying his breath.

Something small moved in his direction from behind the spruces.

Gideon knew the noise of the shutter would scare off any animal.

He had only one shot.

A white bird came into his view, walking toward him.

A willow grouse.

Gideon took the picture and closed his eyes after the horrible mechanical sound of the old camera.

The bird disappeared. But as he let the camera hang freely on his chest, he felt the bird leaning on his leg. Was it sick? He thought of taking a picture at arm's length, but his mind started racing, and a slight chill rippled through his neck.

Are you seeking safety?

He knelt. The bird leaned its head against him, and he gave it a gentle pat on the head. "Don't worry; I'll be your guard."

Gideon scanned the woods. Was there a chance that the bird was choosing the presence of lesser evil between two beasts?

He pressed the handle grip of the camera tighter in his palm.

Fuck it.

He walked deeper into the woods, mustering courage with the idea that an epic picture always involved high risks. As the grip of the trees grew tighter and tighter around his body, he made his best effort to fend off fear. The deeper he delved, the more snow there was on the top branches of the trees. Unflinching, he received a dozen snow showers on his neck.

He arrived at a glade he had never seen before, although he knew the forest inside out. The ground was obscured entirely by fog, which gave a great contrast to an old tree standing in the middle of the glade.

It still bore leaves, silver in color.

The snow-bewigged spruces surrounding the glade shot skywards, and from their divine heights they seemed to study this small anomaly like grand masters of the British high court. For several seconds Gideon sensed the trees in a new way as if he could feel sap moving inside them, becoming packed closer to the tree. And as a result, snow melted down from their branches.

Suddenly blood in his system packed to his front as well; a stronger-than-magnet pull unbalanced him onto his toes until he needed to take a step forward.

Impossible.

Watching the tree through the mingling vapor of his breath, he sensed a strange pulse beating inside the tree, resonating with his heartbeat. As if the tree were a living being.

An involuntary shiver ran down his spine.

For years the photography of stop-motion animations was the closest thing to magic. And magic made life worth living for.

Gideon closed his left eye and took the tree into the viewfinder, amusing himself with the thought of making a career as a Greenpeace activist, saving trees hug by hug.

He relaxed his shoulders, slowed his breathing. As he zoomed and manually focused the objective, a phosphorescent source of light came into view on the bark of the tree.

A hand mark.

Fear snaked into his gut.

The mark wasn't there a few seconds ago.

13

K ONRAD STAMPED THE wet slushy snow from his boots on the banks of a pond adjacent to the university. Passing by a snowmobile, he stepped on the dark ice that seemed not to be ice at all. There were footprints gathered with water. They belonged to a man who was ice fishing.

Professor Lennart Klemetti was a Sámi specialist and notorious 'lifestyle cynic.' Probably much like the rest of the Sámi people Konrad knew, always complaining about their downtrodden rights. Geographically, Konrad knew that the Sámi, or Lapps, were an indigenous population who occupied the northern fringes of Norway, Sweden, Finland, and the Kola Peninsula of Russia. Lennart had been his colleague just behind the wall next to his office for twenty years, although they never spoke to each other. But rumor had it that Lennart's doctor had given him a death sentence. A few months to live just when he was about to retire.

Konrad needed to show him what Ruut and he had discovered.

Troubling symbols.

Konrad cupped his hands and blew them warm, then took steps, fearing his foot going through the ice. The cold water didn't make him shiver. Getting out of the ice was easy with the ice claws hanging on his chest. Only the *suddenness* of the fall cast shivers down to his spine.

Lennart's gray fur hat was pulled low but not against the cold, more for the sake of privacy. He peered over his round silver-rimmed glasses at Konrad. Droopy-eyed basset hound, bloodshot eyes. A double chin, long white nose hair, and a matching unibrow. The man was weak like a thirsty-looking houseplant.

"Now, isn't it the sexual predator of the year?" Lennart shifted to stare at his ice fishing rod. "Why don't you go swing your dick someplace else?"

"I need to ask you something."

No response.

Konrad eyed him with concern. He took a step closer. "How well do you know the ancient Sámi symbols?"

"How many years, Konrad, did we study and plan our stuff in our offices? A stranger to a stranger, aren't we? Little did I know that I was neighboring a freak of nature."

Konrad rubbed the back of his head.

"But you're a brave man," Lennart's tone changed rapidly. "You make and try out new things. Push yourself, challenge yourself, receive setbacks. What would our society be without beloved crooks like you? Would we die of boredom?"

Konrad shrugged. Lennart moved an unlit smoke under his hairy nose, slowly, back and forth. The old wristwatch in his right hand looked valuable.

"Here, I brought you a bottle of wine," Konrad took a bottle from his backpack. "A gift."

Lennart stopped fidgeting. He put the cigar in the package and pocketed it.

"Insatiable cellular tumors are ravaging my body. Even my cancer has cancer. How do you suppose I'm going to enjoy that if I'm not allowed to enjoy a single bloody smoke?"

Dry, persistent coughing followed.

Konrad looked down, feeling like a harlequin clown from the Commedia Dell'Arte. "Is there anything I can do?"

Lennart's eyes narrowed, and his double chin trembled like Jell-O. "Dying is certainly a good thing. It's the only private thing in life. I appreciate kind comments, gifts, and advice, but for fuck's sake! I don't need doctors and charlatans advising me how to live my life. Like everybody's eager to tell their father how to fuck!"

Finding no place to sit, Konrad went into a Slavic crouch and drew out *The Wicked Bible*. He had ripped off the skin following a gut feeling. On the other side of the skin was a cosmos and mystery of its own.

"What book is this?" Lennart asked.

Konrad told him.

An open stare followed rapid blinking.

Lennart spent a full minute contemplating the images that together formed an old mental map or landscape. He smelled the cover and inspected the symbols with the tips of his fingers, ran them trembling on the separated skin. An old drum membrane, Konrad had concluded.

"And you suppose Isaac Newton made this?" Lennart said.

"Hardly possible. He never left the mainland of England. But he was long periods away from publicity..."

"The membrane is made in Finland."

"How can you tell?"

"A shamanic drum is always a precious source of insights into the Sámi cosmos. The Swedish and Norwegian drums were heliocentric, there was the sun pictured in the center of the membrane. This one has a threefold or three-layered picture of the cosmos; taken from a typical Finnish Lapland drum. The Upper World is the world of gods and spirits. The Middle World is the spiritual realm of the material world, the everyday world in which we live. Below is the world of the ancestors and animal spirits and the gods of the Underworld. A third Finnish drum type, fusion, combines these two: in addition to the threefold worldview, there was the sun in the middle or a world tree. Yours is a fusion."

"The thing in the middle, it's the world tree?" Konrad asked.

"There are some artistic liberties taken. Instead of an ordinary world tree, it's like a gigantic Nil; a Sámi food storage hut built above the ground and out of reach of predators. I have never seen this symbol without stairs leading up to the hut. And what is even more unconventional is who is portrayed living up there: Akka, the fertility Goddess, and wife to Ukko, the supreme Thunder God. Sexuality was never described so openly. Like there was a betrayal, Akka having sexual intercourse with a witch *noaidi* who has antlers."

Konrad crossed his arms. "Is the human reindeer strange?"

"The reindeer was the most important animal to the Sámi. Reindeer symbolizes prosperity. Many folktales involve marriages between a human and a reindeer. It's strange that the structure of the hut starts from below, crosses the central world and continues to the sky above."

"What about the surrounding trees?"

Lennart made a knowing grin. "We live with trees in an elemental embrace, both in a biological and symbolic sense. Trees provide a connection to the heaven; they are the symbolic links to the truth. We have always turned to them for shelter and food, medicine and fire, weaponry and tools. I trust you know to what extent trees are celebrated in every religion and pagan worldview out there."

Konrad drew a mental list: Buddha gained enlightenment

while sitting under a Sacred Fig tree; Jews celebrated the holy day Tu B'Shvat, a new year for trees; in Islam Allah's name written in Arabic resembles the branches of a tree. In Norse cosmology, the tree of life was an eternal green Ash tree, Yggdrasil. Jesus's iconic death, redeemed sins on a wooden cross. In cathedrals and churches around the world stone columns towered and curved into arches the way branches extend. Arched passageways in the garden are silent spiritual transformation, rebirth. And what would Christmas be without the China-machined decorations of spruces?

"Does the phrase 'A thief in the night' mean anything to you?" Lennart suddenly asked.

"No. Why?"

"It reads here."

Konrad looked where Lennart pointed. He didn't see.

"Forest for the trees, Konrad. Forest for the trees."

After a while, the letters found their way into Konrad's consciousness, the words masterfully hidden in the surrounding forms of trees. They were Jesus's words, a promise of His second coming at the end of the tribulation.

"It means nothing to me."

"Then we've run out of business," Lennart said, grabbed the bottle and took a swig. "Maybe you should ask your wife's help." He pointed at the ring finger in Konrad's hand and offered the bottle with his right hand.

Konrad reached for the bottle, but it slipped from his fingers. Lennart reached for it, but Konrad was faster and put his left hand on his wrist.

"I got this." Konrad tasted the wine. "Thanks. I'm not married, by the way."

"Yeah, me neither." Lennart showed his ring in his finger. "My wife died a year ago. I can't let her go because by holding her I feel I can still keep her close. Grief uses elbow tactics, but it becomes more translucent when you get used to it. By the way, your ring could tell your future if we gave it a spin on the drum."

"Bone hopscotchery? Are you a shaman?"

"I'm not going to *yoik* if that's what you're afraid of."

Unasked, Lennart stretched the skin to a metal fishing bucket, but he had nothing to tie it down.

"I think I'll pass," Konrad said.

"Noaidis ate seven dotted fly agaric to get into a trance before drumming. Wait, there's another way around to achieve the state of trance." Lennart raised fish from the bucket. "Drinking fish entrails."

Konrad pressed hands against his stomach and shook his head.

"Suit yourself. But be careful if you decide to try it out yourself. The drum was a means to connect with the dead. The Sámis believed that noaidis, the spiritual leaders, could heal a person gravely ill by bringing the soul back or finding out what had to be offered to make the person well again. Inexperienced as you are, you can't be sure what spirits you'll unleash. The realm of the dead is no playground. Beyond is upside down, the dead walk against our feet—and they can drive you crazy."

"I think I'll manage."

"Sure you do," Lennart said, reeling a fish up from the hole. "You're doing so well."

Konrad forced a smile. Time for a smooth exit.

"Take care, Lennart. I owe you one. I'm glad we finally spoke. I wish we hadn't started from the wrong end."

"Yes, weird knowing you. I'm going to take back as much time I have been neglecting myself as possible." Lennart grumbled, mostly to himself. "What an idiot have I been when I tried to deny my old man's pleasures when he was dying..."

Lennart lit a matchstick. Konrad walked away, dialed Ruut, and put his leather gloves on. It was getting cold.

A woman waited on the shore.

KASPAR NYMAN STARED from inside a parked car on the eastern shore, as Konrad walked on the ice. He dumped his cigarette and prepared for action. A cheaply dressed and messed-up woman moved toward Konrad's position on the bank. The meeting was going to be the final proof against the professor. Soon the man would be bombarded with an inferno of questions.

Time to make money.

He considered his options and the risks involved.

A long second sought its end.

Stealing and anonymously selling the Bible would only make himself the target, so he shoved his fake gun and fake patch deep into the glove compartment.

He attached a telephoto lens to his systems camera.

A few deep breaths.

He opened the car window.

14

THE WOMAN WAS a unique cocktail of difficulties.

"Do you have a light, handsome?" she asked.

Konrad evaluated the dark-haired woman, who had appeared out of nowhere while he had listened to Ruut's voice on the line. Her eyes were unfocused in her bony face. In her black tattered pair of jeans and cheap jacket, she looked like an underfed vulture with a drug addiction.

"...Gideon called me," Ruut said, "there's something urgent he wants to show me in the woods. He used the word *miracle*. Not his vocabulary. He adores his father, but during difficult situations, he turns to me..."

"Hello? Light me up, baby," the woman said, cracking an unreadable smile.

"Sorry, I don't smoke."

"Sure you do. I saw you there with your drinking pal." She stepped into Konrad's path.

Konrad gazed at her eyes, confused.

"... and needless to say," Ruut spoke in his ear, "you are carrying a bag of gold with you. Do not leave it unguarded..."

"I'll call you later." Konrad shoved the phone into his pocket. "Look, Ma'am—"

The woman's sharp intake of breath cut Konrad's voice off. Blinking seductively, she moved closer to him, but her face blanched. Clumsily, she crashed to the ground at his feet.

Konrad knelt. "Are you okay?"

The woman looked up, an open wound bleeding from the corner of her eye.

Konrad's stomach clenched in dread. Did she just cut herself?

She backed away on all fours. "Help! A rapist! Help me!"

Konrad's heart skipped beats.

"Are you insane!?" Konrad walked after her, offering a helping hand.

"Stay away from me. Help!"

"I'm not going to hurt—"

"Help me! A rapist!"

The woman fumbled at her face with a trembling hand. The blood spread across her face.

"You did that on purpose!" Konrad shouted.

"Now did I?" The woman asked and flashed a questing smile: what are you going to do about it? "Help! HELP ME!"

Konrad clenched his fists. "Have it your way then."

He threw his gloves to the ground, opened his jacket and took the ice claw around his neck. He hovered it in the air, threateningly. Then he raised the sharp edge of steel higher and lacerated the back of his neck. Hand and the ice claw pooling with blood, he stepped closer to the woman whose face was ghost white. Konrad grabbed her hand, put the ice claw to her open palm.

"Grab it."

The woman looked at her fist in disbelief; the reality shoe-horned into her mental box: her fingerprints on the assault weapon.

"Your move, sister." Konrad watched her scrambling up and collecting herself. She let the bloody ice claw slip to the snow from her hand.

The woman staggered away, her arms creating a barrier across her chest.

Numbness set into Konrad's body and pain in his neck started spreading. A disembodied voice called his name.

"Konrad?"

Ruut—did I forget the line was open?

Konrad put the phone to his ear only to find out that the battery was dead.

Does she think that I attacked the woman?

Exiled into despair, he missed Lennart moving behind him and putting his hand on his shoulder.

That single touch brought instant tears to his eyes, soothed the length of his body.

"That was a low blow," Lennart said.

"Not the first attack."

Concern dug deep lines into Lennart's face. With the jerk of his head, he signaled there was something else to see.

Konrad focused his gaze to the east over the ice sheet.

Kaspar Nyman.

Shit. I'm finished.

"The man talking on his phone and entering his car photographed your confrontation with the woman."

"He's a cop. He'll take me into custody."

"Not exactly. He's a freelancer. Born and raised in Russia, so he knows propaganda. Your improvised maneuver will look awful on you when he uploads or sells the photos. Another goddamned media spectacle awaits."

Dread respawned in Konrad's stomach. "He might demand money for the photos." *Or fool me out of money and still sell them.*

Lennart coughed hard. The double-bent man's pains overshadowed the pain in Konrad's neck entirely.

"I want to offer more than my sympathies. Here are my keys. Stay in my house if that's any help. I would like to see you nailing that guy's ass on the front page. I'm off to the hospital for treatments. I hope I can still be there when you unearth this mystery. Which reminds me, I made a deliberate mistake with one of the membrane symbols. Show it to me, please."

Konrad thanked Lennart for the offered keys and showed him the membrane.

"This symbol in the hut in the Upper World is not Akka. It's Sáráhkká, generally depicted in The Middle World in Sámi arts, but in the lower parts of the drums. Sáráhkká, the Sámi first mother, is a female goddess equivalent of Venus. She's the protector of home and family and especially of womanhood; she grows the flesh around the soul in the womb and protects girls and women from the cradle to the grave."

Lennart paused to grimace at the pains that came on to him in waves.

Konrad found letters in the hut. "Mánná...? As in manna from the Bible?"

"A double meaning perhaps. Manna in the Bible refers to any divine or spiritual nourishment. The ark of the covenant included a jar of manna among others, such as the Tablets of Stone; the Ten Commandments. 'I am the bread of life' Jesus said. Mánná in Sámi language means a child."

"I see."

"I think there's a promise of a messenger, but it could be a morbid prank," Lennart said. "Playing with the dead brings living nightmares. The membrane portrays the world-view of Sámi peoples in the 1600s and 1700s, before the time when the witch trials swept through the northern regions of Europe. The Crusader-priests believed that the yoiking Lapps pounding their magic drums with transfixed eyes were possessed. They burned the drums and anyone with witch qualities. The fuck heads. Thought the runic drums were instruments of the Devil!" Lennart cursed, coughed, and spat in the wind.

The horrible sounds and helplessness drilled a caustic hole into Konrad's heart.

"The Lapps were pushed aside if they didn't convert. They were forced to morph their rituals into less prominent ways to be one with nature. Time passed, and more protesting Lapps vanished. The memory wore thin. The ones who still dared to yoik started to drink heavily. With that, drinking was bound with the practice of yoiking, serving false gods, and not long after there was nobody left to tap into the dead."

Konrad stared at Lennart. "I wasn't aware of your people's plight."

Lennart coughed forcefully. He dabbed his pain-moistened eyes to his sleeve. "I wasn't aware of your plight either. You—the media—poisoned the very depths of my blood like some fucking fat blockage in my heart's artery. Now I know better. The Gods balance everything in the end. Hopefully the times of great atonement is at hand. Whatever you decide to do now or what discoveries you shall make, respect the wilderness. Honor the dead. But piss on all around your enemies."

Konrad nodded.

Lennart gave a handshake, not avoiding the blood in Konrad's hand. The squeeze was nothing less than a juice extractor.

"Weird knowing you, Konrad," Lennart said, his voice growing severe. "Can I get my wristwatch back?"

15

KASPAR LOWERED A GLASS of wine on the table next to the computer screen and checked his phone, pausing the check up on the RAW images briefly.

Seven calls from her.

You played your role well. But you just have to wait your turn...

Car lights strobe through the busted blinds. He stood, opened them and checked the perimeter, confirming it was only the neighbor's car.

It was full dark, no stars. A perfect moment for his new career.

He closed the blinds and pulled in the curtains. The vision of his journalistic firm started to get flesh around its skeleton as he smiled at the pictures he had been narrowing down and processing these past hours in Adobe Photoshop. Konrad's self-inflicted wound was fabulously genius, but it had only raised the stakes. The pictures he had chosen left no room for questions. Konrad was going down. His carefully masterminded plan paid back all the invested hours and shed sweat.

Out of curiosity, Kaspar went through the pictures he had

already abandoned before deleting them. The weather had been on his side, the horizon at the background perfectly balanced. He considered himself a famous artist whose name was on the rising tide.

But one detail made him frown.

The skeptic in him shook its head at the possibility. He scowled at his imagination.

But he made a duplicate and decided to zoom in.

The air around him grew crisp and cold. With a few mouse clicks, he magnified the background.

A man with binoculars he had taken for a birdwatcher who stood behind a black van at the far western edge of the pond held something familiar to Kaspar. Another camera-like object on a stick possibly aimed at the professor and his friend on the ice.

A laser microphone?

It was used to eavesdrop with zero chance of exposure. But it was usually used to hear a conversation in a room that was beyond access or bug. The two men weren't behind a vibrating window that would record spoken sounds. Unless he was missing something.

From another picture, he recognized the man.

A Russian war veteran.

He took a sip of his glass of red wine. A draft raised his neck hair. He remembered talking on the phone with his woman assistant inside his car.

Behind a window...

A shadow flashed in the wine glass on the table, but before he could even react, he felt cold metal pressed against the back of his skull.

A man's deep chilling voice said, "Do. Not. Move."

∾

THE STREETS WERE DARK, wet, and asleep. Gideon strode faster on the road to home, squinting at the freezing drizzle of the night. Tomorrow he would lead his mother to the woods to witness an incredible phenomenon.

He had touched the tree, seen an unexplained darkness. As if it had touched him back.

She had suggested that the maniac university professor might also be interested in the tree because of some related mystery.

Not in a million years.

And to his father, he would say nothing. Maybe after he had taken more pictures, investigated the place and done his first report. He chuckled at the notion of doing something that began to sound like school. Perhaps there was light at the end of the tunnel after all. He occupied his mind with an image of himself boasting with a world-famous photo.

The dream stopped short.

A tall stranger came out of his home.

Gideon jammed his hands deeper into his hoodie's pockets and walked past the path leading to the house. He quickly side-glanced at the man and noted an Easton ice hockey bag on the man's shoulder. Its shape made him think of a body bag.

His heart leapt into his throat.

With the gaze of the dark man in his neck, he took a turn right at the dead-ending street. Walking on the path to his neighbor's house, reading the resident's name in the mailbox— Pantzar—he stole another glance.

The man and the bag disappeared into a big van Mercedes, but another man kept an eye on him via the wing mirror.

The house in front of him was dark. He was not friends with the owner, Iris. The first time he had taken a shortcut across her lawn to a playground, the cranky old granny had accused him of being a terrorist. He had tested her nerves more than he could recall. Once he had raised his middle finger at her, and she had called the cops on him. The cops had come to the playground to address him on false claims about destroying the old woman's garden.

She had vandalized her own bushes, and his father had to pay the bill.

Gideon rang the bell, his stomach clenching.

He started counting to ten and repeated the ringing on four.

Nothing stirred in the house.

The driver of the car came out. Gideon could sense his alert gaze stab.

Another ring.

Please... please...

A reflection in the window of the house sent him into a panic: the driver moved toward him on the street.

A light sprang life inside the house.

Gideon could hear curses behind the door.

Quickly!

Iris's short but quick steps were now audible, and Gideon knew he had only one option to get inside.

The door opened.

"This had better be important—" Iris initiated.

"I'm sorry," Gideon said, teary-eyed.

The old woman opened her mouth but suppressed her hatred. Then something lit behind her cloudy eyes. She yelled over Gideon's shoulder to the man behind him.

"Get your filthy ass off my yard! Now, or I'll call the cops!"

She let Gideon inside and cast a grim dragon's eye at the man, who withdrew to the car and gunned it away.

Fuming, the old woman slammed the door shut and turned to face Gideon. She had to unclench her teeth to get the word out.

"You little brat. You almost gave me a heart attack. Explain yourself, what was all that about?"

16

KONRAD PEEKED OUT of the frost-rimed window of Lennart's old veteran's house where an ongoing battle between wooden tar tools and mold made his head dizzy and stuck to his clothes. Here and there the walls bore creepy antlers of different sizes. There was also a balding and undecorated Christmas tree put into the stand, so he gave it water, but couldn't locate any decorations.

Outside in the dark was Lennart's sauna and a sawn hole in the ice for swimming. He flashed on an icy memory in which he came second in the ice swimming world championships held in Kemijoki in Rovaniemi in 2014. His pride switched to agony when at the opposite side of the partly frozen river, the more-recent memory of the explosion replayed. Oona had shattered his life and reputation all at once.

Now it was Winter Solstice, the shortest and darkest day of the year. The velvety cool blackness engulfing the house caused a surge of mistrust to wash over him, convincing him that everybody had their share in the lie, that the arc of morality had fallen flat.

He switched on the phone that was recharging. As the loading phase went on and on, Konrad tried to reach a consensus with himself whether Ruut was the only one he could trust.

A long, agonizing moment ticked by, then notifications hit the screen one after another.

Eight SMS messages from Ruut.

21.12.2017

10.54 a.m. *Are you okay?*

10.56 a.m. *Did you get caught in a fight? Can't reach you.*

11.00 a.m. *Call me. ASAP.*

11.55 a.m. *Netta is sick. I have to pick her up from school. Quality time, yay!*

12.15 p.m. *Sorry for bombarding u with these. Worried...*

15.12 p.m. *Konrad???*

16.20 p.m. *Gideon called. His father's house hit by burglars. Father missing. Going to check the house.*

17.34 p.m. *What a glory hole... Men... My old neighbor who likes advising me in upbringing methods said that she had called the cops after Gideon...*

THE CLOCK READ 18.00 P.M. He dialed her.

"Konrad!" Ruut's answer was instantaneous. "Thank God."

Konrad laid out the conversation with Lennart and his encounter with the woman.

"What the hell was she thinking?"

"Tell me about it. There was also a freelancer immortalizing the whole episode. I met him in the hospital when I woke up from the coma."

Ruut paused. "You were immediately questioned?"

"It turned out I was scammed. Kaspar Nyman was the guy's name."

"Excuse me?" Ruut said with a rise in her tone. "Kaspar Nyman?"

"Yes. I don't know how he fooled the guards and the system. Perhaps bribes."

"Jesus."

"Not your problem. But Jesus is."

"You always deflect sympathy like this?" Ruut said, concluding the funny games. "I remember seeing a picture of you in the media taken in the hospital. You were unconscious on the hospital bed. So, it was Kaspar..."

"It doesn't matter... wait.... What? You know him?"

"He's my ex-husband, Gideon's father. I'm at his place as we speak."

The schmuck's name boiled Konrad's blood. He counted to three in his head. "What's going on there? Anything missing?"

"Nothing's gone. Only Kaspar. Wait... you said he photographed you today. I'll check his computer. I'm sure he hasn't changed his password. Stay on the line."

Konrad probed his memory. He returned to the moment of stealing Kaspar's watch. The carving—abracadabra.

"Is a woman named Julia there?" he asked.

"Wait, I'll put you on the speaker."

"Is Julia there?" Konrad heard Ruut stop writing with the keyboard.

"How do you know her?"

"Kaspar mentioned her."

Pause. Keyboard noises. "Liar. Kaspar never spoke of her. He harbored everything about her. Not even after she caused our marriage to break up did he talk about her."

Third wheel. Crap.

There was no hint of sourness or condemnation in Ruut's voice. Konrad gave in, "Alright, I confess. I—"

"You stole something from him."

Unable to conceal surprise from his voice, "Actually—"

"Kleptomania. It would explain why you pocketed that silly saltshaker at the university while playing table chess."

Konrad shook his head. "It's more like the thrill-of-the-act kind of thing."

"Uh-hm." Ruut's unarticulated comment made it clear she didn't buy his explanations. "If a teen steals, it's a crime and a perfect reason to demonize the youth. If an adult steals, it's an illness and reason to feel sorry. But hey, it's a fucked-up world, so who cares. Okay, I've checked the computer. There's no trace of pictures being processed on the computer. It's strange because Kaspar practically slept with a camera under a pillow and memory cards on his eyes."

Konrad doodled on random papers and started tapping a pencil he found against the table. "What the hell is going on?"

"Wait a minute. Gideon said he saw a black Mercedes parked in front the house. I remember seeing one at the university when I commented on someone's hobby of looking at porn in broad daylight."

"I wouldn't condemn," Konrad said. "Pornography has existed throughout recorded history, in every culture, in every civilization—"

"So, you don't find it problematic that men's brains are on porn everywhere? It starts with scantily clad cheerleaders in every sport you can name, women on sportscar hoods, weather forecasters with low cleavage. Do you know how many men feel trapped by their inability to stop consuming pornography?"

"I didn't mean to pick up a fight or dig into this topic."

"Is it okay for you that a naked female body hijacks your brain, hypnotizes you, and makes you incapable of making good decisions? How many times did you put your marriage at risk for videos of couples having sex?"

"This has nothing to do—"

"Pathetic. You don't give a shit about young minds whose brains are most vulnerable to exploitation. Their closest sex partner is a machine. They warm up faster and are more reliable. Digital gadgets seem to beep more realistic sounding orgasms. And after masturbation, she can be turned off with a press of a button. No wonder teens don't care about sexually transmitted diseases."

There was a long pause on the line. Then a few mouse clicks.

"Konrad?"

He frowned at her voice, which vibrated on a whole new frequency. "Everything okay?"

"I think we're not getting anywhere like this," she said in a sudden 180-degree mood swing. "You know, we haven't considered what the broken commandment of *The Wicked Bible* urges. Besides, I must make a confession. Gosh, how can one get so emotional—I'm beginning to like you, Konrad."

Konrad tried to form a sarcastic comment.

"Spend a night with me," she continued.

"What are you talking—"

"I knew you liked me. I'll be right there. Your address?"

"Raevaarantie 4. But—"

"See you in thirty minutes."

Ruut hug up.

Konrad stared at his phone in utter bewilderment.

What are you up to?

He glanced outside at the moonlit view. A plunge into the black icy water would make the circulation kick and get his head on straight. For as long as he could remember, he had always started the work day with a little dip, in the river or shower, but not because of the day-long energy boost and skin care it provided.

He explained the need to himself as the ritual of being macho.

17

HAIR DRIPPING WET off the back of his head, Konrad opened the front door. Ruut walked straight into his arms, planted a wet kiss on his lips, and forced him to back up to the first bed she could find.

Ruut closed the door and turned off the lights. She was coughing, but before Konrad managed to say anything about the mold, she jumped over him, knocked him on the bed.

She was on top, gazing down at him while removing her jacket, slowly. Seductively.

"Ah, I can feel your erection against my belly," she said, her voice raised an octave. "It's already so big!"

"It's nothing yet, but—"

Ruut placed a hand over his mouth. "Let me find out." She suddenly took a pair of handcuffs out of her pocket and threw the jacket aside.

"Do you trust me?"

Bondgage cuffs? Konrad nodded. *But I'm sure you're bluffing...*

Ruut closed the ratchet rotating arm around Konrad's right wrist, took the chain around a metal bar of the bed frame and secured the other one onto his other wrist. Meanwhile, Konrad let his eyes study her up and down: long-legged, slim and a sexy smile that shamed the moon. But he was ready to stop.

She moaned and roughly turned Konrad on his stomach, placing something next to the pillow.

A weird sensation spiked through Konrad's body as Ruut took off his belt.

"Ruut?"

She kissed his neck and gently pushed the middle of the leather belt into his mouth; and she pulled his head back, holding the belt in one hand, the other finding a way under the clothes of his back.

The phone started to speak. Ruut's ecstatic voice was easy to extract:

"Oh, kiss me, Konrad. Let's make this a night to remember!"

Konrad was unable to speak.

What the heck is this? A recording?

The voices from the phone continued. But atop of him she spoke without words.

Her finger moved rhythmically on his back.

She was writing a warning, letter by letter...

We're in danger.

18

PATRICK PRAYTOR POCKETED his phone at the gates of the forest road that wound down to the old veteran's house where Konrad and Ruut shared a bed.

The Veteran had insisted on getting rid of the insects.

Neutralize the targets, Patrick played back the command in his head. An understatement of the force of the six killing machines at his disposal. Even among the world's special operations elite, his team enjoyed near mythical status. Behind the blacker-than-black backdrop, they changed the course of history. They preserved the ground of life, prepared the way to everything that was good.

One of the soldiers broke radio silence, the voice coming from Patrick's coin-sized subdermal embedded behind his ear.

"Green sniper... sights are hot."

"Blue sniper... you too, Green."

"Green sniper... screw you."

"Blue sniper... already."

"Red sniper... Green, Your Tango is Down at 6 o'clock."

"Blue sniper.... what're you? A priest?"

"Red sniper... your father."

"Blue sniper... don't fuck with me!"

Laughs.

"Alpha. Get your shit together," Patrick said.

In three times, "Copy that, Colonel."

Patrick stretched his neck in his sailor's solid black wool coat that kept his body functioning in the cold and kept him focused.

He looked through his night vision riflescope and took aim at a Rottweiler. The dog was looking in his direction from a cage near the old house.

Scenarios began to rush through his brain. One after another the most dangerous men in the world collapsed in front of him, just like the goal of every responsible hunter to kill or incapacitate an animal—to drop-it-where-it-stands with a single bullet.

The dog initiated a deep growl, but Patrick squeezed the trigger before its alarming bark. Without noise, the dog dropped dead. Beautifully.

His men, from their positions, heard the woman reaching the peak of her sexual excitement. Each one of them knew that only by finishing this mission could they earn lasting peace and return to their families. The Veteran had guided them all on the only path to end all wars, to reach the higher domain of existence. A puppet was free only if it knew its strings and could fully control itself.

You two have nowhere to run.

After spearheading the war on terror for ten years in the top-secret US Army special operations unit, fighting proxy wars on both sides of the ideological fence and preventing many behind a myriad of codes names, he had grown tired of the endless battles, the endless vicious circle of revenge and soul-poisoning hatred.

New world awaits.

The front door opened. Patrick mentally prepared himself, then whispered to the microphone under his sleeve.

"Get ready."

Patrick heard the woman voice in his ear clear as the cold night sky.

"...to McDonald's and then we rent a movie..."

He watched the woman slipping behind the wheel of her Volvo. The man was about to sit next to her.

The beams from the car lit up the house's edifice.

"Damn, I forgot my wallet inside," Ruut said. "Could you pick it up while I'll turn the car around?"

Konrad was making his way inside as the car started reversing. But it stopped. The lights went out and the engine shut off. A few ticks later the car lit the house again, reversing. The path was long and narrowed by trees, and for that intention, there was a short side extension to the road that allowed a car to turn.

"Wait for my command," Patrick said.

The braking lights indicated that the car was slowing down.

It was starting to turn to the side, the lights sweeping along the woods.

But then Patrick saw something unimaginable.

No driver in the window; the car swerved a hard turn back on the main road, launching a full-speed reverse.

Impressive. Ducked with a reverse camera, are we? "Tires!"

A split second later, bullets whizzed through the air from behind the surrounding tree trunks. One tire flat, the car smashed its side against a tree.

Glass shattered.

Patrick looked through the scope for a target. He needed only a glimpse of a head to put it down in a crimson haze.

Bullets flew, the tires exploded on all sides.

The car slammed into a tree with a thud that sent shock waves. Snow fell like a drapery of white fireflies. The tires spun, the damaged wheels shrieking. The car plunged forward from under the snow.

Patrick inhaled the sweet intoxicating smell of gunpowder and started walking the path toward the house. "Finish them."

Raging spurts of fire came from the darkness. They pierced and sliced the air like the reaper's random scythe. The metal frame of the bouncing car was soul-torn by sparkle and flame.

An explosion.

The car was on fire like a medieval battering ram of war. The car slammed through the wall into the garage and buried partly under the snow falling from the roof. A whoosh of flames resounded.

Patrick stopped and made a quick analysis. Could the car have been remotely controlled?

He stood at ease, the sphere of future in full control.

"Alpha, hold your position. Bravo, proceed."

19

KONRAD GAGGED ON the smell of gasoline fumes and gray smoke inside the garage. "Nice driving."

Ruut had sneaked in through the back door. She closed the steering wheel screen on her smartphone app and pocketed it. "A malfunction..."

Dodging the flames, she reached for something through the broken windshield.

Two Glock 17 firearms.

"Take this," Ruut clicked off the safety.

Konrad's ears rang. "What are we going to do?"

"Kill yourself along with your stupid questions."

She was already shooting through the cracks in the wall into the darkness and receiving scores of bullets in return, curses bursting from her lips. Konrad jolted back to his senses. He tightened the shoulder strap of the medical bag and picked up the fallen keys from the floor for Lennart's Arctic Cat snowmobile that he had been trying to start.

Beats skiing by a mile.

The growing flames lit the dark garage orange. Bullets tore

through the wooden structures like they were made of paper. Konrad fired up the engine.

In the left hand of the side rear mirror, someone attacked Ruut. A knife flashed at her throat. Konrad whirled and heard the attacker whispering something in her ear.

"Ruut!" Konrad tripped and fell shoulder-first on the cement floor. He reached for his slipped weapon and pointed at the two shadows now struggling.

He closed his non-dominant eye, locked his hand and shoulder, and squeezed his hands around the grip.

Bang!

The bullet lodged inside the attacker's heel, sending his face up like of a howling wolf.

Konrad kept a white-knuckled grip on the grip of the gun.

I shot at a man...

Ruut took the knife out of the attacker's hand.

"*Chyort voz'mi!*" the man shouted as the blade shot through below his jaw all the way up to the upper part of his mouth. He gargled blood bubbles. Ruut pushed the man until he stood outside. A quick rain shower of lead exploded the man's head, splatters of blood and brain matter sprayed Ruut's face. He dropped dead onto his knees like a limbless doll.

Ruut gazed at Konrad, her eyes wide, both sharing the same question.

Russians?

The reality sent a bolt of anxiety up Konrad's spine.

Someone barked commands outside; a voice to chill bone marrow.

The car caught on fire.

"Here," Konrad said to Ruut, pocketing the weapon, he jumped on the Arctic Cat.

Ruut ran over, sat behind him and knotted her hands around his stomach. "Go!"

Konrad aimed at the wooden back door, gritted his teeth, twisting the throttle. With mounting terror and a horrible sound of wood exploding around them, they reached the backyard. The car and garage blew up into the sky, lighting up the riverbank before them. Konrad riveted his gaze on the far side of the river, but the ice cover didn't reach that far.

Ruut started to shoot to their left.

Konrad glanced sideways at the neighbor's backyard.

The huge muscle-bound man he had seen at the university stood on a forsaken and partly-crumbled pier, a big sniper rifle nestled in his arms, his head down as if meditating or praying.

"Faster!" Ruut shouted and fired at the man.

Ducking and blinking wind and water from his eyes, Konrad accelerated on the ice full throttle.

Ruut had run out of ammo, but squeezed the trigger repeatedly in some moment of paranoia. A bullet whizzed past Konrad's ear. It broke through the bag strap. The Bible half slid out as the strap loosened, bouncing on the ice. Konrad pulled the bag, the strap tangling tight to his clothes, but he got only the lightened bag.

"Shit!"

"Let it be!" Ruut said. "We still have the membrane."

"There's water up ahead," Konrad screamed. "We can't make it."

Ruut took the second Glock out of Konrad's pocket and shot behind.

"Don't slow down!"

A bullet flew past his temple.

The edge of the ice rushed toward them. Konrad eased on the gas.

"Ruut! We're going to die!"

She reacted instantly, pushed his head down and took the controls.

The engine revved like a demonic beast.

Something burned in Konrad's thigh, and the engine started spilling white smoke. He glanced down, and an intense burning sensation kicked in.

A hit.

He managed to bite through the pain. Luckily, it was only a scratch. He desperately searched for safety in the veils of starting snowfall.

Nothing.

Only black nothingness ahead and below.

"Ruut!"

She pressed her body tighter against him, bullets whizzing past and overhead. Water splashed up in the air, cloaking them with freezing embrace. The transition from the ice to the water happened smoothly, like butter sliding onto a frying pan.

They were too heavy; speed decreased.

Fortunately, they reached an underwater layer of ice. But the snowmobile came to a neck-breaking halt, catapulting them, flying on the ice. They rolled, ducked low, bullets still filling the air at random pulses.

For the span of three skipped heartbeats, Konrad took a mental inventory of his pain and injuries. They were bruised, badly wet, soon freezing to death.

She shot at something.

Once.

Twice.

Konrad had just turned his head when a statue of fire rocketed skywards. Ruut had shot the gas tank and blown the old piece of shit into oblivion. For their protection.

"Crawl," Ruut shouted. "Behind the fire!"

Konrad noted the bullets had stopped flying; either the enemy waited for a clear shot or had withdrawn to circle the lake by car. Ruut's lips were blue; she shook badly. Konrad's body was functioning perfectly. He pulled her slender body behind him.

"After this, you will eat cake to get some warming fat around you."

"Shut the fuck up. We're not safe yet."

The second Konrad raised his head too high a bullet penetrated the flames and the top of his hat.

"Come on! My favorite hat!"

"Lucky bastard."

A voice drew their gazes skyward. Konrad remembered his father had described such a voice before.

"Get down!" he said.

A grenade landed twenty meters in front of them. The explosion sent a myriad of tiny shrapnel all over. As the smoke blew aside, a gigantic hole in the ice appeared. Veins of breaking ice grew closer to their position, and upon reaching them, the ice creaked under their weight.

"For the love of God," Ruut whispered.

They sank through the ice.

Konrad could feel the semi-strong current in the water. Fighting against the pull, he kept his eyes opened and fumbled for Ruut's hand.

Gotcha!

Konrad brought her to the surface. Ruut hyperventilated with the Glock in her hand.

"I can't swim!"

"What?" Konrad took the pistol. "You go ice-fishing with a snowmobile, and now you tell me?"

"I'm going to kill you, Konrad."

"Save your last breath for them. Keep yourself moving because—"

"Hypothermia, I know."

Konrad brought Ruut near the beach on the edge of the

blown-up ice cover. He couldn't get on top of it; the ice either broke under his weight or forced him to slide back.

"I can't breathe," Ruut said, her voice fainter than a whisper.

"You can. Relax." Konrad looked at the beach. Ten meters. So near. Yet so far.

"Stay with me. Keep your hands on the ice. Do not let the current pull you under the ice."

Ruut nodded, her eyes closing and opening like a sleepy-head on watch.

"Count to ten," Konrad said. "Loudly!"

"Yes... to keep me awake... One... two..."

Konrad dived under the water and the ice cover, his head exploding as if he had just received a bullet in the head, a sense of hot blood pouring out of his mouth, nose, and ears.

Excruciating pain.

He took a few breaststrokes and relaxed as much as he could to keep his oxygen storage as full as possible. With but one breath he was part of that dark, desolate space that gave no room for error. After the slide of the third stroke and a kick he hit bottom. He crouched into fetal position and gave a push to the ice on top of him with his back.

Nothing.

He tried again.

Nothing.

There was a hand-sized rock on the bottom. Konrad picked it up and tried to hit the ice with it.

A slow, moronic attempt.

He breathed out.

I'm running out of time.

Panic started taking over. He tried his fists, head, and legs.

The ice didn't budge.

A flash of a Nazi gas chamber hit his vision as he felt his nails leaving scars on the ice. There was no way to blast out of the walls. He looked at oxygen bubbles lingering in the ice and sank to the bottom when he felt it in his jeans...

The Glock.

Konrad aimed, closed his eyes and pulled the trigger.

The recoil hit his jaw hard.

Click, click, click...

Empty.

The mirror of ice shattered. He sprang up from the bottom through the ice out into the night.

"Forty-five," Ruut said, faintly crying. "You said count to ten..."

Konrad circled the hole and went to her rescue, hearing her repeat the line in a stupor. He took off his jacket, crawled the last meters and threw it at Ruut.

"Come on! Take it!"

Her eyes were closed, her breathing shallow through blue lips. Konrad took the gun and threw at her with it.

"Auch! You broke my nose. I'll kill you!"

"That's my girl!" Konrad grinned and threw the sleeve of the jacket at the length of her arm. "Grab it."

Pulling Ruut out of the water was easy, getting her on the beach a bit more complicated as their combined weight defied the fragile ice. They reached solid ground, both blowing out cold steam. Ruut panted.

Konrad tried to annoy her to keep her warm.

"You know, you sure can fake an orgasm."

"Konrad... " Ruut said, "I'm sorry to disappoint you..."

"I was just kidding."

Ruut spoke between breaths. "No, you don't understand..."

"I'm going to take you to the hospital; it's just behind the hill."

Her breathing wheezed.

"Ruut?"

"I've got... Asthma..."

Konrad stopped. His tongue withdrew to his throat and dried out.

Ruut continued, "No hospital. They'll find us."

She collapsed. Konrad barely prevented her from hitting her head on the forest floor they had just entered.

"I'll take you to the hospital."

For a second Ruut's eyes stared back at him, calm but intense as the breathing glow of an ember.

"Take us to the woods. I need to know if that Russian soldier was lying."

"Ruut, whatever that evil man said to you, I don't think—"

"They had captured Oona a year ago."

"What?"

"The soldier said..." Ruut whispered. "They've extracted the *information* from her. She was the *Divine Messenger*. They are like gods now. Soon they'll do... horrors beyond any measure."

Somewhere within his shattered mind, Konrad found a thin logic. Ruut was right. They would have needed them alive if they wanted them to do the job of finding and locating the prophesied one.

"Stay with me!"

"Leave me, Konrad." Ruut fell unconsciousness in his arms.

An oppressive stillness descended.

Konrad gently combed her hair back with his trembling hand.

"Don't die on me. I'll take care of you this time."

He ran.

He ran for their lives.

He ran for the sake of unknown destiny buried ahead.

The air was suddenly thick with mist. Cold trees rustled like living things, and the forest floor bore so many holes and traps and small rolling rocks that it begged for a broken ankle.

Carrying the limb, light-weight woman in his arms, he fled into the woods like a thief in the night.

A thief in the night...

Konrad slid into the ranks of dark trees standing sentry like soldiers on around-the-clock standby.

20

O FFICER THEO KRAFT gazed out of the window of Finnair A350 flight from Helsinki to Rovaniemi and rested his thoughts on the black runway. Welcome shone out in four languages from the embedded screen: *Welcome to Christmas Land!* As though that left any room for error, there was a giant screen outside with double confirmation: *The Official Airport of Santa Claus.*

The airport itself was small and cozy, but the weather was as bad as thirty years ago, just like the old historian sitting next to him had told him. The day that gave rise to the Christmas stories that still span the globe was probably the most anti-Christmas moment imaginable.

But the world bought the tale.

"*Summa summarum,*" the old historian with a facial tic in his eyes continued, "Santa is here because of beer talk. Santa came here to stay thanks to a Concorde flight from London in 1984, planned by two travel agents in a pub. The pilots pulled elf hats on, landed the beaky-nosed sonic boom beast here, and the hundred British guests were treated like kings and queens in a remote Lappish inn with lavish foods and presentations. They drove circles with a few rare snowmobiles partly on grass and met a poor man's Santa Claus. The trip made headlines everywhere; an overnight sensation for the gloating British. Nobody even knew that Rovaniemi had a permit of exception from the government to open the airport because until that Christmas Day it was closed, like all the airports in Finland. The airspace belonged exclusively to Santa and Rudolph and the other flying reindeer."

The man paused briefly to lean closer as if whispering a secret: "Apart from the Northern Lights, Santa is the only thing that brings tourists and their money here. Santa used elbow tactics against Alaska, Greenland, Norway, and Sweden to get Finland Santa Superpower Status. Our government funded his PR world tour from Bollywood to Beverly Hills."

Theo smiled at the historian. "Wonderful story."

"Pleasure." The historian sighed. "The war left an unforgettable memory. Luckily, we have Santa removing the worst traumatic shadows. Even the official airport is a former Luftwaffe base, and the woods surrounding are scarred with dark and consuming history: scattered remains of railroads, barracks, and trenches. They remain uninterpreted for the tourists who come to meet Santa. I wish my story gives a new perspective to look at things. My grandchildren always want to hear the story of how Santa came here to safeguard his secret hiding place. I tell them that if being in the right place at the right time is impossible, one can always study and learn from history."

"Being in the wrong place at the wrong time happens to other people, not me."

"I'm not sure if I understand what you mean, son."

"Let's just say there was only a stain of white in the ground thirty years ago. I still remember how it felt under the snowmobile. And under my feet."

The old man revealed his bad line of teeth. "You were there?"

The plane came to a stop.

People started to remove seatbelts; the air filled with the cacophony of metal clicks.

Theo said, "Add a little snow to your story. It always saves the Christmas."

The historian rose to his feet and shook his head in disbelief. "My wife isn't going to believe this. I acted as the first Santa Claus ever, and I told my best story to a man who happened to be in it. Maybe miracles do happen after all."

"They surely do." Theo offered his hand, and they shook. "Never doubt it."

The historian paused as if weighing Theo's words in his mind, and then he walked away with the others.

Theo sat still. He looked outside. Whispered, "Never. Doubt. It."

He took his phone and stared at the screen.

No contacts.

Where are you, Patrick?

He glanced at his mirror image in the window, liking what he saw: a rested man with determination in the eyes. As the latest Supreme Allied Commander Europe in the fine line of men starting from the European Theatre of World War II and first positioned by Dwight David "Ike" Eisenhower, his was a seat that belonged only to real leaders. They all excelled with one distinct quality: being the first to act. Only a few times had he doubted his motto of acting first and asking questions later. The interrogation of Oona was still a ghost in his mind. Torture was unnecessary. They got answers to every questions they asked.

Moral questions.

Technology issues.

Intelligence problems.

As if she was not born of nature.

A high-ranking Finnish military officer Eric Pantzar entered the plane to discuss with the pilots, the man's lips pressing into a white slash every time he glanced at Theo. Troubling talks loomed up ahead and around the corner. Everything said would remain between the two of them. He wasn't worried about letting this man enter the loop. Oona troubled him. She had somehow regained her erased memory back. What she could remember before she died might manifest itself in her willed *Wicked Bible*.

Eric marched at his direction, his clenched fists already demanding a thorough explanation. Fortunately, they shared a common enemy.

The Russians.

Theo rose to shake hands.

"Eric Pantzar... it's been a while."

Gazing with focus and drawing to his full height, Eric replied, "What are you doing here?"

"Rallying the world to act."

"You haven't come this far to discuss NATO."

"Absolutely not."

"Why then?"

Theo smiled as if sitting on a treasure chest. "A little brain teaser. You are our vassals or our enemies—which twisted country am I talking about?"

Eric's eyes narrowed. "Fuck you, Theo. You're like a mouse chewing through the insulation. Go home. I don't want to hear the word or any NATO shit."

"Speaking of mice," Theo said. "I'm offering you cutting-edge technology against Russians. Did you know that just like human babies, mouse pups calm down when carried around?"

Eric rolled his eyes, inhaled deeply. "Go on."

"I'll tell you why you'll never need to think about joining NATO again. I can make Russians calm. You know why it's the best possible moment to rub shoulders with your twisted big brother?"

Eric crossed his arms, tilted his head. "Why?"

"Because they are making a move on you. Tomorrow Santa Claus meets his Russian counterpart Ded Moroz for the first time ever in Finland, in Santa Claus Village. And that meeting, my friend, is loaded with agendas."

"Don't take my deliberate shortsightedness for blindness," Eric said. "You deserve a punch in the face."

"Let's exchange punches at your office, shall we?"

Eric paused for several beats. He jerked his head. "My fist will be the first and last thing you'll see on Finnish soil."

21

KONRAD KNEW THAT a soldier's survival was based on staying tactical, being on a knife's edge. There was gunpowder within ammunition, but extracting it without proper tools was a fool's errand. Luckily, his Trabant's key fob had a mini flashlight with one AAA Duracell battery. He had only needed a thin piece of metal from Ruut's pocket to connect the battery's ends to light a fire.

The gum wrapper.

He lit small twigs in a hole he had dug, a smokeless fire pit, just like his father had taught him. The roots formed a cavity under a spruce and needed only another hole for a draft of air. When the fire burned from the top downward and dragged air from the air hole, it became a safe heating system. The tiny puffs of smoke were dispersed by the tree above.

He made sure she got all the warmth.

The string of luck continued with the surprise of sphagnum moss. The little swathe of land under the spruce bore excellent water retention properties. The moss had been used in Lapland in insulating mattresses and toddler's nappies, and during the First World War field hospitals in Europe used it as a bandage.

"Antibiotic properties," he whispered his father's words as he blanketed her body that he had to strip. He stayed close beside her.

The mist hung low, shrouding them with an extra blanket. After a few minutes, as he peeked to check, the color was returning to her lips. There was a tree in a glade, bearing a hand mark on an old tree behind a pond. Its frozen-looking leaves made him forget all of the calamity lying ahead. Was this the miracle Gideon referred to?

It was strange how he could produce so much heat. But then his hands started becoming numb, and his legs lost power. His mind desperately sought a way out of his shame and agony.

Shit, shit. Not now.

Ruut opened her eyes and frowned over her shoulder.

"Do I look like I want you so close to me?"

"You're always so close to me, so I thought what the hell."

Ruut's elbow dug into Konrad's ribs. His stiff body produced a few seconds of dull delay as he started getting up.

Ruut grabbed his wrist. She squinted. "Why is your hand shaking?"

Konrad glanced at the pond where the fog was on a dispersing withdrawal and went to fix the strap of the medical bag.

Ruut made a quick analysis. "Cold treatment? What's your diagnosis?"

"Misdiagnosed."

"Multiple sclerosis?"

"You tell me you could see through my MS in fifteen seconds? You doctors are always so far from emphatic in sharing your kisses of death."

"It's not a death sentence," Ruut stated.

"But it's a constant limbo. I'm not ill and not well. Soon I'll be in a wheelchair and become bed bound, being log rolled into diapers."

Ruut gave her best sympathetic smile. "Why do you find it so hard being vulnerable?"

Konrad said nothing.

"Stress makes the symptoms worse, doesn't it?" Ruut studied the muscles in Konrad's arms. "Sudden changes in temperature also. Heat intolerance is often the leading cause of worsening symptoms. Maybe you should take the dip in the water."

"I've been thinking... I'll expose us if I go."

"Liar. You were thinking about the sex we didn't have."

"You are wicked. How can you tell?"

"Hardly rocket science. Your eyes tell." She shoved Konrad aside, reaching for her clothes on a branch.

"By the way," Konrad said, "how did you know we were being followed in the first place?"

Ruut was unable to breathe for a second as she put the moist shirt on her. "I noticed an empty wine glass on Kaspar's desk and got suspicious. He never finished drinks nor his coffee, forget them everywhere. I searched for his camera but couldn't find it. Then I searched his computer. He had a habit of deleting pictures that were for his eyes only, but emptying the Trash is never enough. Every file has a second life; the erased file continues to exist. I recovered the pictures taken on the day you were staged on the ice. I found normal pictures deleted, knowing well that Kaspar never had the time to sort out his exponentially growing galleries. I put two and two together and found a picture that should never have been taken."

"What did you find?"

"Russians. Eavesdropping. Following your every move. And Kaspar's."

"Russians?"

"I think there are Russians teamed up with Americans. Might be a black op."

Konrad rubbed his brow. "It doesn't make any sense."

"Actually..." Ruut looked up into the clearing sky. "I think my boss is also involved."

"What?"

"Let me gather my thoughts. Take the dip. I'll watch your back."

Konrad stifled a shudder. They listened to the woods; then he trudged naked to the pond.

He felt her gaze on his back.

22

G IDEON STUDIED FIVE autographs and monster
handprints embedded in concrete on a monument
stone in Lordi's Square.

He took off his glove and put his hand flat in a monster man's
hand and imagined himself on a stage with an electric guitar
and rock-god hair. The renamed avenue and hand marks were a
tribute to the local Eurovision Song Contest winners Lordi,
much like the footprints and handprints of Hollywood Stars and
Starlets on the Walk of Fame.

This was supposed to be the heart of the A-rock-alypse, but
for the most Finnish people the winning song, "Hard Rock
Hallelujah" offered only a shared sense of shame.

He gazed to the east where the fenced street was being
prepared with storage snow for reindeer speed race and lasso
competitions. Christmas spirit was literally in the air—even
though tower-tall snowmen and rows of ice lanterns were
melting—but Gideon was not in the festive mood.

He had a murder in mind.

The street behind the fenced area dipped down to the river,

and behind it the misty Ounasvaara beckoned him with a reverent silence. He saw a peek of Belvedere, a tower build for birdwatchers, but a place he and his friends used to get drunk every weekend.

"Retardo."

Gideon turned toward his best friend, Ville Kaitio. His large, intelligent eyes behind Harry Potter eyeglasses smiled at the new invention of his favorite football player, Ronaldo. He was small, a touch shyer than a raccoon, and his nerd's forward head posture amplified his sensitiveness. Sometimes Gideon wondered how Ville, who practically and exceptionally lived his life in books instead of steam and screens, could hold himself upright while walking.

"Yes, Decamoron?"

"Is Ruut coming to the meeting today?"

"I don't know."

"Can't you call her?"

"Her phone is dead."

"Where is she?"

Gideon shrugged. A fisherman selling fresh-caught fish found Gideon's eyes. The man forced a smile on his face and waved. Invitingly.

Gideon sighed and turned to Ville, who poked his glasses up on a prominent bone on the bridge of his nose. He was waiting for an answer.

"Let's go to Hemingway's Bar."

"I can't. My mom will find out."

"She's working." Gideon took his fake IDs out of his pocket. "Come. Just for one. Like last time. I'll order while you pick us a table."

"I can't." Ville took a smart phone out of his pocket.

"Since when have you owned a phone?"

"Since my mom decided to track my every move."

"What? You hardly breathe fresh air. Cut the umbilical cord already."

Ville stared at the ground.

"Give me that," Gideon said and snatched the phone. "We can hide it or shut it down. Say it went off in your pocket."

"Even if I did, there's also a GPS-tracker in my backpack."

Gideon made a nervous laugh, staring at him openly.

A girl with red hair took them by surprise. "Hi there, bone balls."

"Hi Rebecca," Ville murmured.

Gideon frowned at Rebecca Kreivi's new polka hairstyle pushed to one side. She was a thin girl with wide-hipped build and hair-trigger reactions. Any verbal or unpronounced insult might set her off.

Apparently, Ville was careless with his tone of greeting, for they were caught up in the fight. Gideon focused his attention on a man buying fish. The shoulder-line under a black battered leather jacket was familiar.

Flashes of memory assaulted him: vigilant eyes looking at him on his father's porch.

His mind and heart racing, Gideon faced Ville and Rebecca.

"...And you," Rebecca snapped at Gideon, "Call your mother so I choose between girls' movie night or her spiritual sessions."

"Shut the fuck up," Gideon hissed. "Speak normally. Don't look. The man on my left buying fish murdered my father."

Ville poked his eyeglasses and remained cool, but Rebecca tried to turn around. Gideon caught her wrist with a force that hurt.

Rebecca glanced at her hand. Then Gideon. She yanked her hand away and lit a cigarette so fast that Gideon and Ville thought she took the tools out her sleeve like a poker player. Practically every fiber in her emanated: 'Play with me, and I'll fucking rip your head off.'

Gideon glanced at the man with dark skin color now leaving.

"I need your help," Gideon said. "Let's tail him. I'll pay you. Whatever it takes. Give me your phone number so that we can go separate ways and nail this guy's ass."

"I can't. My mom told me not to give the number to anyone."

Rebecca placed her hand around Ville's throat. "You heard the man. Money. Got it?"

Ville forced a nod.

"Quickly now," Gideon said.

The man halted. He looked at his watch, then entered the Sampokeskus shopping center from the north entrance.

Gideon ran after and said over his shoulder. "Rebecca, send me Ville's number. We can tail him one at a time. Go west."

Gideon speed-walked inside the building through the first pair of sliding doors of the east, knowing the man might cross his path. He hid behind a Christmas tree and cursed at stumbling into the big empty gift parcels.

He waited.

The hall was deserted. And quiet. Except for an old man snoring on a bench, the hum of two escalators, and the heat pump above the entrance.

Gideon walked inside.

Santa with Rudolph, a giant plushy, hung lower from the ceiling than usual.

His phone vibrated in his pocket.

A text message.

After Ville's number, Rebecca had written:

Murderer follows us!

Gideon felt his heart relocate to his throat. He exploded into a run. The corridor to the north entrance was blocked by big machines and three workers hammering the floor, removing tiles.

Gideon sent a message back:

Comin.

He ran all the way to the west entrance, passing more elderly people—seriously frightened—who supported themselves with the walls.

Gideon hit his shoulder at a slowly opening sliding door and slipped out.

He peeked to the north.

The man had just disappeared behind the corner, and Gideon took his phone:

Go straight. I gotcha.

He bolted and thought how badly this could end. He stopped at the corner the man had just passed, spotted all three of them at the lights and took the Canon out of his backpack. Rebecca held Ville's hand among a gaggle of tourists.

I'm just a bird spotter, Gideon calmed his nerves.

Rebecca and Ville walked over the street and steered away to McDonald's.

Gideon followed the man walking over a bridge, past his friends taking a seat around a table with a sad look on their faces. He sent a message.

You did great.

The man walked through a park. Gideon took a few pictures at a delicate layer of snow resting on the branches of trees. He took one shot at the man's back and continued.

The man left his bag of fish with a driver in an RV and walked down the road toward the north.

Gideon memorized the registration number and model, taking a shot while the driver began reading a newspaper.

He walked past the RV and soon saw the man entering Arktikum, a museum and science center on the riverbank. According to Ruut, the building's iconic glass tube represented the frozen finger of the north, the direction it points in. But because it was so close to the water she referred to it as *Water Damage*, the biggest aquarium tank in Finland.

Gideon followed the man inside. All the way to a room full of stuffed northern wild animals and maps and scale models and tourist groups marveling around in blue and red thermal padded overalls. The room had only one access, so Gideon wrote another message to Rebecca.

GPS-tracker. V's bag. Need it!

The man paused before an old scale model. He watched it, unmoving, hands resting at his sides.

The phone vibrated.

V's shocked. Rebecca wrote. *Doesn't like the idea…*

Gideon wrote back.

Money. Doubled.

The man was still silently staring at the model. Gideon waited for the answer. He would have a clear shot of the man's face, but the sound of the camera would expose him. Then it dawned on him what the man was staring at.

Burnt bridges and buildings.

The city of Rovaniemi was demolished in 1944 after the Nazis' scorched earth tactics in Lapland. The brothers-in-arms turned their weapons against each other because Finland was forced to break all diplomatic ties with Germany and drive the Nazis out of the country. The havoc had been masterminded by a man in Moscow, whose successor today was every bit as merciless and cold as a raging bull.

Joseph Stalin.

The screen of Gideon's phone lit up.

Rebecca.

Persuaded him. Coming. Better be worth it!

Gideon pocketed his phone and walked away. He invented an idea of how to get the tracker to the RV without going too near.

Snowballs.

Little prank.

Everybody hates teens. Carrying the mad professor's words in his mind, his declaration of war would either seem like vandalism, or would go unnoticed.

The first ball, however, would land on the roof, including the GPS.

23

FROM HIS ELEVATED viewpoint, Patrick Praytor peered down from the bird tower at teens he had evicted. Drunken, middle-fingers-up and openly cursing at him as they stumbled down the hill.

Soon your pathetic lives will have a new meaning...

He hummed a tune under his breath with the emotional input the view had to offer. Would the snow return before Christmas Eve?

Arkadi Alexander, one of his Russian allies, most trusted comrade and the best tech, worked with his pad. His oxidized copper green eyes flashed.

"I have located them."

"Well tracked." Patrick gave him a biodegradable nanodrone. A bee. A stealthy airborne camera for tactical spying and assassination. It was so natural looking that once a recon mission of an enemy identification was blown in Yemen when a bird picked one up. "Make your country proud."

Arkadi pocketed the machine. He tightened a silencer in place, reloaded and nodded, and went to his mission.

Patrick viewed the teens disappearing out of sight below

him. Soon all the parents of the world would have the tools to ensure that their children didn't grow up mean-spirited, depressed or criminal. That would be the everlasting impact of their mission.

A small sapling pine tree, beaten and bent by the teens, caught his attention. So much stupidity and lack of intelligence. One of the teens yelled, threaten to knock over his gravestone. He balled his fists.

You'll never get a chance at that.

Seeing the tree conjured memories of the times of interrogations in Baghdad while hunting down Saddam and questioning his bodyguards. Without a reliable power grid, torturing in makeshift electric chairs left behind men either dead or shell-shocked for life.

His mind returned a decade back to a honeymoon in the Alps. He saw his wife... drawn at gunpoint by mercenaries, a hand pulling a fistful of her hair, a knife on her exposed throat...

They made him watch.

Gang rape.

Inhumane torture.

Then feeding her to the dogs...

They burnt the house and vehicles. Left him to die in flames.

He recalled crawling out, in the snow, bleeding, walking down the slope to a village. Phantom pain in his lost little finger reflamed. He had had to chew his little finger off to keep frostbite from turning to gangrene. But losing a little finger means losing over 50 percent of grip strength and holding everyday small objects. While the index and middle fingers function, with the thumb, in pinching and grabbing—zipping zippers, buttoning buttons—the little finger teams up with the ring finger to provide power. He became left handed with firearms.

Patrick pocketed his hand and mentally locked the memory away.

I must direct human evolution.

Why wait for natural selection, which was not progressive or directional? Man had governed the evolution of so many animals and plants by far. People self-medicated every day in developed countries. Raising the bar of morality would not only meet the basic needs of the suffering and needy and do the job faster, but there would also be what the majority was praying for: The Kingdom of Heaven. Rearchitecting humans' biological moral heritage was to be the new foundation for human flourishing. Self-sabotaging all the good efforts for the betterment of the world would cease.

Divine Civilization—I'll build it.

A MATCHSTICK LIT BEHIND ERIC PANTZAR'S eyes. "You fuckwad! You're working with terrorists!"

Theo was impressed. With his booming voice, Eric found a way to make calm vanish from his face. First time since his boot camp. "Russia is not a terrorist government."

"Cut the BS," Eric said while trembling in anger and pinching the bridge of his nose. After the span of six full heartbeats, Eric grabbed his phone and dialed the president of Finland. "Your maneuver is a despicable crime against humanity."

Theo crossed his fingers on his stomach. "I strongly advise you to hang up that call."

Eric shot a glance over the table at him, his face a solid mask.

"The operation can't be stopped," Theo continued. "Otherwise, the geopolitical clock will rewind to 1939. It's only a matter of time. You do want to eliminate the martial spirit in the human condition."

"President Dufva," the voice said on the phone, but Eric

slammed the phone against the desk in such a fury that the glass exploded in all directions.

"Where's your team?" Eric said. "Tell me now, or I sure as hell am going to make your life difficult."

"My boys are everywhere. Even in your ranks. Seeking them out one by one would take weeks. The mission will be accomplished long before that."

Eric's stare was full of disgust. "You're bluffing."

"I'm doing your country a favor."

"A favor?" Eric let out a mocking laugh. He walked to a window and opened the blinds. "See those three men out there? They're Russians. Evaluating and inspecting our firm from bottom to the top according to the Vienna Document. Only this fucking glass stands between a cocksure war with Russia! A few millimeters! You don't even know how often those maniacs insult our airspace! Every single-motherfucking day. Including Christmas! And we don't have the money to keep our Hornets in the sky!"

"I assume that's classified information."

"Fuck you. Fuck your dignity and your protocols! You guys know the real situation on the borders better than our ministers, let alone the public."

Theo shrugged.

Eric closed the blinds. He sank to his chair with hands over his face, still screaming curses.

Eric's phone beeped on his desk. He answered, pieces of glass falling on his desk like hail, and cut his finger in the process.

"Dad," Eric said. Then he showed a bloody middle finger at Theo. "Okay. That's fine... I understand... I'll be there. Bye."

"Is Ilona sick?"

"Fever."

"She's a brave girl. I remember how strong-willed she was as five years old. She's more like you than Iris."

Eric said nothing.

"Hear me out. President Viktor Vodyanoy knows that Russia is founded upon one principle: the country is exceptional, and its task is Messianic..."

Eric's phone buzzed.

The president of Finland.

"Frankly," Eric said, not picking up the phone, "I don't know how that differs from American politics."

Theo leaned closer. "The power in Russia isn't based on institutions or laws. The power of Russia is one man. The people worship him as long as he creates unity either through economic growth or conflicts. Viktor takes personal pleasure in cruelty, just like psychopaths and murderers and school bullies, and Russians are in awe of a man who shows heroic defiance. The country has to have a conflict as its primary uplift of team spirit. Although many Russians like western products and visit the West, those in power make sure the country's inferior complex prevails, so the West can stand accused as enemies who have created all of its problems."

"The American people suffer from the same double standard," Eric said. "You hack the world and spy on everybody while you deny that right for everybody else. Dropping one man out of the chain of command doesn't break their Great Mission's aim. Besides, you're not neighboring a psychopath who thinks his country's borders don't end anywhere."

The phone rang again.

Theo leaned in, hand on one knee. "The President of Russia is coming. Think of it, Eric. Right now, on the other side of your Finnish-Russian border, the children are being raised exactly as in the Soviet Union during the Cold War, in confrontation against the US. They have already changed the course of history in schoolbooks; it's totally biased. Russia will stop at nothing until the country is back dictating terms to the rest of the world."

Eric considered the painted bleakness.

Theo thrust his chest out. "Viktor has a new lady who has softened his heart. He is at his most vulnerable state of mind. He knows it. He has doubled his personal guards."

"What do you want me to do—smile at all the clusterfucking possibilities?"

"I'll give you the specifics later. We have a consensus. You want to end the tension at the borderlands as much as I do."

Eric glanced at his phone ringing again. He cracked his shoulders and picked up the phone. He let out a breath and pressed the answer with the bleeding hand. Then he said to Theo, his voice like the growl of thunder:

"You're dismissed!"

Theo stood up and brushed a few shards from his uniform. Glass breaking underfoot, he exited the room with a wide grin.

His phone rang.

Seeing Patrick's name on the screen tickled his skin with excitement.

24

KONRAD COULD HARDLY breathe. He cursed his swollen, snot-clogged sinuses while evaluating the hand mark on the tree.

The forest had always been a place for hiding and games, growing up. All those times spent in the woods made him feel privileged. Hunting small animals with his grandfather's juniper-longbows, spending time in a self-made tree house, reading comics and doing experiments with gunpowder (and burning down the tree house), carving wood vessels and playing Pooh-sticks on old bridges. Thinking of shooting blueberries with a blowpipe at people's clothes took him back instantly to his childhood.

When did I get so old?

"A penny for your thoughts," Ruut said.

Konrad turned to her. "It's getting cold. Soon we'll get snow."

"You can predict the weather?"

Konrad pointed at his right eye. "A believer once hit me when I was fourteen. That's the reason my eyes seem mismatched. The pupil in my right eye is enlarged. Permanently open. Every time the air pressure shifts, my eye subtly aches."

"Not possible." Ruut took a long close look to tell the difference. "You're kidding, right?"

"My eye doesn't lie." He glanced at the woods. "Any idea why they haven't come?"

"They might be waiting for our next move."

"Who are they?"

Ruut leaned closer and traced Konrad's forehead with the tip of her index finger.

"Worry lines again?"

"I thought I saw the sign of the devil," Ruut said. "Maybe they fear you."

Her eyes went wide at a sudden realization. The phone in her pocket had sprang alive by itself.

"A message from Gideon," she said, "'I know who murdered Dad...'"

The screen died.

"Oh my God, is he going after someone?"

"Hold on," Konrad said, "We have to figure out what we are going to do."

"I'll do some scouting."

"Don't you think we should talk first?"

She was already jogging away.

Konrad said after her, "What if they capture you?"

Ruut glanced over her shoulder, uttering a laugh, one of contempt. She pointed at her bicep and planted a kiss on it. Then she disappeared into the thicket like a shadow after a sunset.

Fear and disbelief slithered through Konrad. She was like the most active force in the universe, but her stubbornness would get her killed.

He sat under the tree to think through the sordid saga that led them here. How did he fall in love romantically with Oona in the first place? What the hell was he thinking? He wondered how far Julia had gone. Yes, their marital sex was occasionally infrequent and unexciting, but not always. He didn't recognize himself in that morally gray area he had for so long lectured on and loathed in human nature. He wasn't incapable of shame, as Julia had often insinuated, especially not in this case.

He buried his head between his knees, wanting to shrink down enough to travel underground tunnels, curl up into a ball and be no use to anyone.

But if Oona had already been questioned, what did she have to tell? What made her so valuable? And how did they find her in the first place?

The idea that she could be a divine teacher was still a stretch. A software glitch of the brain, like the notion of afterlife. Some rare people possessed enough charisma to fit 'exceptional human being' category, but that was it.

Oona's smile had not been flirtatious, merely a suggestive line, like some bed-goddess of Victoria's Secret, glossy, a passive doll of a human being. Where did the overwhelming attraction come from?

And the more he thought about her, the more he had to look at things through the lens of Zen: Did anyone see Oona during all those mornings when they passed by each other? What if she came into being only on the day of the incident, after she had been questioned and probably killed?

There's no such thing as resurrection.

He took the medical bag between his legs. A drop of water fell from the tree, flicking in a prism's colors before landing on his hand. Trying to combine all the riddles and colors, he thought of sunlight he hadn't seen in a long time. He thought of Newton, how the prism worked, and the essence of light. The seven-fold spectrum.

The rainbow.

An idea broke free. God created the world in seven days. The

Newton riddle was hidden in the seventh commandment. In the colors of the rainbow. A rainbow represents the transformation of the God of wrath of the Old Testament into a God of love. Rainbows and God—they both beckoned ordinary people, but were not located at a particular place or distance. Neither was an object, neither physically approachable.

Konrad took the membrane from the bag. Lennart's words spoke to him:

For the true Noaidi, the drum was a means of connecting with the dead.

Was he supposed to connect with Oona?

A gust of bitingly cold wind hissed through the trees. Konrad stood up. A snap of wood. He bolted around and saw Ruut in the tree line.

She made a squeezed throat sound as if she had stepped on an iron bear trap and repressed her pain. Her paralyzed face was a blue-white mask, drowned and expressionless as if it were sculpted from ice.

"Did you get lost?"

She held her empty gaze at nowhere point, stupefied.

Konrad closed in on her. "Ruut?"

"For a moment I couldn't see you," she managed. "But now I can't hear you."

25

ONE OF THE DEEPEST of silences met Konrad in the woods. Misshapen branches densely weaved a canopy. The temperature was above zero now, no snow in sight.

He had to leave Ruut in the glade to rest after she had mumbled something about impossible distances and a manifestation in the woods, something he had to see. According to her, they were trapped, somehow unreachable.

Then she had started hyperventilating and repeating: "I need to find Gideon..."

In the glade they were just sitting ducks waiting to lose their heads, any action was a better alternative.

The oddest thing was that he couldn't distinguish Ruut's footprints trodden into the gray lichen. An eerie feeling also suggested that someone paced alongside him behind the overgrown and impenetrable wall stretching to his right.

Armoring his heart against the unknown, he gained a small hill, but the woods gave way to harder obstacles: blackthorns and diabolical fish traps of juniper. Seeing traces of trenches made him think of the silent graves of war heroes and unspeakable memories of the veterans. Traumas were cruelly persistent; they lacerated areas in the brain that weren't for communicating.

Once again something stirred on his right. Probably the shadow of his own fear.

Konrad strode through the tangle and came to a temple-sized boulder rock, relocated by glacial ice sheets during the Ice Age. The rocks would remain in their original position through infinity, for no man possessed the strength or interest to remove them. Only water could break one down into smaller pieces as it froze and expanded inside.

The branches of spruces embraced his body softly, almost apologetically, like his mother's sensitive mimosa plant, a shy touch-me-not species that folded inward on touch. Their long evolution shielded them from predators, re-opening when it was safe. Humans were much like such plants: not until an absolute guarantee of safety would they let down their guard.

He had little problem with that too.

Somewhere a woodpecker drilled into a tree.

Tat - tat - tat.

The sound came in groups, the sustained fire of a rifle. The sound was a hollow echo as if the tree's spine were but sawdust.

Konrad wanted to make sure he was walking in the right direction. He checked his pockets for pieces of metal and produced one from his broken reading glasses, and then heard his father's voice inside his head. A memory came through his eyes. He saw his father placing a needle upon a leaf plucked from a birch and lowering it inside a hollow stump. Slowly, the needle and the leaf calibrated to point north.

Taking the metal and a plucked leaf, he walked to a small water pocket in the ground. He took his case for reading glasses and plucked out the piece of silk fabric. Then he started rubbing and magnetizing the needle.

It demanded about a hundred twists. The improvised compass confirmed that he was in the right direction.

He trudged forward, knowing it wouldn't be a long walk now. The familiar place was suddenly more foreign and different. Like a home after a divorce.

Tat-tat-tat.

The path wound slightly to left, to a small alley. Konrad knelt, lowering the leaf and the metal to a puddle. He checked his clothes for metal that would confuse the compass.

The leaf spun.

A foul, rotten stench wafted to his nostrils. A ripple of intuition stiffened the length of his body.

Something dark was keeping an eye on him.

A dark and cloak-ragged horse rider stood still, drawn from nowhere else than the red abyss.

Konrad experienced full body tremors.

The rider's racked-yellow eyes were fixed on him, studying him quietly. From their narrow slots under the hood, the eyes had no humane message to deliver. The horse was older than a curse, skinnier than a death spell, and its death-seen eyes twice as mean. Steam rose from its nostrils as the horse exhaled.

Konrad took a step backward, hyperventilating, but the rider clenched his fists and pressed heels into the horse. Retrieving the compass was an invitation to an open grave, so Konrad whirled and bolted toward the glade.

He ran.

The twigs and branches tore through his clothes into skin. The hasty hoof beats were gaining the slippery, leafed ground, the horse flying like a sin on the wing of the past world. Only a few leaps separated Konrad from the glade, but the spreading shadow closed in behind him, engulfing the trees.

A heartbeat before it would run him down, Konrad threw himself through the last remaining spruces...

His lungs howled, and his teeth clang together with an audible crack as his head hit the ground.

Quickly, he covered his head with his arms, shielding himself from claws and blows. The moment melted, flew past.

The door to the woods stood still, opened, only wind-twisted branches. On his back, Konrad scanned and listened to the bushes, hearing Ruut's vague footsteps approaching. Her calling of his name felt like a distant dream. But despite the dizziness and his relocated heart racing in his throat he understood what he saw.

The ground around him was littered with twigs and brown and yellow leaves as if the horse and rider had exploded and vaporized.

26

THE LOOMING RESULT of Gideon's plan wrenched at his gut like barbed wire. Crawling on a pipeline under a bridge, he balanced himself on the slippery, icy metal. There might be no return.

His cell phone buzzed, probably the tenth time in the past hour. Ville's parents took him for a criminal mind and bad company.

Only Ruut knew the place where he positioned himself on a rocky pylon under the bridge. A hiding place he found years ago with Ville. He had called the police and the emergency teams to get them to safety.

He couldn't see what triggered their interest in the place. Perhaps the stories that the worst scum, heroin addicts, and drunken teenagers spend their time below the bridge, drawing them like it was an exciting show. Some illusion of detachment. He worked to keep himself sober, but couldn't resist a dose of cannabis when it was offered. His loneliness was partly caused by his refusal to drink.

Breaking sweat from his forehead, he yearned for a relaxant more than ever.

The enemy car stood by the shore parked next to a blue house. Through his camera's viewfinder, there was occasional movement of light and shadows. Surrounded by stone and metal almost doubled the sense of freezing, so he thumped his feet and shoved his hands into his jeans. The coldness gnawed his energy. His stomach protested with intensifying growls.

A light appeared outside the house.

An engine fired up.

Gideon looked through the camera and saw only one head-light moving.

A snowmobile.

In the light that shone toward the river, Gideon saw a shape of a man that stood guard. The man gestured in Gideon's direc-tion, giving orders to the driver on the snowmobile.

All of the sudden he didn't feel cold anymore. His legs went weak, and his heart raced.

The snowmobile moved on the ice with the steady speed of a train.

He looked at the route back over the pipelines; thoughts of fleeing rose and he sought a realistic timeline to leave. But the closing sound froze him still. As far as he could estimate, he had only thirty seconds. He texted to Ruut:

They killed dad and now they're coming to me!

Gideon reconsidered. Erased the text, and called Ville. But, realizing the stupid choice and loss of time, he called Rebecca.

Pick up, pick up...

"Gideon!" Rebecca exclaimed and suppressed her voice to a hush. "Ville's dad is furious. He has been calling me all evening, sending threat messages. I told him that you jumped on the train to Helsinki."

"Listen to me," Gideon said. "I'm in trouble. I can't speak much. I'm at the Bridge, and the killers are close. I'll leave the line open. Record the call."

"Shit. What have you got yourself into? I'll switch on the voice recorder app."

"Do it."

Speaking with Rebecca brought him to his senses. The more Rebecca would hear, and hopefully record, the more it increased his chances to stay alive. He would scream every detail—clothes, tattoos, scars, accents. It was a combination of Ruut's paranoia and criminal catechism of how to survive a while longer in the hands of the enemies.

Whining through the whirling fresh powder snow the snowmobile moved like a torpedo on a destruction course with the bridge. The driver parked it to a blind spot and killed the engine. The man quickly worked on the trailer with a black cover.

Acid burned a hole in Gideon's stomach.

Dad's ice hockey bag.

Thickening pulse hammering at his temples, Gideon shifted on the pipe to the other side and stared down. The man hardly made a sound as he effortlessly carried the bag under the bridge near the stone pylon. He left it two meters from the dark waters. Then he disappeared from Gideon's sight, only to return with a long piece of wood.

Gideon wanted to scream in horror.

A man's voice carried out of the bag as though his mouth had been taped.

The driver gave the bag a push with the stick.

Panic spread in Gideon's body.

"No!" The second his words came out Gideon pressed his head against the pipe in tears.

"What is it?" Rebecca said.

The man in the bag and the driver fell silent. Tears fell down on Gideon's cheeks. Then the driver gave the second push. And the third.

Splash of water.

An inhumane muted scream sprang out, black and cold.

Then silence.

Gideon waited for the driver's next move. The engine fired up again. The driver stared into the blackness, then studied his wrist watch.

Gideon took his camera, clenched his teeth together and took a photo. The noise of the shutter made him swear.

The driver turned his snowmobile and sped off. While Gideon stared at the red tail light behind the rising spray of snow, he took his camera and studied his photograph on the screen.

Zooming.

The picture was mostly dark, but a line of text at the side of the snowmobile was familiar.

Ounasvaara ski team?

Was there a place left where they hadn't infiltrated?

The battery of the phone had died.

I have to find my mother.

27

THE SKY WAS sleet and snow with no sun peeking above the horizon. Konrad tried to avoid thinking of it as their destiny ahead, the stage set for black.

Ruut made a rope out of black willows, cutting, weaving, and lashing them together with bare hands. She tore the willows from their place by putting a stone next to a willow, then bent the stem upon the stone, and hit it with a sharp rock. Ceaseless determination. The sound of the horse's hooves returned to haunt Konrad, but it didn't seem to bother her.

Repeatedly looking over his shoulders, Konrad let out a heavy sigh of exasperation. Their escape options came down to a few powerful words: tunnel, lock picks, disguise, sheets, fire, fake seizure... Usually he enjoyed prison break-out stories, carving a prison officer's key from memory or squeezing through a tiny food slot. It settled warmth into his stomach to hear that some people escaped from maximum security. But now the rope of sheets for a vertical escape was to be, as she put it, 'the line of willows for a horizontal escape.'

"Help me out." Ruut dropped him a bunch of willows as if he were her squire.

"What are these willows for again?"

"You mean Black Mauls. They are not just willows; they have specific names. Black Mauls are suitable for ornaments and furniture, but also make the skeleton for domes, tents, and arches."

"Wait a sec. If a child asks you how babies are made, obviously you don't share everything that you know about fucking. You just answer the question."

Ruut concentrated on testing the hold and strength of the knots. "Escaping."

"Are you planning to spank the enemy with a thirty-meter whip?"

"Fifty-meter."

"You're just going to ignore those things prowling the woods?"

Ruut tested the knots. "I take it as a sign from God. A test of our faith."

"You're testing my faith. One of the horsemen of the apocalypse comes knocking at your door, and you're like, 'Oh, nice to see you, Jesus, you look exhausted, would you like a cup of loose leaf tea?'"

"Exactly why we'll not regard its presence as nothing new. *The Wicked Bible* forecast all this." Ruut's hands made a quick hangman's noose. "Unless you have a better idea?"

Konrad spread his hands.

A bee flew through the thick air hanging between them. Ruut leaned back, quickly hid behind Konrad's back. She clutched at her necklace.

"Fearing bees, are we?" Konrad said over his shoulder.

She flushed bright pink. "You said it was going to get colder. I didn't expect to see one." Then her face hardened like a stone, void of expression. "Follow me."

Darkness fell already. Konrad walked behind her to the dim

solemn wood, past the wall of spruces. They stopped when they could still see the glade behind them. While Ruut tied one end of the willow rope to a short and boughless, but robust and erect, pine; the trees around them bore an aura of foreboding and unease.

Ruut released a sigh. "Here goes nothing." The wheel of the rope ran over her shoulder as she strode forward.

They made slow progress. Despite the overhang of the boughs and spiked whip-splashes, he followed her determination as she chose trees by circling once around them. The idea started to come alive. They needed the straight line. The woods gave no room for error; orienting was impossible.

"I feel we're supposed to find something back at the glade," Konrad said.

Ruut's body language spoke otherwise.

Konrad frowned. "Why do you care about teens so much?"

"Because of the *Freudian* slip." Her voice spat the name as she brought her face close his. "Everyone hates teenagers. We can thank Freud for that. And all other experts and scientists, who put forward negative conceptions."

Ruut marked another tree with the rope and strode on.

"You may be onto something," Konrad said, walking a pace behind, "but most teens know only to snooze and booze. You must at least admit that Freud was on to something. The young are different. And indifferent. Go Goth—that's their overall contribution."

"Defaming and underestimating," Ruut retorted, "exactly what causes them to riot. If we see them as rowdy provocateurs and fail to see them as a reservoir of creativity and energy, they just sink to meet the low expectations we give to them."

"What do you even teach in your gatherings?"

"Love. Care. Camaraderie. Chance. Respect. Anything for balanced growth. The young hate lists of rules, but the ideas of self-discovery and what's important make their faces shine. Meet their needs with possibility, and they are more willing to contribute to the betterment of the world than most adults. It's not indifferent where our horse gallops and what fields it starts to plow to become healthily independent."

"Sounds like Sunday school."

Ruut held a bough from slapping across Konrad's face. He acknowledged his gratitude with a nod, but she released it. The bough-spikes whipped his cheek numb.

He grumbled a curse.

"Sorry. But you saw it coming," Ruut folded his arms. "By the way, don't you think it's odd how much ahead of his time Newton was?"

"The crowning achievements require the right brains. But physical truths change when condition change. At high speeds and strong gravities, at the extreme circumstances of traveling the speed of light, Newtonian physics breaks down. It took Einstein and his Special and General Relativity theories to go beyond the limits of Newton's ideas. We expand our awareness by building upon one another until one day we realize we did everything ourselves."

"You can't expect to approach God with a map of perception and a compass of analysis," Ruut said and started talking something about a theory of nothing, but Konrad felt heaviness on his tongue. Two crows in a tree were staring at him. A chill passed over his skin. The air around him became crisp and cold, for he expected the birds take to the air, to make the shriek darker than their wings.

A bee flew past Konrad's head and collided with a tree with an unnatural loud bang.

"Konrad?" Ruut asked.

Halfway through the sound of overstretched rubber breaking in half, the blast of a handgun exploded behind them.

A jolt of impact passed through the rope up Konrad's arm and numbed it. His fingers lost all sensation. Another boom brought up unintentional gulps. Something tightened the length of the rope.

If there was a way to comprehend the pain in his hands, nothing could explain the tightening of the rope. Did the distances do the impossible? There were more explosions. Konrad grit his teeth together as he sensed blood—as cold and sticky as truth—oozing from his palms. He didn't know why, but an image of an old grand piano visited his eyes. It brought familiar warmth and memories, refueled safety, but they were taken from him as if a sudden missile blasted it, the white keys torn apart under his fingers.

The rope slipped through their fingers, disappeared.

Konrad turned to Ruut. Face wide and white, a shadow of her had bounced to run like a wild antelope, but the shock had numbed her still. Her asthma resurfaced.

The blood on his hands made blood escape Konrad's head. He fell to his knees.

Passing out wasn't an option for there would be no coming back. The truth hovered on the outskirts of his consciousness, lying just out of reach when he saw a shadow approaching at great speed.

Ruut's icy hand slapped across his face, carrying a dire warning of alarm.

The enemy was close.

28

KONRAD'S VISION ELECTRIFIED with black specks. Ruut crouched next to him. Her hand was on her windpipe, and she labored through her thin and wheezy breathing.

Something moved behind them.

A stab of panic made Ruut's eyes bulge.

Konrad scrambled up and turned toward the noise. A bright red color that looked like a flashlight was pointed at them.

"Hands up," a voice rang out.

Ruut spun around and squinted. Konrad had already figured out what they were looking at, but not what was wrong with it.

A gun's laser.

Konrad saw a silhouette of a broad-shouldered man trying to track the laser across his head, but the beam spread, engulfing him and Ruut in the light. The man's voice didn't shake.

"Hands where I can see them!"

Ruut gave a nudge with her leg to Konrad's shin, and they bounced to run in opposite directions.

The red flash turned to Konrad. The man fired. Konrad saw

the flames and flinched, but there was no sound. The trees flashed around him again.

Still no sound. Not even a whisper.

Ruut screamed something from behind.

Konrad made a full 360 and saw the agent aim at Ruut and squeeze the trigger.

Flash of light.

No sound. No bullet wounds.

Ruut acted swiftly and attacked the agent. Her directed punch landed on his ear, throwing the mountainous man off his equilibrium. Forced to his knees, the agent received another strike to his chin.

A knockout.

Konrad raised his hands over his head, feeling tremors in his fingers. The punch rewound in his eyes, the agent in an awkward wobble-fall. His mind combined the bits of information. She was dragging the agent to a pine. She hit him again.

Blood started seeping from the corner of the man's eye.

Konrad's voice shook. "Ruut?"

Being unnaturally quiet and decisive, she fetched the rope from the last trunk, returned to the man and tied his hands behind the tree.

"What are you doing?" Konrad whispered. "Let's go."

Ruut ignored him. She untied and pulled off the agent's shoelaces. She combined them, tied his legs together.

"That won't hold him forever," Konrad said.

Ruut swiped her hand across her nose. She explored at the bee between her thumb and forefinger. "A nanodrone?"

She was hovering the bee's sting close to the man's eyes. Surgically.

Pocketing his hands and scratching his head in turns, Konrad walked around back and forth, keeping distance. Ruut dug a pad out the man's pocket.

Konrad stopped.

Ruut looked at a lit-up screen. "Konrad, are you checking on me?"

"What's that supposed to mean?"

"Look at this and say you don't want to hurt him as much as I do."

Konrad stared down at the screen in total confusion.

"An infinity mirror?"

Ruut scrutinized Konrad's eyes. She plucked something out. "Contact lenses with an in-built camera. I thought you were only wiretapped."

Konrad experienced a loss of coordination.

"God knows what else they have done to you."

Konrad couldn't look at the bleeding man without instant dizziness. "Wake him up."

Ruut started slapping across the agent's face without any intention of being gentle. Konrad walked away. At fifty meters distance or so he kicked cones and pebbles on the forest floor. His racing mind didn't register the presence of another soul until they stood face to face.

"Gideon?"

Gideon looked past him, avoiding eye contact. "Who's she beating?"

"Some bad people want bad—"

"Don't talk to me like I'm a child. They murdered my father. If these cases are linked, I won't interfere. She can do whatever she likes."

Konrad swallowed.

Gideon continued. "And hitting is what she likes."

"Has she hit you?"

"Her husband beats her," Gideon replied. "She tries to save the world and kids so much that she forgets herself and her needs. She thinks she can change Jake, because she cares about Netta so much. She blames herself for the death of my real sister eight years ago. Why do you think she serves in the army anyway?"

Konrad digested the news quickly. "To keep you safe?"

"In war civilians die more than soldiers. She knows the army is the safest place to be. And she can take me to the army cave, should war break out."

"Cave?"

"Classified."

"If Ruut has told you to keep quiet on the matter, I respect that. But we're in the middle of illegal operations. Any information would be welcome. We don't like each other, but maybe I could help you find your father's murderer."

"Yeah, right." Gideon looked like he was ready to spit on the idea.

"I stole a watch that belonged to your father. I threw it out the window in the hospital. With luck, you could find it at the southeast corner flowerbed. It may contain valuable information."

Gideon frowned.

"I'm sorry. But please, tell me about the Cave."

There was deep adolescent defiance in Gideon's body posture. "The place is below Santa Park. The entrance is hidden near the civilian entrance. There are firing ranges, lots of computers, wires. They test new weapons and bullets. Ask her. She's the one who works there."

Konrad nodded. "I'll discuss it with her."

"I'll check for the watch," Gideon said. "By the way, one agent has infiltrated Ounavaara ski team. The ski center is closed tomorrow. Something weird is happening there."

Gideon turned to leave.

Konrad said, "That morning... You saw the collision? The police haven't heard your story yet."

"You carried the explosive."

"What?"

"The bomb rolled on the road from your suitcase and detonated. But she rolled onto it. On purpose. She saved you."

Fear crept into the pit of Konrad's belly.

"My friend heard his police officer father saying a low-tech wristwatch was the mechanism behind the bomb."

Konrad made no comment.

Gideon prepared to leave. "Your Parabellum is buried under the tree in the glade."

"I don't think I want to have it back."

"Suit yourself, oldie. By the way, if you ask Ruut's opinion, she thinks it was you who planned to suicide that day, but the woman got in your way."

"I assure you I never had such intentions. I didn't carry any wartime bombs. They're highly unstable."

"And you aren't?"

"Sorry to burst your bubble, but it was Oona who screamed *allahu akbar*. She thought she was committing a righteous act. That it's a good way to die with Allah on her lips."

"No," Gideon said. "She didn't say anything."

Konrad's world twisted. "How am I supposed to trust you?"

Gideon said nothing as though to emphasize that Konrad wasn't listening to him. He walked away.

"Gideon!" Konrad felt cold sweat dripping down the back of his neck. "I've questions!"

He saw danger symbols in everything; the experience of a complete break with the reality. Could it be true he had jumped to illogical conclusions about Oona? Did she really manage to roll herself upon the bomb? But where did the explosives come from? And why had Ruut left matters unspoken when she claimed to be so straightforward?

Konrad felt the pad in his hand. He weighed the technology inside the machine. How much did these agents have control over him? Konrad considered all options. Then the most frightening yet utterly insane question formed in his mind.

Can they make people commit suicide?

29

ANGER LACED THE VETERAN'S words as he heard Patrick's status report through his cell phone.

"You were supposed to put them into the grave—without caring who goes after."

"This development wasn't a risk factor."

"Your job includes risks and constant risk evaluation, but it is not limited to them. Getting rid of any threat is the priority."

"As I have reported before," Patrick said, "the woods put our gear in great distress. We're still working on understanding the phenomena. There has been a delay in the video feed since the two ran into the woods. They've got Arkadi. You know the skill set of this man..."

The Veteran knew well the man's reputation. As an assassin, he had liquidated high American and Russian agents and was none other than one of the top five secretly most-wanted men by the world's alphabet agencies. The resources and burned money just to get a word to him was a taxpayers' nightmare.

"Oona warned us not to intervene in God's plan," Patrick commented.

"Don't talk me about her. Just put a lid on this."

"I trust Arkadi. He knows how to proceed."

The Veteran sighed inwardly. "See that it happens."

"We'll prevail. But if you don't want to take risks, we could offer Konrad a deal."

"What kind?"

"Profitable."

"Go on."

"Konrad has the twist of divine irony. He has exactly the opposite worldview as we do. Offering a meaningful role in the inevitable future world might work. He's by his own definition a man of the dark side."

"And?"

"The immoral man knows morality," Patrick said. "His calculated, provoking performances and journalistic investigations have spawned a rabid fan-base mainly because of the global fire and shit storms among believers. The more he reasons, the more reason people have to abandon their faith or defend their stand."

The Veteran made the deduction, and indeed saw the need of a public speaker, but grew reluctant. "The future world has no gods with many faces. Nor will it have idolized men. Where does he fit?"

"That's the thing. He makes people feel they are the authors of their lives. When people are truly free, there has to be something that roots them to the former world. Quarreling and debating and fist fights will never disappear, no matter how moral we make the man. We'll only tend the fever of the climate change, not the virus causing it."

The Veteran hated the risks involved. Russia, as the world knew it, would cease to exist. The people of Russia would learn to inhabit their actual characters, stripped of lies. "Although Konrad has all the signs of the perfect puppet, I disagree. We're too close to our goal. It took me the best half of my career to come to terms with what must be done. I will not let anything lead to unexpected complications."

"Understood," Patrick said, his voice emotionless.

"Any other troubles before the showdown?" The Veteran asked.

"No, sir. Who will deliver the package?"

"I have a Finnish general in mind."

"Is he any good?"

The Veteran heaved a peaceful sigh. "As good as it gets."

"Fulfilling his dream of getting rid of the Big Brother?"

"Hell yes."

30

E AVESDROPPING FROM A distance, Konrad saw blood in his vision with every hit Ruut landed on the agent's face. The agent was surely a strong mind to break. It could take days to make him speak. But before that, his partners would arrive and make them disappear as fast and effortlessly as piss melts snow on a grave.

He had to withdraw to the glade for another cold dip. The air was suddenly at least ten degrees colder than it had been an hour ago. The madness of having to move around to keep his muscles warm and get cold treatment to keep his body functioning was worse than a prolonged torture. He was the condemned, ready to trade places with the torture master.

The pond was frozen shut. Konrad left his clothes on the bank. He walked on the ice, stood there in the middle for a few seconds. Not having put much weight and pressure on the balls of his feet he fell through the ice, and let his body regenerate itself. He thought of Jesus and his miracles, how he never walked on water as the legend had it, but on thin ice during a cold night. The darkness and coldness surrounding him squeezed his heart smaller in his chest before it launched itself to a pounding like a panicky bird bursting out of his rib cage.

The cold shock took him out of his reverie. Adrenaline flowed through his system. It was ages back when he hadn't been able to contain the internal responses, keep calm and pulse rate in check.

Above the surface came a flash of light. Knowing that panic was the first enemy in water, he considered his options. Rising might mean an instant bullet lodged inside his skull. After ten seconds, the one-way ticket was about all the options before him. He thought of the hole above him, contemplated the contrasting colors, the hole darker than the snow-covered ice surrounding it, and kicked off.

A gasp of air. There was nobody in the glade. Where was the source of light?

The easiest way to get up was to imagine the ice as water, lean over it and swim with a kick, while getting the body as horizontal as possible. Konrad rolled over until the ice felt more solid. He quickly redressed himself and fought off the body vibrations.

There were footprints in the frozen grass, not his size. His eyes followed the prints approaching the tree that backed up the same way. The shoe size seemed bigger compared to his. Under the tree at the base, dirt spread over the snow. Someone had dug something up.

Ruut screamed curses far behind the trees.

Screams of pain.

Konrad wasted no second and sprang after the footprints that seemed to lead directly in her direction.

His heavy breathing drowned out all other noises. He ran with a new adrenaline surge, closing the gap between them, stopping short at what seemed impossible.

Ruut hung his head between her elbows as though her head was too heavy to hold upright. She was resisting something painful with every fiber of her being.

"Ruut?" Konrad said.

She aimed her weapon at the agent's head and took off the safety mechanism.

"NO!" Konrad ran to her, but she guided the barrel to face his forehead. He backed up. A chill raced its way up his spine as he raised his hands. "It's me. Konrad."

Her eyes were transfixed, some thoughtless imitation of a killer.

"Speak to me, Ruut. You're not yourself!"

"I'm sorry, Konrad. We're just obstacles standing in the way of the inevitable."

The agent locked eyes with Konrad over Ruut's shoulders. Konrad looked down and found another bee on the ground. He picked it up, stifling a shudder.

"You're poisoned!"

"Man can't make the right sacrifices unless forced to do so. I need to perish for the sake of progress. They've already won."

"They represent an idea that is genocide. Please, put the gun down. You can still choose."

"No," Ruut said. "I can't." She aimed the gun at her throat.

The agent began pulling his hands and legs apart.

"He's getting away!" Konrad shouted.

"Good-bye, Konrad."

A sour taste of iron flowed into Konrad's mouth, muffling his voice.

The agent freed himself, but a weapon was placed on his temple.

A quick finger pulled the trigger. Like a puppet cut of its strings, the agent fell face down on the ground.

Konrad fell to his knees at the spray of blood.

Ruut spun around, taking aim at...

Gideon.

She released her fingers and dropped her weapon. A chasm stood between Ruut and Gideon. Konrad held his breath.

The Parabellum that was supposed to be disabled.

Ruut turned to him, and pieces started filling the puzzle. The weapon had been loaded and working on the day he collided with Oona. He had been going to his own funerals, never reaching his destiny that was set up.

Gideon threw the weapon at Konrad's feet while Ruut was still reasoning the shock, and Gideon bolted. As Ruut ran after him, she yelled and begged her son to stop with all of a mother's means of love. Konrad picked up the Parabellum.

The enemy was planning something big. Why else would they use such an advanced technology?

He missed his office. The Parabellum belonged there on the shelf. He missed lecturing and the students reaching the state of intellectual excitement. The dryness of chalk on his fingers. The innocent chalk-talks.

The Russians could not directly invade Finland without a major conflict at the borders or if the Finns oppressed Russians within their borders. They couldn't invade Europe. NATO would respond. Unless its weapons were somehow made useless. Again, all weapons still worked at the command of the human mind. If those human minds were somehow turned against themselves...

A clench hit him in the pit of his stomach.

Was Newton's bestial warning concerning the end of morality?

Konrad glanced at the dead Russian agent, who had probably killed more people than the average human being meets and greets. His father's words about Russians echoed in his ears. After tons of enemy contacts with no end in sight, still rising to his feet in battle after battle, the ultimate question pierced his father's mind like a hollow bullet.

Don't they ever learn?

31

"NO SIGN OF HIM?" Konrad asked back in the glade.

The empty gaze in Ruut's eyes was a driftwood in an ocean. A woodpecker was flying above her, settling itself on the limb on the alder tree.

"For all my adult life," Ruut began, "I have been trying to keep Gideon on a safe path. How could he just take the man's life...?"

Konrad was the worst at giving consolation.

"...I have been living in a lie, Konrad. Netta isn't my biological child. I have been taking care of her more than my boy, whom I forget to hug any more now he's grown taller than me. His father provides the only sense of touch he has. Kaspar was his gate to the world."

"You still are the other half of it."

"He doesn't even take part in my youth group."

"Maybe," Konrad pondered, "maybe it's the truth that there's distance between you two. But you're reaching him through his friends who you're teaching."

She paused for a moment, forcing courage into her voice.

"I'm not used to bleeding my heart out, but I need to share something with you."

Konrad nodded.

"I'm not a doctor. I do care for and tend people, but my work in the army is a bit more complicated. I design weapons."

"No shit. The way you handle weapons..." *And even as a student, you were a hell of a mathematician. Addressing the questions of weight and shape, velocity and aerodynamics without effort... It wouldn't surprise me.* Konrad folded his arms. "But how much of the stuff we went through did you already know?"

"I wanted to hear those things from you. I still view you as my teacher. I hope you didn't get offended."

"You're about to be the definition of 'full of surprises.'"

Ruut blushed. "I've always been on this particular job because I thought I was securing the future. Hunters need ammunition to keep wild animals in check, and law enforcement is all about having reliable firepower. Only a handful of people knows how unregistered money is diverted to army weapon maintenance and inventing ways to hit the target more efficiently with less collateral damage. But men are motivated by the smell of gunpowder. Every bullet shot makes men thirsty for more. Adrenaline junkies think missiles rival God's dick."

"How serious an addiction are we talking about?"

Ruut gathered her thoughts. "I'm building a donkey bridge to what we are probably facing. You and I could be prototypes for the next generation of warfare. I don't believe the agent could make me aim the weapon at myself with poison. Why did it lose its effect? What if we have been compromised by nanotechnology?"

"Elaborate."

"Our body and brains are circuital systems. When there's only us inside us, we're in control. Even when cancer's spreading in our brains; it is still part of us. Cancer wants to stay alive. Cells are programmed for survival. But we also consist of bacteria, and we need most of them. When a bacteria-sized nanobot moves inside us, it can be either an ally or an enemy. For our enemy, the thing that might be flowing inside us is their ally, responding to particular stimulus as wanted. Consider the world if such technology falls into the wrong hands."

"No one possesses the knowledge of such technology. Even the material decisions..."

"What if Oona was forced to share her knowledge? What if she knew the requirements for such technology?"

Konrad folded his arms. "We would need a blood test in a lab to verify any intrusion."

"You think we would find any traces?"

"Men like silicon. I'll bet they would be made out of it."

Ruut riveted her gaze. "What if it is biodegradable?"

Konrad rubbed the bridge of his nose.

"Suppose," Ruut said, "that the assisted suicide is the extreme of the nanotechnology. What would be the ultimate good?"

Konrad noted a black woodpecker edging near the alder, looking for a place to slam its beak.

"Moral enhancement," Konrad said. "Humanity lacks morality. We're weak. If the technology could bring people up to the level where the most morals are, that would put an end to the cycles of violence. A total rise above our animal bonds."

"See any side effects?" Ruut asked.

"Don't even get me started." But before Konrad managed to sort out even the smallest disaster on wheels, the woodpecker slammed its beak against the trunk.

A dull clang.

Their foreheads puckered into perplexed frowns.

Clang-Clang-Clang.

"Is that tree metal?" Ruut gasped.

The woodpecker tilted its head on both sides, tried to hit tree again, then took wing.

"Isaac Newton," Konrad said with great satisfaction. "I'll be damned for the Giant of the Occult. Newton wasn't tinkering blindly!"

"What?"

"In the cold metal burns. Now we are getting somewhere." Konrad grinned. "I've always preferred looking into an exceptional scientist's mind than God's."

The woodpecker screamed.

"That bird freaks me out," Ruut murmured.

"No wonder, for the Finns the black woodpecker has been the foreteller of rains and cold and beautiful winter weathers."

"Any negative meanings?"

Konrad released his words like the blade of a guillotine.

"Only the bringer of *death*."

32

D ISCOMFORT IN THE silence of the woods drilled a gaping hole into Gideon's heart. The thought of being a murderer pained him with every step he took. Had he felt like this when his father disappeared, he would have gone to take his enemies all out, even though he didn't stand a chance in pure combat. Nothing mattered anymore. Nothing helped him to stop his mind reinforcing the idea weighing down on him.

I'm the enemy of the society.

He deserved this slow torture, being a conflicted stranger to himself and others. The way he treated himself was unjustified, but he couldn't get rid of it like others could.

I'm wired up wrong.

As he started hearing traffic noises behind the trees, he realized there was no reason to help his mother and Konrad. He couldn't lose his mom's acceptance. Her love was solid. It was painful to admit that he could never trust his father's acceptance in the same way.

The headlights of the cars danced with tranquilizing melody. A police car whizzed by, sirens on, and he quickly stepped behind a pine. From the shadows, he stared at the spray of snow rising at the taillights.

Gideon hit his fist against the trunk of the tree, leaned against it and leveled his gaze down.

"Gideon," a powerful voice surprised him from behind.

Before even moving a muscle, he heard a safety mechanism taken off a weapon. He found himself looking into the black hole of silenced handgun.

"Who are you?" Gideon snarled. "If you're the coward who killed my father, I'll kill you."

"I'm sure you would."

"Did you kill him?"

"Your father's very much alive."

"At the bottom of the river?"

The man lowered his weapon. Nothing changed on the man's stern features.

"My name is Patrick Praytor. I'm an American elite soldier. If I had wanted you dead, you wouldn't be standing there toughened by blind hatred. My team pulled a play that we assassinated your father. He had enemies on his trail and would have been killed if we hadn't reacted."

"Don't you taste the shit coming out of your mouth?" Gideon asked.

"When a man hears or sees things that aren't in accord with his core beliefs, logical thinking shuts down. The brain prepares for battle. Believe me; I have witnessed it too many times."

"Did it happen to you too? When you ate ape shit and killed child ragheads?"

Patrick closed his eyes for a second. "In the Middle East, some men prefer using kids' headwear as a good place to carry explosives. I disagree."

Gideon gulped.

"Believe me. Taking a man's life for the first time stays with you longer than your first kiss."

Gideon blew out a noisy breath. "What do you want from me?"

"I want what you want."

"I have no fucking clue what I want."

"When the pain is most extreme, you'd rather die," Patrick replied. "Part of you is doing so right now. Silent screams. Self-hatred is even worse than loneliness. Everything seems ugly, dark, and uncontrollable."

Gideon dropped eye contact. Then pointed at Patrick with his finger. "You killed my father and are after my mother. I'm going to either walk away or scream if you take any step closer."

Patrick reacted like a shadow coming into life, closing the distance between them in a second.

"I'm in your personal space," Patrick said dryly. He offered his weapon, the grip up for grabs. "If you speak the truth, you'll never hesitate."

The weapon in Gideon's hand felt lightweight, perfectly balanced. He took aim at the lone, arrogant soldier.

"Gideon," Patrick said. "The world we're living in is growing darker with each passing day. You see it, you feel it, and you hate it. You also want to make it better. But deep inside you know that pulling the trigger would never make that happen. Hatred makes more and more people draw their guns."

"What makes you so *different*?" Gideon said.

"I happen to know that the man and the machine are becoming one in heart. Missions that once were handled by Special Forces' soldiers are now handed over to machines. There's no honor, dignity or loyalty anymore. But there's a solution to all our problems."

Gideon leaned back, creating space. He looked away. "What difference does it make? Why should I care?"

"The exact reason why you don't pull the trigger," Patrick said. "You do care."

Gideon stayed quiet, then aimed at Patrick's forehead. "You're trying to manipulate me."

"Yes, I am. But only to help you stop denying the truth."

"No. Life's a bad game. Maybe it's better that it ends."

"There's a way to change the course of humanity," Patrick said. "When moral and psychological barriers to killing are about to vanish, it is better to hand love and care over to the machines as well. The world doesn't care about right or wrong anymore. It's all about power, arrogant abuse, and dominance. But in the world I'm building, none will be in control anymore. Humans can't let anyone pull strings in the shadows if they are to thrive in harmony."

Gideon tested the metal of the trigger.

"Gideon, we have been fighting this war so long we don't feel comfortable in our skin anymore. My mentor who calls himself the Veteran knows how to end the war, all war. There can be a fresh start."

Gideon aimed at a pile of snow. "I'd rather kill myself than become your slave!" He pulled the trigger.

The sound of the hiss of melting snow made him angrier. He pulled the trigger again, and again.

Until the *click*.

Patrick took the steaming weapon and hid it inside his coat.

"Come. I'll show you how to recreate the world in seven days. We are on the sixth day, but what separates us from God is that we don't rest on the seventh."

Gideon swallowed rapidly. "Prove that my father's alive."

Patrick produced a pad, danced his fingers on the screen. It took several seconds to register what Gideon was looking at.

Kaspar was in a dim room in a hospital bed. Somebody

carried a laptop or pad closer to Kaspar who looked weary and ghost pale. His lips barely moved when he spoke.

"Gideon?"

Hiding his total mayhem inside his body, Gideon quickly wiped off a tear falling onto his cheek.

"Dad?"

33

"THE TREE OF DIANA," Konrad said, his palm flat against the rough bark concealing metal. "Philosopher's Tree."

"You don't look convinced," Ruut noted.

"This only grows in a solution of silver nitrate in a glass jar. Under the right conditions, metallic crystals build up a treelike structure. It's simple chemistry, but in the eyes of the alchemists, this was nothing less than magic. Metal growing like vegetation, tiny, twig-like branches of solid silver. Newton believed that metals could be made to grow, and from the Tree of Diana the alchemists concluded that life existed in the kingdom of minerals."

Ruut grew confident. "Unusual divine powers are at work here."

"Let's think this through," Konrad said. "Three fundamental physical laws are off-balance. *Time*—when the agent tried to shoot us, the noise came with delay. *Space*—when the rope started snapping. *Light*—the laser in the agent's gun, it shouldn't have spread."

"What if this place is a parallel universe?"

"Multi-universe theories are media tricks for the masses," Konrad deflected. "It's possible they do exist. Like it's possible we are living in some Mad Konrad's computer program. But what's drummed up by the media has nothing to do with science."

"Nothing?"

"Zero value."

"I thought science was about being arrogant, aggressive, and radical. Playing with ideas. Even if ideas are just ideas, they might prove useful later."

"Are you challenging me?"

"You made yourself stupid enough already," Ruut said. "I'm beginning to see that Alchemy and God have much in common. A blacksmith forges a piece of shapeless metal—useless becomes useful, nothing becomes something. Like the Big Bang Theory. If God didn't plant this tree here himself, it was one of his Messengers who knows the human mind. First message is expressed, then repressed, but expressed again."

Konrad exhaled an ugly laugh. "Explaining everything away with God?"

"I'm not the one explaining anything away. Clearly, Newton's study of nature and Scripture were two halves of a whole: the discovery of the mind of God. And the mind of God manifests through Messengers. They have taught about love and potential of man and substance. We have been invited to take part in something no one has ever done before. God's creation needs our protection. That's why He bends the laws of physics around us. He had sent Oona to prevent something bad."

"Before your ecstatic prophecy finds its way into fortune cookies," Konrad said, "how is Oona's death going to help us?"

"Self-sacrifice. It's the ultimate expression of love," Ruut said, her voice pearl and jade. "My best guess is she didn't leave *The Wicked Bible* only for you. It's a will to the world. Oona must have seen your potential. She's backing you up."

Konrad recoiled but bit through the internal ache in his stomach. "Let's move on. 'Menstrual blood of the sordid whore'... According to Lennart, one can get the color on the drum map from an alder tree like this."

"If you look at the skin map," Ruut said, "you can't help think what a rainbow a human being is. Feelings of rage and uncertainty are mottled in red on it. Blue for coldness. Organ failure makes skin color blossom in yellow and green. You turn white at the sight of..."

"Blood..."

"Skin color gives clues to health, but in your case, it doesn't apply. Whether you liked or disliked what you saw, the reaction is beyond your control."

"White light into a prism, sending in the mixture of all colors..." Konrad said. "And if we trail the rainbow back to the prism, we'll get white light again."

"Thinking what I'm thinking?" Ruut asked.

"The skin." Konrad said. "It needs to be placed on the hand mark. I'll do this if you tell me why you and Gideon have such a troubled relationship. You're strangely interested in certain aspects of medicine. Where does it stem from?"

Her upright posture slumped.

"I accidentally killed Gideon's sister."

Konrad gave her time.

"It was sunny, warm summer holiday, and we had gone swimming in the Mediterranean Sea. We wore elf hats just for fun. Gideon and Alina were excellent swimmers, going deeper and competing back to the shore. But on one race Gideon got a cramp in his leg, and he came to the beach. Alina got tangled with water reed. She got water to her lungs, started panicking..."

"You went in?"

"I dived into the water, swam as fast as I could. I managed to cut her loose and bring her in. Gideon came to hug her, a few people cheered, and a lifeguard also. But then something happened. We walked for ice cream bar, talked about returning to the water afterwards. Alina ate her ice cream complaining she was sleepy. We all thought we could stop at home, and take a nap, return later. Gideon, Alina and I slept in the same big bed. That was when she drowned."

"I'm not following."

"It's called *dry drowning*. Even a small amount of water in the lungs acquired from a bath can be lethal. I misinterpreted the signs, which were hardly any apart from the drowsiness. It was hot, and she had been running and swimming in the heat for an hour before the incident. I thought she was just tired."

"And Gideon accused you of her death?"

Tears dyed her eyes red. "Yes. A small amount of water in my little girl's lungs broke our family. Gideon blamed me for not taking care of her, but even though he was just handling his mixed-up emotions, I took the mantle of guilt. I drifted black, reading all kinds of medical stories. It was the darkest period of my life. Gideon tried to drown himself from a bridge in the winter. But I saw it happening, and I knew cold protects the brains, so I managed to save him with a rescue team. After thirty minutes, we found him and rushed into the hospital..."

Konrad noted how her hands folded in and out in a biological ache, the memory causing a great urge to protect a child.

"He's a walking miracle," Ruut said.

"I'm sorry, I had no idea."

Ruut flashed a smile. "It's okay. Will you look what's behind the creaky doors?"

Konrad turned to the tree with the drum skin in his hand. Unable to control the pulse of his hyperventilating heart, he positioned himself before the hand mark, reaching for the heartwood.

"Here goes nothing."

He felt the relentless burning of ice on the skin. But as if struck by lightning, something tightened around his heart, stopped it. His body stiffened, his lungs not functioning. His consciousness remained in a paralyzed, useless body, when a twin manifestation arrived.

Gideon was an avatar of destiny. He wore an explosive vest among a crowd of people celebrating Christmas, the flames of destruction burning all human flesh. And he saw Ruut betraying him. She turned her weapon toward him.

She pulled the trigger.

34

VIKTOR VODYANOY WAS a smaller man than Eric remembered, but the handshake was a powerful pull. The president paid much resemblance to Stalin himself. Nobody could meet Stalin without trepidation, not even one who was held in history as one of the greatest wartime leaders of all time.

Winston Churchill.

If western civilization still allowed Viktor to lead Russia with his iron fist, the nuclear mushroom cloud would be stamped in everyone's backbones.

The toxic footprint of war.

Because of the presence of the press in Santa Claus Village, he kept a forced smile. He wanted to launch all his fury and frustration with unbridled bitterness. Viktor was nothing but the embodiment of reversed progress in the global affairs.

Ded Moroz, the father frost in blue clothes shook hands with Santa Claus, and Eric. As Eric was ready to give the present to Santa Claus, he drawled:

"Please accept a small present as a gesture of companionship."

Viktor's blue eyes were callous and calculating. But upon opening the present, his face revealed a small boyish signal. The narcissistic smile building on his face after reading the note proved Theo's theory right: the man was a megalomaniac wielding too much power.

Out of the blue, Eric's mind repeated Albert Einstein's famous saying: *I know not with what weapons World War III will be fought, but World War IV will be fought with sticks and stones.*

<hr />

LOWERING HIS BINOCULARS on the table in the restaurant Ensilumi a hundred meters away, Theo closed his eyes and sighed. The Plan was running smoothly with its unstoppable momentum. The historically long and bloody moral arc of man was finally bending toward freedom and justice.

Theo felt his own eyes crinkling at the corners almost without a care in the world. No nation was able to fight against their invisible weapon. So many times, the wars were fought with kids in the battlefield, the generals using them as pawns. For the first time in history, the first casualty of war would not be the truth. There would be only one simple, single sacrifice.

Viktor Vodyanoy.

<hr />

FIVE KILOMETER SOUTH of the Santa Claus Village, Gideon's foot jittered against the floor in the passenger seat of the black van. Behind the dark, frosty window in the street lights, the line of trees falling behind seemed to jump closer as though they were passing through a lightning storm. Briefly, he held his hand on the window. But he couldn't thaw it.

What's happening to me?

He closed his eyes and leaned against his seat, his scalp itching with nervousness.

A road sign up ahead read *Ounasvaara ski center*.

Gideon noted that Patrick's right hand missed a little finger. Had he encountered a wolf or some wild animal? Patrick's bright-eyed look was engaging with the environment. Not even the buzzing of his cell phone broke his solid concentration.

"Affirmative, sir," Patrick said. "The light is green." Then, as he hung up the call, he stayed quiet for a moment, until he turned to Gideon. "The president of Russia will arrive at our training ground in thirty minutes. Our Russian colleagues have replaced the original skiing teacher. You'll know what to do."

Gideon started imagining what might happen. While over-thinking the outcomes, his father's words gave him the boost and determination he needed.

I trust you, son.

35

"**A**RE YOU OKAY?" Ruut asked Konrad who lay on the ground unmoving.

Konrad took a deep breath. His brain was stunned into inactivity, and when he regained normal sense of balance, his heart double-thumped, then began a tap dance of panic in his chest.

"Give me a minute."

Ruut held her cheek against Konrad's temple and held him in a one-arm hug.

"I thought I'd lost you."

A few seconds later Konrad managed to give her his most winning smile. She helped him up to all-fours on wobbly knees, guiding him back against the tree.

"What did you see?"

"Not much more sense than in palmistry."

"Spit it out before you forget anything!" Ruut's voice rose with authoritarian gusto.

"It's nothing uplifting."

Ruut sat on her knees.

"Please, Konrad. Speak. If it were like a dream, you'd forget it soon."

Konrad knew he would never forget nor understand what he experienced.

"I saw Gideon."

"You saw his future?"

"I saw... you might say... his potential."

"What?" Her voice first dropped only to bounce up. "You could see? You mean like... as if you were... a substitute for a Messenger?"

Konrad felt his stomach clinch. "I saw only the flash of a scene where people were celebrating Christmas. Gideon stood among them. He detonated a suicide vest."

Ruut's eyes were wide in search of 'I beg your pardon?'

"Ruut. Don't make any hasty judgments. Gideon doesn't seem a bit suicidal."

She let out a hollow laugh. "You're kidding, right? Tell me that you are making this up."

There was a strange vibe of unprecedented pretension in her voice. Did she know something he didn't?

The membrane was in her hands.

"What's in it?"

"The membrane is now complete," she said and rose. "But you wouldn't value its teachings."

"Let me see."

Ruut pocketed the membrane and produced the Parabellum. "I'm sorry, this information is not in our jurisdiction." She took Konrad's face in her aim.

"What are you doing?"

"Oona told me to take care of you."

"No, she didn't," Konrad said. "This is not you. What's going on?"

"I care about you, Konrad. I truly do. But people like you...

you are anti-everything. If Gideon blows himself up, it's because of the shit he's gotten all around from evil people. Those fuckers want to study him and hinder his potential. They'll use him, like Oona. And get rid of him. But not on my fucking watch!"

"But I'm on your side. I didn't mean to cause harm. Ruut!"

"End of discussion."

"But... this is so wrong," Konrad pleaded, "I saw you too—"

BANG.

Skyrockets of pain went off in his head, and all turned black.

36

THE WHOLE DOWNHILL was closed to the public. Gideon saw Russian security men surrounding the president like spiders placed around an entire web. All were protecting the man like he was the mother queen.

Up along the hill, there were agents and more security on both sides in the tree lines. Did they honestly expect any threat coming from the woods? At any rate, the ability to carry any attacks on Viktor was zero and below.

They exited the lift and looked down at their own, secured downhill.

"You," Viktor said and pointed both at Gideon and the open road. "First. You."

"I'll go a hundred meters down and wait for you," Gideon said. "Is it okay?"

Viktor was nodding.

Gideon tied his legs to his board, and waited for the president to finish his. Then he went down, trying to look calm and relaxed but his knees were feeble. Not wanting to show any trembling, he sat in the snow, looked over his shoulder at the president.

Viktor Vodyanoy was known for his Aikido skills, and as the man started coming down, and falling after every five meters, Gideon thought the man should have stayed in the Dojo.

A black belt won't make you a master on snow.

After a minute, the president found some balance and came down thirty meters before stopping his speed with a skillful *ukem* rollover. From the snow cloud surrounding the man, his smile reached Gideon. "Good?"

Gideon nodded. "Magnificent, sir."

Viktor pointed at himself, then the hill.

Gideon said, "Go ahead. Take it easy. The hill gets steeper." Gideon showed the degree of tilt with his hand, but the president was back on his board, sliding down like a speed-junkie without brakes.

As Viktor fell and got up, Gideon couldn't fathom how anybody could harm him. The security was impenetrable. Also, he was being watched and probably targeted with a weapon from somewhere, should he attempt any aggressive move on the president.

FURTHER DOWN IN the tree line, agent Bruce Moodyson saw Patrick Praytor's hand signal at the bottom near the skiing cafe. A Russian agent accompanied Bruce. A muscle-build goon, who smiled at him as they were able to see the president coming tumbling down. Bruce did nothing, but looked at his watch and said: "*Abracadabra.*"

The Russian agent faced him. "*Prastite?*"

Bruce smiled and waved his arm: don't worry. The agent suspected nothing. As Bruce activated the weapon in the president's direction, the moral enhancement began in all its glory.

The machine made the Russian agent only smile brighter his crooked, stupid smile.

Smile, for tomorrow your service won't be needed.

37

THEO KRAFT OPENED a champagne bottle in the car outside Santa Claus's Village. He filled two plastic cups and offered one to Eric.

"Potential uncorked," he said, raising a toast. "For the better future of Finland."

Eric evaluated the liquid in his cup, waited for the foam to settle.

"They now have the Messiah, who's not tempted to invade, command and tell the rules to others," Theo stated. "All we have to do is to watch God's word come to pass."

"This is wrong," Eric muttered. "The moral enhancement was not Viktor's choice. This was purely moral enforcement."

"I like you being analytical, Eric. And I know that as time passes you'll understand you made the right decision. Think of your children. Their future. It's all that matters."

"There's no turning back for humanity."

"Let's face it. We were biologically and genetically doomed to cause our own destruction. Not anymore."

"Philosophy has never been your greatest strengths. If you

haven't done the groundwork well, then all hail the Russian reaper and soon-to-be ground zero Lapland."

"Oh, we have the philosophical ground covered," Theo said. "Our greatest mind in the team has accessed the inaccessible. I can't go into the details, but our source knew the potential of the matter better than the genius of geniuses."

Eric shot Theo a look of disgust.

"Trust me," Theo said, his voice hard and piercing, firm as granite.

"For fuck's sake," Eric said and handed over the cup. "Give me the bottle."

Holding two cups in his hands, Theo waited for Eric to drink the bottle empty.

Eric opened the window and threw the bottle out. He pinched the bridge of his nose and closed his eyes. "You should be crucified."

"I take that as a compliment from a good friend."

Eric's eyes widened and rolled in their slots. "I wouldn't. Jesus H. Christ..."

They stared out of the windshield and spoke nothing in a minute.

"Eric," Theo said. "I still need one favor."

"How about that. A friend who speaks like an eloquent gentleman—yet has no intention to get permission—wants to do as he pleases. What can I do for you? Find you a whore house so that you can indulge in a final act of lust before you leave?"

"Actually." Theo paused to consider his words. "There's this Santa's Little Hideout I would like to clean up."

Eric blinked.

"There's a secret laboratory I would like to seal."

"Cleaning up the crime scene where you produced your weapon? It's *here*?"

"Don't look so surprised. Surely you had done the math already."

"Who the hell do you think you are? Bringing some fucked-up presents. I have no fucking clue about any secret laboratories."

"Even though you have your personnel working in there?"

"Do I look like a football manager? Like I keep an account of my players, who parties and fucks whom and where?" Eric leaned his head closer to Theo. "Who?"

"Ruut Stark."

"She works below the level meant for tourists in the Santa's Cave. I know all about that, and their current progress."

"Give me clearance to go down there. And below."

"Below the secret level? There's nothing."

"If you say so."

"Fuck! If you want to hit your philosophical bedrock with your dick and expect a new majestic discovery, please do that."

"I will."

Blood pressure rose red high on Eric's face. "I recognize that fake-friendly look. You are not ready yet. Russia was never the actual target, was it?"

"Viktor Vodyanoy was a top priority."

"My God." Eric erupted in ugly laughter. "You've got balls! What are you truly up to?"

Theo took a deep, satisfied breath. "We have the balls of the world's leaders in a tight squeeze, why stop now?"

Eric's nostrils flared. "Whatever I try to make you rethink or disagree, you say: 'Think of the children.' You can't blackmail me."

"We are in this together, setting up the guard rail for the path of humanity."

Eric quickly took back the steel of posture of his bent spine.

"Then I want in. If you're truly ready to sacrifice your career for this, I want to know exactly your next move."

"It's not how this game is played."

"What if I went to your home in the US and slept with your wife, and you would know nothing when you came back?"

"You're comparing *sex* to *war*?"

"One simply can't exist without the other," Eric said. "If you're going to fuck with people's minds, you're not going to do it without me."

"Eric. You have no pressure points to apply pressure."

Eric signaled his weapon holster on his hip. "I can still put a bullet in your head in a blink of an eye."

Theo tilted his head. "Do you honestly think I didn't take that option into account?"

Eric's eyebrows collapsed. "You. Touched. My. Weapon?"

"Sure."

"I have had this with me all day. You're bluffing."

"You obviously don't know how skilled Ruut is. Let's discuss more when we get back to your base."

"My. Base."

"And your country."

"Do not forget that."

"Or you'll rip my head off?"

Eric said nothing and sped the car away from the Santa Claus Village.

38

THESE PROFESSIONAL SOLDIERS *are my family,* Gideon thought. *And I'll see my father in a moment.*

Since nobody bothered to blindfold or cuff him, Gideon granted the elite soldiers the authority they deserved. He was a member of a mission greater than them. It was only two months ago that the police captured him for shoplifting, put him in cuffs in the back of a police car, and dumped him in jail.

Patrick Praytor spoke on his phone, and Gideon concluded from the 'Yes, sirs' that he was receiving orders from someone outranking him. He just realized that nobody in the team wore any buttons or decorations that would have revealed their rank. Then again, his father had once said that in the battlefield it was suicide to use the insignia. He heard his father's distant whisper:

Wear the medals on your chest, and you are already beef on the plate of the savages.

The car drove into a rock that was a hidden entryway for cars. Gideon had been inside this underground network twice; once with his class and once with his father. Santa Park was a Christmas theme park in the hill where Santa could welcome friends and visitors. A big picturesque nature sign with Santa Claus smiling his Coca-Cola smile in the wall read: 'The Home Cavern of Santa Claus.' A bit misleading. Overflowing with Christmas spirit, Santa was never seen hanging out there. His real home was his chamber a few kilometers away close to the airport.

Gideon wished Santa Claus's death for Christmas. He hated the whole concept of fooling generations of children.

As the car came to a halt in a small parking lot, Gideon realized nobody had congratulated him on his successful mission. The appreciation and respect were probably hidden on the soldiers' stern and stone-cold faces. The mission was teamwork. Top-notch. Nobody did it for thanks.

They walked down a tunnel wide enough for two buses. The walls and roof were bare stone; the air was cold but moist. At the dark end of the tunnel was a big metallic door that slid open with a horrible rattle. Behind the door Gideon saw somebody working with another car and filling it up with grates. There were more army men, but in Finnish uniforms. Everybody greeted each other without a shared word.

Patrick reserved an elevator. Gideon waited back against the wall, staying away from marching soldiers. He noted standing in a pool of water, whose source was high in the wall, and that the pool was frozen. He didn't know how, but the temperature didn't seem to be at water freezing point.

The elevator arrived as the light sprang in the hall lantern. Darkness swallowed the team. Extra light appeared in the floor designators.

Down in the hidden depths, the doors opened to a long bright white corridor with similar looking plain doors. Patrick chose, perhaps, the fifteenth on the left, behind which a silver spiral staircase led to an intricate corridor of a sophisticated laboratory.

Instead of thinking where his dad might be, Gideon missed his mom. He shook his head at the thought that when soldiers were severely wounded they always screamed for their mothers.

He didn't have that weakness.

39

KONRAD HEARD WHISPERS in his hallucinogenic stupor, and his eyes flew open. His body was on fire with intense phantom pain as if his body parts were pulled off from their joints. The déjà vu moment reminded him that his body was designed for discomfort.

The sky was dark. As his vision came into focus, beacons of light sprang alive, as though they were mankind holding candles aloft. His head was about to crack open from the searing pain.

He moved his fingers, felt the wound in his skull. Blood. Lots of blood.

What the hell did you do to me?

The Parabellum was on the ground. Konrad rolled onto his side, drew breath and snow whistled into his lungs like flour dust. He coughed his throat clear, then started crawling to the pond. He wanted to see the wound in his head in the reflection of the water, although light was scarce. Crawling and vomiting along the way, the growing pain sent endless nauseating shock waves through his body.

Why am I still alive? Am I a machine?

Konrad managed to bring himself to the pond with elbows

and knees bruised. He put his head down. The world saw what kind of filth and wicked creature he was. He had been anti-everything for too long.

Every sin has a price.

Konrad stared at the dark water. The stars gave a bit more light, his face still a gray mask of shadow. He wished he would see Oona's face. Not because of her smile, but for answers.

But she never showed up. The pond turned darker, taking away the picture of his face.

He undressed, dived into the dark water, floated alone on the surface, then began to sink. But he opened his eyes at a sudden question.

How does a weapon designer fail at a point-blank shot in the head?

His muscles tingled. The automatic breathing reflex kicked in. The numb tension in his body produced an overreaction. His lungs were giving way for cold water to dash in, but he wanted to put the flawed design of his body to work—he plunged up through the red darkness a way back to the living.

And grabbed his Parabellum.

40

GIDEON MET A man who introduced himself as Aslan Said. It took him no more than a single question to affirm the man was Russian. Gideon remembered seeing him on the downhill slope.

"Basics," Aslan said. "A soldier must know the number of bullets in the clip."

Gideon felt the difference as Aslan masterfully added or reduced rounds in the pistol on the table.

"You know what this is?"

Gideon nodded at the green ball of metal. "A hand grenade."

Aslan pulled off the pin. "This is how you set it up. When you throw it you've got three seconds to get cover." Aslan put back the pin and offered it to Gideon. "If you throw this baby and see it land... bye bye to your pretty face."

Gideon nodded.

"Remove the pin."

Gideon triggered the grenade as showed, now realizing the true terror of what it was like to hold an actual one in hand with the fuse burning and counting. He quickly tried to put back the pin...

Aslan slapped the grenade away from Gideon's hands, and the heart in Gideon's chest froze; the grenade stopped in the corner of the small room. Instinctively he jumped over the table and shoved Aslan from the back toward the grenade, covering himself against the floor. He closed his eyes and held his ears.

After a long silence, he heard hands clapping, cruelly.

"Good. A strong survival instinct makes the best soldier." Aslan went to pick up the grenade. "A training grenade."

"I want to see my dad." Gideon swallowed his fear and tears. "I won't do this anymore until I meet him."

"This is what your father wanted. Go through the training and reunite with your father. He needs time to heal his wounds."

"He is wounded? How?"

"It's better to hear it from himself."

"I'll kill you if you're bluffing."

A smile spread across Aslan's scarred face. He signaled Gideon to take a seat.

"This is a flash bang. The blinding effect lasts for..."

Gideon stared at Aslan's fingers dancing on the surface of the gray can of soda and drifted away to somewhere else, fighting his internal war against the self-accusing questions.

What the hell are you doing?

RUUT EMERGED FROM the woods in front of a taxi. The driver stopped the car in a chorus of brakes and horns. He jumped out, lips snarling with rage as he shook his fists and yelled at her.

"I'm sorry," Ruut said, "but you're wasting my time."

She spun behind him and brought him down in a solid choke hold. She applied pressure but only enough, hopefully to keep him out of the hospital.

The man lost consciousness in less than ten seconds.

Swallowing down her adrenaline rush, she took his phone and dialed Gideon. She jumped behind the wheel. Gideon's phone was dead. She tried Jake's number and got through.

"Where are you?" Ruut demanded.

"Netta and I are at the playground," Jake replied. "The one close to Gideon's father's."

"You're not safe. Get out of there, now!"

There was a pause. Something was wrong. She accelerated to fetch firepower from her home.

"Ruut," Jake said finally. "I think you'll need to come over here..."

41

HUNGER CHURNED KONRAD'S insides and his vision tapered.

Where did you go?

The bleeding didn't seem to stop on his head; he kept a snowball attached to it, and made a new one every two minutes. He could barely walk straight, swaying as if in a narcotic fog. But there were temperature differences between areas of the air like warm spots in cold lakes, so he fumbled for warmth like a snake with extra-sensory perception.

Finally some artificial orange light appeared. The amount of snow increased as the trees grew less dense. The air was getting colder. And he was getting vicious pneumonia.

There was a house ahead. He cut across the backyard and concluded he would realize his whereabouts from the roadside.

"Terrorist!" A voice mocked.

Konrad spun around. An old granny peeked out of a window.

"What's the problem with you youngsters? When I was young, I respected the older folk!"

"I'm sorry," Konrad said, "I was lost and I..."

"Always making up excuses! Get off my property, or I'll call my husband. He'll drive a tank turret up your ass!"

She launched another tirade before she slammed the window shut.

Konrad sighed. Fog began to lift.

A child laughed nearby. Konrad went to a playground, where a father played with his daughter. Only thirty meters down the road leading to the city center he saw a man dressed in black, gazing at the father and daughter. Konrad hid behind a pile of snow, barely in time.

Could they be Jake and Netta? Could he have been so lucky? Ruut might be close as well. Konrad gazed up along the steam of his breath dancing in the streetlight.

Shit!

His breathing could reveal his whereabouts. Quickly, he shoved a piece of snow in his mouth to neutralize the steam from rising. He checked the magazine of the Parabellum only to find it empty. The hair in his back and arms shot up as he peeked over the snow, keeping his head down and the snow tight against the palate.

The agent reloaded a silenced gun.

Then a taxi appeared behind the agent without headlights on. It approached fast, almost as silent as a tiger, and hit the agent's legs. His head cracked against the windshield, and sent the body windmilling in the air before falling on its head.

Konrad watched the scene in utter disbelief.

Jake and Netta froze.

The driver of the car slammed on the brakes. Ruut rushed to the playground with a pistol in her hand.

As Ruut ordered Jake and Netta to take cover behind a children's slide complex, another car curved into the scene. Two more agents appeared out of nowhere with tactical silenced rifles used in direct raids to end a bloodbath.

Or to start one.

Konrad started circling the park, crawling as fast as he could so that he could maintain the element of surprise. He shoved the suicidal signs of the mission to the back of his skull. The only environmental ally was that the snow wasn't frozen but soft, it didn't cause a sound to move on it.

Taking a split-second glance at what was happening, Konrad increased speed.

Ruut took Netta and Jake behind metal trash bins while luring the agents to herself. She managed to hide behind a massive pine. The bullets striking the bark sounded like giants bees swarming behind a wall. Ruut fired counter shots from behind the tree by leaning back against a tree and shooting over her shoulder. Her chances of surviving were slim at best if the agents flanked her.

BULLETS BIT INTO the bark behind Ruut's spine. She reloaded her weapon. The shots sent sharp wood splinters at her eyes, and she almost lost eyesight. Netta and Jake were on her left; Netta held her ears, and Jake hid behind her.

Coward.

Now or never she needed a lucky shot, a miracle. Something. There was no way she could continue fighting half blind. Suddenly the world seemed surreal, empty and cold. As though God had turned a blind eye on her. A bullet sank into the tree from two o'clock. The agents were circling her.

She fired below under her armpit. Barely managing to hide, two bursts of bullets hit the tree again.

I'm dead.

Denial was futile, as was her feeble resistance. But if there was something she had learned in the army among men, it was what she always told herself: don't play the game if you can't stand the pain.

Suddenly she saw movement on her right. The other agent had her head in the crosshairs. Someone hit the agent in the head with something metallic, but as she raised her weapon, fire pierced in through her teeth and out of her cheek. In the inhalation of blood and loss of balance she aimed and pulled the trigger.

Got you, you son of a bitch.

Someone called her name.

Konrad?

Ruut turned to her left, blood escaping from her head and sending her to her knees. The sight shattered her world all at once.

Netta and Jake—unmoving in snow in pools of blood.

"No. No. No."

Ruut dived and stumbled toward her family, but Konrad and the agent were fighting. Konrad took a huge blow to his right eye socket, and the agent stepped behind him, pulling Konrad into a tight strangle.

Ruut trained the barrel of her gun on the middle of the enemy's eyes.

"Stop. Lower your weapon." The agent put more squeeze on Konrad's Adam's apple.

Konrad face was red, veins bursting.

"Konrad!" Ruut yelled. "Look at me!"

He didn't pass out this time but played it as best as he could, which gave a bit leeway for Ruut with the agent's head a little more exposed.

Ruut fired.

The bullet hit the agent in the neck.

Konrad found a knife to his hand from the agent's sheath and pressed the blade into the muscle of the agent's thigh, but he resisted the pain and swung the pistol, connecting it with Konrad's head. He took balance from the ground and swung his fist, landing only at the clip. But the agent's finger squeezed around the trigger, and bullets flew directly at Ruut's chest.

Ruut squeezed the trigger without breathing. But she could breathe no more. As she fell, she saw from the corner of her eye how Konrad managed to wrangle the agent's head into the line of fire.

She smiled.

Got you, too.

42

KONRAD CRADLED RUUT in his lap. Despair telescoped inside him as heavy as an extension ladder.

She traced her bloody forefinger on his forehead, forcing a smile over her pains. "Your eye's hurt. Put an eye patch on it and update your dating profile. Women will love it."

Konrad's earlobes went warm. "You still try to take care of me. I realize it now. You always leaned in, offered help."

"Servitude is love." Ruut coughed. "The only sacrifice that matters."

His brain finally put it together: the bee's poison had still affected her thinking and caused paranoia in the glade. The enemy had the tools to reduce all inhibition and stimulate extreme aggression.

"Did Oona tell you that you were going to shoot me?"

She gasped for air, then held her lips together and nodded, eyes closed.

"What was in the bullet?"

"Progress."

"Your design?"

"I tried to create peace, not grudge and revenge. Some bullets had optical sensors in them. If they don't to curve away in time, the nanomachines inside repair the damage done. They know the value of human life when the shooter forgets it."

"But Gideon killed one agent."

"No. I finished him when you weren't watching."

Dumbfounded, he nodded.

"Take the membrane from my pocket," Ruut whispered. "I think Oona left you a message." Konrad located it and put it in his pocket while Ruut continued: "Get to the bottom of the conspiracy. Be careful. But don't worry about me..." Her words caught Konrad off guard.

Resurrection?

Trying to mentally reduce his high expectations, Konrad quickly glanced at the membrane. Disappointment flooded his limbs.

"Empty?"

"No, Konrad," Ruut said. "The message is obvious: you must have faith."

A cold sting of metal landed on the neck of his head. Konrad raised his hands up.

"I knew you were a terrorist," a woman said.

"Iris," Ruut sang. "Thank God!"

"Miss Ruut? What has this piece of shit done to you?" Iris contemplated the surrounding massacre. "Don't you worry, I already called the cops. I can shoot him if that's what you want."

"Don't." Ruut winced her head to signal for Iris to stop pointing the RK-62 at Konrad. "I'm sorry to say this, but your husband is involved in a horrible plan that might turn into a global catastrophe."

"I doubt that. Eric has learned decency the hard way after I discovered his relationship with an army officer."

Ruut coughed. "You've got an army rifle. You must own Eric's clothes. Disguise Konrad and take him over to the base. There's not much time left..." The length of Ruut's body stiffened. "Konrad. Tell Gideon I love him. I never said it to him. Please, it's all I'm asking."

"Of course."

"I'm ready." Ruut's voice was weakening to a whisper. "Sleep is taking me."

"See you on the other side," Konrad said.

Ruut coughed a laugh. "And there's my atheist..."

As Ruut's final breath vanished out into the sky with her glazed stare, Konrad closed her eyes. He gave her forehead a kiss and laid her hands on her stomach, tears obscuring his vision. "Go gentle, dear."

They heard the sound of sirens.

Iris threw the rifle over her shoulder and helped Konrad up.

"Come on. War is not over yet. I'll call my husband on our way."

"Everything I touch falls apart," Konrad reasoned. "I can't do any good."

"Right, wrong—forget it. You'll do what's *necessary*. Besides you promised her. Gideon might not last for long."

"They've got him? How do you know that?"

"What do you think? That I have forgiven my husband?" Iris shook a menacing finger. "I've bugged his office. Gideon is there somewhere. But that is not the least of your problems. Not that I know what's going on, but the top brass of NATO, General Theo Kraft is over there. Those two sound like they have a recipe for chaos in their hands. They've attacked the president of Russia here in Rovaniemi."

"What in the name of—"

"I'll explain on the way," Iris said. "Now, let's dress you up like a soldier."

43

GIDEON TOUCHED THE sergeant triple-triangle insignia on the chest of his army uniform. Although skipping ranks, it meant he was taken seriously, capable of doing anything. Breaking walls or go through a stone if needed. The respect he had gotten from Patrick was as immeasurable as it was liberating. The feeling of being someone meaningful filled his heart with content as he recapped the task Patrick had given to him.

A checklist of equipment and arms.

The objects in the storage room varied from binoculars to C4 explosives. He went through the list and let no item past him without touching it first. Then at the last word he frowned.

Bulletproof vest?

He looked around while keeping a pen on his lips.

"Gideon," Patrick said, holding something in his hand.

Gideon quickly did his best salute.

"Stand at ease, soldier. We don't salute the rank nor the man during a mission, is that clear?"

Gideon nodded. "I couldn't find this last item..."

"Put this on." Patrick handed the vest and helped dressing it.

"Come." Patrick started walking along a long corridor whose end Gideon knew nothing about.

"Where are you taking me?"

Patrick kept walking, kept his silence.

They came to a room at the end of the corridor, where a door stood open.

"He's expecting you."

Gideon's heart started aching in his chest. He entered the room that was half-lit. At the end of the room's one side was Kaspar.

"Dad?" Standing next to his father, who had been mostly wrapped with bandages and was emerging from sleep, Gideon felt his eyes were deceiving him. "I thought you were dead."

Kaspar opened his eyes, took stock. He blinked, trying to focus on Gideon. His speech was a slow slur.

"Son... My God. It's you."

"Are you okay?"

"Seen better days. Are they taking good care of you?"

Gideon nodded.

"Are you ready to go on the last mission with them?"

"I'm not sure what that means."

"Taking Viktor out was only the test phase..."

"Are we going somewhere?"

"Where do you want to go? What part of the world do you want to change first?"

Gideon shrugged. "It's not my decision."

"Don't sell yourself short. Ultimately it all comes down to one question you must ask yourself to know where you stand: Mankind—divided or redefined?"

"Dad, it's not that I wouldn't want this, as I understand the higher purpose of it all, but I feel strange. I feel I'm not getting all of the information."

"Nobody ever gets to know everything. That's why you have

to base your action on a certain amount of knowledge. Future missions secure that no gears of war can be shifted anymore higher."

"You believe I'm up to this?"

"Absolutely. Just like you're in the process of shaping your identity, it's your destiny to shape the world's. The old world is crumbling under our feet, and hell awaits us all if we don't march on. Besides, I know war. War never changes, only its actors. War never changes things because not everyone can be your ally."

Gideon said with an attempt at humor, "You sound like mom with 'keep your friends close and enemies closer'—bull."

"Words can't describe your importance. Humanity will be more divided than ever if people aren't guided. You are the new messenger. The actions you take will be the teachings the world will need to stay in the books of the living."

Gideon stayed quiet.

"The people around you are all killing machines, pure and simple. But humanity's best interest is at their heart. Never question that, no matter what you'll see, hear or feel. The wrong kind of care clouds your judgment."

"Messenger..." Gideon said perplexed.

"At the beginning of creation, we were all meant to be prophets. We are to be repurposed. That is our destiny."

"Dad," Gideon said. "If the team is humanity's best hope for the future, if you truly believe so, I'll dedicate myself to it. I'll stick together with you."

"Good. We'll discuss later," Kaspar said. "Go and rest. I need to gather strength too. Then we'll work. Remember, this is all about becoming one in heart or letting beating stop. We are *The Continuists.*"

Gideon took a deep breath. He had the proud feeling that he knew exactly what his father meant.

44

ERIC PANTZAR RUBBED the sweat from his forehead as Iris spoke to him on the phone. Iris's tone, although calm and decent, revealed she was using the tactics of applying pressure on old wounds.

"Don't you care about your child?" Iris attacked. "Do I have to spell it out for you? She's in the hospital, and she might die. I'm coming to get you. And do me a favor—open the Goddamned gates when I get there."

"Iris," Eric said, but she had already hung up. Eric felt Theo's inspective eye on him. "Sure. I understand. See you."

"Troubles?" Theo asked.

"You know women."

"Touché."

Eric took his winter jacket from a hanger. "I need to leave for a few hours. It's urgent."

"Your daughter?"

"I don't know what's going on. Iris is dead worried. Knock yourself out while I'm gone. There's vodka in the drawer."

"A typical Finn."

Theo took Eric's place and sat. "My last favor, Eric. Can you get me to the Cave with Iris?" He placed his elbows on the table and crossed his fingers. "We both know your daughter is not in peril."

Eric nodded. "Iris is overreacting."

"Is that all?"

Eric scratched his cheek. "I guess this is her weird attempt to add firewood to the cold hearth…"

"Marriage is all about the intimacy, Eric." Theo leaned back in the chair. "About the timing of touch. After all, on the grander scale, intimacy is our last chance as a species. People have lost their touch."

"Easy for you to say, you probably see your wife every two months. You don't have to fight when time's so precious."

"Intimacy is not about how much. It's about timing and how you do it. And that's what I'm good at, thanks to God."

"I don't want God in my office. God is a perverse Beast. And nature is a serial killer."

"Burdened with an internalized conflict? You've got a secret lover?"

"I stepped into a huge pile of shit once."

Theo cocked his head. "May I ask room service from her?"

"I thought intimacy with one's wife means honesty and trust. You lied to me."

"That's the other thing that is the requirement for a man to attain this job," Theo said, his chin up. "Master timing and lying and you'll never lack women to keep you warm."

"Thanks for the tip," Eric said. "But when it comes to my soldiers, here I'm in charge. Arrange your own company of whores. I'll send someone to take you to the Cave."

"Can I least get a handshake, a salute or a hug?"

"I'll salute you when you're officially retired. When I see your god damned plan hasn't turned into a nightmare."

"Don't lose your sleep."

"No, I won't. It's not my job to worry. Bracing myself for the worse is."

Theo folded his arms. "You need a new motto. *Si vis pacem, para pacem?*"

"Easy for you to say," Eric chided. "But I can't prepare for peace when your ugly face is still around. Good-bye."

THREE ARMY TRUCKS stood idly as a lonely Lada appeared on the military grounds. Some Captain was cursing at soldiers who had forgotten equipment in their rooms. "Beat your goddamned faces!" He threatened revenge on another group to shave up their faces in thirty seconds, "...or I will put you to shovel feed your own testicles to the bears in the woods." One private panicked and cut his face, falling to his knees. The Captain came shaking his head and slapped a backhand across the private's face, demanding, "Fifty push-ups!"

Konrad sat in the back seat of the Lada, remembering well the time of his own army year, always in a hurry to be somewhere to do nothing at all. He felt the uniform Iris had given to him, and the beret and the eye patch that barely held the bleeding trickle of blood under it. He saw how Iris squeezed the wheel tighter as her epically tall husband approached the car. Thinking of the fiery debate ahead, suddenly for Konrad, this car that no one could heat enough was suddenly as hot as a sauna.

45

KONRAD SENSED THE dagger-sharp rage cutting at Eric's temples. Fortunately, Iris kept her husband on a short leash.

"That's why you will give this man your access card and keys he'll need. Or I swear to God I will turn you and your big shot NATO friend over to the police."

"You know what," Eric said, unable to look at her. "I thought we had gone through this issue, but no! You still twist the blade, using my mistake as leverage. As though you never made any?"

"I don't make mistakes! Have I ever been anything but a loyal and trustworthy companion, who thinks only of what's good for her husband?"

"This is not companionship! This is..."

Konrad witnessed the flaming conversation and pressed his back tight against the seat, thinking it was the safest spot to wait. While listening, he revisited fights his parents had had.

"Give me your weapon," Konrad said to Eric, shocked to the core at his sudden act of courage.

"What?" Eric turned around.

"I need a weapon."

"I'll give you shit, you piece of—"

Iris slapped Eric with an open hand. "Do not curse in my fucking car!"

Eric held his cheek, his big eyes sad and wide like a little boy who had just received an unnecessarily harsh punishment.

Silence settled in.

Eric took the phone and started looking for a number. "I need to call a friend who will take Theo to the Cave."

"Give me that." Iris grabbed the phone.

Eric pressed his lips into a white slash. "I should have brought your ass to the shooting range years ago."

Iris connected her elbow to Eric's stomach, and he let out a painful yelp. Tears reached his eyes.

"Now that you've reached cooperative mode, you'll give Konrad your keys." She took something out of her purse for Konrad. "Here, take this headset."

"What is it for?"

Iris gave Konrad a little earplug and told him, "It's a mini electronic sound-canceling earplug. Your ear defender against explosions and gunfire. It's transparent, so no one will notice. It's designed so that you'll hear conversations and orders, everything needed."

"Ha!" Eric snorted. "A true soldier, my ass."

"You'll be his guide." Iris signaled the headset. "Wear it."

"I will not let this gormless douchebag on my base. He's a rat. And I don't like rats. I will order my soldiers to kill him with Mortal fucking Combat fatality."

Iris leaned in, grabbed Eric by the clothes and pulled his head in a few centimeters from hers. Konrad couldn't see what else Iris pulled from her pocket, but whatever she placed on Eric's groin made the big man whimper.

"I could use some fresh air," Konrad said.

The intensity in Iris's menacing stare at Eric continued over the better half of ten seconds before Eric nodded.

Konrad let out a silent sigh while pulling the beret over and back on his sweaty forehead.

"Good," Iris said. "Now call Theo that General Elvis has left the building. Colonel Keloneva will escort him to the Cave shortly."

"What? Who?" Eric said.

Iris gave Konrad a sticker where the name was. "I always wanted to put my private time name in use." She smiled at Konrad, then turned to Eric. "And don't you think I'm not planning to take my own surname back when this is over!"

Eric seemed now to keep his hatred inside. "A guard is standing outside. A good man. But won't let anybody in my office."

"Then call Theo and save your tears. I'll handle your guards just like last time I went inside and wired your room."

"What are you going to tell him?" Konrad said.

"That Colonel Keloneva is here to call the shots. I will tell him that he never saw or heard a thing."

"How do you think you're going to pull that out?" Eric asked. "You can't just persuade him."

"Nancy-boys. Do you honestly think I don't know who has fucked whom on your base?"

With that Iris stepped out and approached the guard.

Konrad listened to the stillness inside the Lada and thought of all the things that silence hides.

46

ONRAD'S EARS WERE ringing from the conversation as he answered the softened, fearful guard's salute and entered the building.

The familiar stench of mold hit him in the face. The structures were rotten to the core. Mandatory army service was not only a sacrifice of precious time, but also health. Nobody left the military without some degree of silent lung trauma.

On one side of the corridor were the many portraits of high ranked officials who looked like they would get spooked out at the sight of a gun. On the other side all the Finnish presidents evaluated his intentions as he came to Eric's office door.

"Knock and enter," Eric said in his ear. "Beware, Theo is full of booby-traps. His own narrow brilliance seduces him. Especially in philosophy."

Konrad landed a fist at the door and went in.

The small intense man hunched behind the table seemed to have stopped his meditation. "Colonel! How's war treating you?"

Konrad found no answer to address the question.

"Your eyes tell me that you have witnessed a death of children, seen bullets wreaking havoc in their bodies, twisting tissue, and splintering bone."

Konrad nodded. He noted how Theo's eyes spoke of years' worth of worry, but now gleamed as if they'd struck gold.

"Where did you come from? Let me guess. Afghanistan? Ghost paleness sticks to you in that country of dust and sand."

"I came from the woods," Konrad said. "I played the part of Rambo, and my soldiers tried to locate me and get me killed."

"Survival in a hostile environment. Sounds important. But doesn't make a lick of difference. You just get on the wrong side of a board and bull."

"Excuse me?"

Theo placed his tongue between his teeth—a lizard's tongue soon springing for a fly. "War has no place in my heart anymore. I would rather get those boys of yours around a campfire and tell ghost stories. I would persuade them to quit the army."

"Who would then do the work that has to be done?"

"Colonel..." Theo tried to see Konrad's name tag.

"Keloneva."

"Colonel Keloneva," Theo said bombastically, "what if I told you that soon you don't have to prepare for war anymore?"

"That would be a fairytale."

"What would you do if you didn't have to continue waging endless war anymore, practicing and preparing for it in the cold?"

Konrad evaluated Theo's what's-the-rush body language, as impatience gnawed at his insides. "Honestly, sir, although it would require one crazy step of faith from nature toward the infinite... I think I would explore space. And time. Discover extraterrestrial intelligence."

Theo frowned. "A soldier and a philosopher. A rare combination. Are you a religious man?"

"Irrelevant question."

"What do you believe in then?"

Konrad cleared his throat. "I believe in the potential of humans."

Theo paced with metronomic regularity. "When I retire, I'm going to plan a shuttle integrated with a virtual machine that will spin the world we can live in as conscious beings. The hazards of space can only be circumvented if we can remove the clock and hide in intangible information. Then, as space-traveling time loses its meaning, the captain-robot of the ship will go through resurrection files and print us out."

Is this man for real? "May I suggest, since you started pondering, that shouldn't the long-term plan be to manipulate the structures of the universe with our intelligence? Since human intelligence is already moving mountains, we could command natural laws. The only reason I can think of why God is giving guidance is that He wants us to grow so that we can decide the destination of the universe. Gradually our power grows, as does our freedom to choose."

"My thoughts exactly, Colonel! Where did Eric find you? I can hardly mention God or an ism to him, or he looks like a bull had horned his ass."

"I think Eric speaks with vodka."

"You know what, Colonel?" Theo's voice turned liturgical. "You just gave an old dog a new bloody bone to feast on. God didn't create us to be his image. We are meant to become Him. I always become struck by the sheer grandeur of our possibilities. Replace his supremacy and re-create the universe with better possibilities for life. The new universe fine-tuned for life will be the Garden of Eden. It's true we can't create something out of nothing. But the universe is full of something. Our destiny is not to travel around the galaxies, but to re-create conditions where we can flourish!"

Say something neutral, say something neutral. "That is if we don't strike ourselves down with the tragedy of unrealized potential."

Theo spread his hands. "But you're watching history in the making! You've got to ask yourself: do you want in, or are you out?"

Are you offering me a job? "That's a good question. But shall I take you to the Cave?"

"Ever heard of Plato's allegory of the Cave?" Theo pressed on.

"One of my favorites," Konrad said and saw a glimpse of his students, their tired eyes begging, 'Stop torturing us.'

"As we are prisoners, chained to our limitations of senses, I've begun to drag us out of the cave into the world above. I'll keep returning back to shadows and free other prisoners from bonds. And the only question remains, who am I?"

"The Good Shepherd?"

"Exactly! Intelligence has its way of putting the right minds together at the right time to crack cosmic secrets. That's the formula for the atom bomb. Even though we never become God and omnipotent, we can be messengers to ourselves. The shocking, seismic shift will crack down the Cosmic Cave, and everybody will earn salvation. When we have broken down and beaten the laws of physics that dictate that all intelligent life within the universe will necessarily face the ultimate death."

Konrad nodded. "It's called evolution, but we don't know its direction. The law of evolution says that when the environment changes life must leave, adapt, or die. If our universe freezes, there aren't many options left. It's always a choice between adapting and moving."

"You Finns are smart," Theo said, glancing at his wristwatch. "A bit savage for my taste, but smart. I'm glad you had time to listen to an old man's testimony. Let's get a move on."

Konrad listened to Eric's voice in his ear. "Good. My car is parked outside. Green Volkswagen. The key is in its place. It's not an Aston Martin, only a piece of shit I happen to love more than my wife..."

There was distortion from a verbal fight in the connection.

A solemn silence ensued.

As Theo was putting winter clothes on, Konrad's eyes locked on something invisible. He missed Ruut. Her death was like a stone grinding between the hemispheres, utterly incomprehensible.

Why did you promise to return?

47

GIDEON LOOKED FORWARD to more basic training that qualified him to be ready for anything. But this was the first time 'anything' meant the risk of getting killed. Since there was no action in sight, he walked over to Patrick Praytor who tinkered with a digital display on a giant telescope.

"What is that for?"

"Stargazing. My father taught me everything about the night sky. My every question mattered, he never failed to deliver a satisfying answer. We are all children when we turn to the night sky's gloomy enigma. I'm going to do the same for my child. We all communicate with a reality beyond human perception every day. The universe is not dark and full of a void when you realize that no matter where you look—it's light all over."

Gideon crossed his hands. "I'm an exception. Stars don't mean anything to me."

"Then you haven't yet grasped that we are all light collectors like this telescope: the more light you collect, the further into space you'll see and the further your understanding of yourself increases."

Gideon leaned forward.

"Man is only a wolf in a sheep den without reasonable future in sight, other than killing. We are animals, but spiritually something much, much greater. There are two kinds of people—the ones who illuminate the path of humanity and the ones using darkness to divide humanity from itself."

"I don't believe there is no possibility to muffle the human horror story," Gideon said.

Patrick cocked his head left and rolled his eyes to right corner of the ceiling. "I'm going to tell you a secret. The wood where you and your mother and that professor went is one place you should have paid more attention to. I have been there. I found there someone who brought much joy and meaning to my life. I remember I had to shield my eyes against the sun's floodlight between the knots of branches. Those who reach there are privileged. While the grown-ups take paths and paved official ways, the children and young people use back routes and shortcuts, which is why you managed to move quickly and undetected. The Dark Forest Floors may seem evil and inhospitable, but every trap hides a treasure in its labyrinthine core. The forest studies us also. Do you know what that place is?"

"Tell me."

"Heaven. Eden. No matter the name, that's the place we'll arrive at when we grow spiritually."

Gideon shuffled his feet. "I have spent half of my life there. It's no heaven."

"You must see the forest for the trees."

"What does that even mean? That I should be intelligent enough to see something invisible? Intelligence isn't seeing a forest for the trees. It's looking at the other way."

"There are hidden meanings in the woods that dwell beyond our conceiving eyes. We can learn to see them just like man has learned to see the universe by crafting the grain of sand. Our planet earth is blessed with land and sea in just the right balance because technology requires land to prosper. Would we be launching rockets into space with Hubble-eyes if there were water everywhere? Just like the way humanity has mastered glass, by seeing higher meanings in a grain of sand, we seek the very truths of the universe. Through the grain of sand. The distant and the close have become deliciously tangible with telescopes and microscopes. Sand is our magnifying glass to the universe. And what does this all mean in your situation? You, Gideon, have already begun polishing the proper instruments, which could hold answers to your questions. You are the instrument of life and death."

Gideon stayed quiet for a while. "I don't know where to start. I don't know who to trust."

"Reprogram yourself. Do you think there are desperate situations in war?"

"Hell, yes."

"No. There are only desperate people. Do you think there are learning problems?"

"I believe so..."

"No. There's only bad teaching. You are the teacher of yourself. The whole reality is that we are the teachers and prophets of ourselves. Do you think there are good or bad people?"

Gideon considered the question. "I guess I see what you're trying to say..."

"Right. We aren't good or evil; it's just the way we are."

Gideon sank into a thought, tracing his temple back and forth with a forefinger. It crept up on him, an emotional wound, devouring his skin's heat with an icy blow, invisible and less substantial than the wind.

"My life is a ghost voyage."

"Everybody suffers," Patrick replied. "Focus your life on what fuels you, what engages you, what fulfills you, and you'll find your meaning." Patrick examined the telescope carefully, wiped off dust. "God, The Glassblower of the Universe, knew immediately the scale of failing as matter spread out into space, and man came forth and started to play with it. He has always been helping us so that we could find Him."

"Who gave you that idea? Your father?"

"My dad is a huge fan of stop-motion animations. As I grew up, he always reminded me how bringing dead puppets to life was the closest thing to magic. You could play God, create worlds and laws and characters as you liked, and dictate the plot. But deep inside he knew that his passion wasn't in bringing puppets to life, rather in band-aiding his mind's scars, which gave the feeling of control. He wanted more. In the war zones, he saw drifting ruins of souls, and he realized that he wanted to blow life on the same kind of heartless objects, who had jinxed themselves on the different forms of Jihad."

"I would like to meet your father one day."

"I'm glad to hear. He'll be here in ten minutes."

"Cool. But what's your big plan?"

"Shedding light, of course," Patrick said. "Stars are falling tonight."

Gideon pretended he had understood. "Where?"

"Israel. They have been waiting for their savior with tongues in their cheeks too many years. Meanwhile, killed quite too many because of the expectations."

"We are going to the Middle East?"

"We're assembling the team and equipment."

"Is my father coming?"

Patrick looked down. For the first time Gideon saw some hesitation in him.

"Gideon. Your father is dying."

"What?"

Patrick placed a hand on Gideon's shoulder.

"I know this is difficult. A parent dying is always a terrible blow, I can tell it from experience. But he is waiting for you."

"What's going on? He can't die just like that."

"I'll give you two some privacy."

Gideon stared at the wall.

"Go," Patrick said. "Your father has some interesting things to say."

48

IN THE CRADLE of dusk, a blue moment shrouded the world. Time seemed to stand still as Theo and Konrad exited an army Volkswagen and gazed at the sky, where an airplane flew overhead, heading east.

"There goes your Savior," Theo said.

"Finland's?"

"Let's put it in perspective and anti-clockwise: Norway, Finland, Estonia, Latvia, Lithuania, Poland, Ukraine..." Theo took a quiet sigh. "All around to China and North Korea. Russia shares borders with more countries than any other state in the world."

"I'm not following."

"When that plane lands in Moscow, new winds will blow inside the Kremlin. His visit to Lapland changed him quite profoundly."

"Did something happen?"

"With one handshake, we achieved more than all the leaders of the world combined. We agreed we would not throw our world into darkness for the sake of the children and the planet."

"Nobody buries the hatchet that easily," Konrad stated.

"Never in the history of all humanity has East and West come together and agreed on a solution to war."

"Solutions to one problem must be solutions for all. Global challenges require global solutions. Answer them accordingly, and we ascend."

"I have no idea what you are talking about."

"Want to have a sneak peek?"

Konrad lifted an eyebrow, theatrically.

"War has changed. You'll notice the effect in the news of how one man can affect world peace."

"With all due respect, is this a concern for our homeland security?"

Theo entered the Cave and started walking down the road. Konrad rushed behind.

"Humor me," Theo said. "Tomorrow you'll wake up, and you'll feel freedom unlike never before. The Russian fighters will have stopped insulting your airspace. Tension isn't mounting by the minute. You have more time to spend with your family. I see you have a ring on your finger. Do you have children?"

Konrad didn't answer.

"Now it's the best time to create a big family. Like it so far?"

"What's the catch?"

"Devil lives in the detail," Theo said. "Saving the planet isn't done in suits and ties on negotiation tables. It's putting efficiency before bureaucracy. Ignoring long-term global problems is what leaders are most skilled at. But now the genie of morality is out of the bottle, and it's not going back in. It will make our most desired wish come true."

"Which is?"

The elevator's doors opened.

"Heaven," Theo said.

Konrad scratched the back of his head. "You mean global unity?"

"Correct."

As the elevator descended, Konrad contemplated the flash behind Theo's eyes. Like he was saying, 'You can agree with me or you can be wrong.' And that was an understatement.

Theo's smile was crazed and carved to kill.

KASPAR'S ROOM WAS quiet and dark; only a candle burned on the table. Anxiety blossomed in Gideon's chest. He wanted to cry, but gathered his strength and frowned his concern.

Kaspar's chest was calm, almost like he was asleep. "Hey, son." His voice was eerily quiet, and his soulless stare made Gideon's heart flutter.

"I'm not going to last long, so listen carefully..."

Gideon gulped.

"I'm proud of you. I feel terrible that I never said how much I loved you. I guess showing my real emotions is my greatest weakness."

"Why are you proud of me?" Gideon asked. "I haven't achieved anything in my life."

"A man's value is not his achievements. It's about being ready to act for the greater good. Patrick praises your attitude. You'll make an everlasting impact on the world affairs. You possess a great gift. Use it with great care."

"Honestly, Dad?" Gideon felt his father was delusional.

Drops of dark wax crawled down the sides of the candle. The waning flame set deeper shadows in the hollows of Kaspar's eyes.

"It's not the first time you've communicated with the dead," Kaspar said suddenly. "You've done it before, haven't you?"

A paralyzing chill passed over Gideon's skin. He tipped his face toward Kaspar. "Dad, are you dying?"

Kaspar's eyes and mouth opened as if enthralled by a ghost. Before Gideon jumped back, he could hear his father's last whisper: "Bring back the dead."

An emotional shock stopped Gideon's breathing. A hand landed on his shoulder. He spun around.

Patrick Praytor.

"Stay the hell away from me," Gideon said.

Patrick took a step forward, his hands up.

"Don't come any closer." Tears ran down Gideon's cheek. "I don't... I don't understand."

Patrick closed the space between them and took Gideon into a tight hug.

Gideon trembled, he tried to protest, but then the emotions came on to him in waves. "Do something! My father can't die."

Patrick held him tight. The last emotional trigger went off in Gideon's chest, and he let it out. After a minute of crying his breathing was stabilizing.

Patrick spoke. "I'm sorry you had to go through it, but our enemies left no choice. That was an example of what they're capable of. They have invented a way to steal identity and affect the stream of consciousness."

Gideon felt like a total mess.

"Don't worry, crying is good. You defuse your anger and regain control over yourself."

"What happened to my father? Who did this sick thing to him?"

"Russians."

"But we just prevented bad things from happening, didn't we?"

"Gideon. You need to understand that what happened to

your father happened a long time ago. You only saw the last remains of him. The ghost in the machine."

"He said something about bringing back the dead, and that I possess a gift."

"Part of his speech was a genuine echo of your father. Something triggered vivid memories. Words people have said to him, music he has listened to, his most painful experiences, traumas... all that have haunted him and what he hasn't thought in years, resurfacing. Little glitches of the brain. It can be very confusing and disorienting, believe me, I know. But..."

"What?" Gideon asked.

"Your father was right about you. You can bring back the dead. Finish your training, and I'll show you the actual depth of the rabbit hole. You have, after all, made it possible for other families to carry on their lives in Russia. Their lives have been as miserable as if they were dead. Now the rest of the world awaits you."

Gideon's scalp prickled.

"Come," Patrick said. "Get past this, for your dad died long ago. We have no time to waste. Let's meet my father."

THE MOTHER OF *all distractions,* the Veteran thought. Every piece was in its place against all the odds. It was time to rise on the stage, and throw the true voice and captivate the audience.

And reveal the future and role for each of us.

JULIA LOKI STRAIGHTENED her black, tangled hair and white coat in front of the mirror. Her eyes were exhausted, pulled down by heavy bags, and homebound paleness made her look already dead.

She never overcame her fear of public speaking. Many times, her career seemed disrupted with sleepless nights, tears shed or held back. But thank God Patrick helped her through her anxiety.

She had helped him to create a New Neural Interface with preset parameters. It was a challenge of the far future, but they were centuries ahead of time. Patrick had provided her valuable information about the distinctive potential of different matter and insights into the human brain and body. From those blueprints, she could solve utterly miserable human problems and forge the next stage of human and moral evolution. Just by directing magnetic energy into the brain, she could incept fake memories, affect cognitive processing, and even remove God from the belief system.

With light, she could take one brain cell at a time into full control. Photoreceptor cells existed in nature everywhere, but humans had them only in the eye. Through them she sent a rich diversity of biochemical messengers, bringing in the Word, and making specific cells responsive to light. *Shedding* was all about delivering pure light deep into an organism.

Patrick's commitment and faith impressed her. He never tried to convert her to think like him. She felt free because of that. People didn't like being told what to do. All advice given to people was hard to take in. Even harder to act on it. But any advice suggested, rather than insisted upon, fell easier on open ears.

She snapped her fingers in front of her face and reiterated to herself why man needed behavioral discipline.

"Love can't grow in the foundation of violence."

Konrad had a point with his claim that man was unfit for love. That was, now in retrospect, the primary catalyst that had helped her through the worst self-doubts of the process. She had buried their marriage fiasco with a senseless streak of work.

But it was all worth it.

51

KONRAD SAW JULIA with another man. In a flash, he recalled seeing the man at the university and on the shore at Lennart's house. Despite his disguise, Julia could nail his ass in a blink of an eye should she cast a glance at him. Konrad pulled back his shoulders, stood more erect and pulled his stomach in, steeling his nerves.

"I think I ate something bad," Konrad said. "I'll go to the toilet."

Theo nodded and walked toward Patrick, saying, "Come back quickly."

Eric spoke words to Konrad's ear: "There's a corridor on your left. Take it."

Not knowing where to look to avoid exposure to Julia or Patrick, Konrad tried to break his unconscious habits of walking. He focused on his in-toeing so that his toes pointed away from the mid-line during gait, which became naturally slower. But what the hell was Julia doing here?

"Now, open the door to the restroom," Eric said in a stream of white noise. "Close it. Proceed undetected to the end of the corridor."

Konrad did as told. He looked back at the gathering—nobody watched him.

"Behind..." More distortion on the line, "...the room where Gideon might be..."

The signal broke down completely.

Heart jumping in his chest, Konrad stopped. He continued, angry for freezing up, mentally ordering himself to calm down. It would have been Eric's advice as well.

Konrad peeked through a window and saw him.

Gideon was in military uniform with his head tucked between his knees. Was he brainwashed?

"You did it, son," Theo boasted. "I knew I could trust placing the operation in your hands."

Patrick cracked a half smile.

"I have a surprise for you," Theo said. "Someone who might be a great asset in the building of the future."

"As a matter of fact," Patrick said, "I have a surprise for you, too."

Theo quickly rubbed his hands together and turned to Julia.

"Everything ready, darling?"

"We are green," Julia assured.

"Superb. I feel like a child at Christmas again." Theo kept glancing at Julia and Patrick. "Not only have two lovebirds found each other, together we'll give the world the greatest gift it has ever received."

"The children deserve it," Julia said.

"How's our boy? Any word from grandmother?" Patrick asked.

"Fine. Such a lovely child. They'll visit Disneyland tomorrow."

Patrick took Julia under his arm and pulled her closer.

"We should celebrate!" Theo said.

"Let me," Julia said. "I'll get the champagne."

"Bring the kid with you," Patrick added.

52

"**G**IDEON," KONRAD WHISPERED.

Gideon reacted by drawing a weapon. "Go away, or I pull the trigger."

Konrad was too shocked to lift his hands up. "I'm here to save you."

"You're wrong. I've made up my mind. I want to change the world, not to turn my back on it."

Konrad took a step closer. "We don't have time—"

Gideon removed the safety. "I'll fire."

"No, you won't. Your mother is dead. They killed her."

Gideon's eyebrows squished together. "You're lying."

"She wanted to say she loves you."

That single word cracked Gideon's defiance.

"Have you seen any explosives or anything that would cause destruction?"

"No."

"This is important. Anything sticking out of the ordinary?"

"Patrick said that we're going to Israel. He wants to show me the sky over there. Something about a Second Coming of the

Son. He has got a big telescope here. But other than that, nothing unusual."

"Damn. Put down the gun and let's get away from here."

Forearms camouflaged with snake patterns folded themselves across Gideon's chest.

"No."

Konrad attacked, switched on the safety, spun behind Gideon and took him in a chokehold. "Don't resist, or I'll add pressure, and you will lose consciousness. I'll carry you out if you don't comply."

"Let. Me. Go."

Behind the window, something moved. Julia dashed in the room.

"Konrad? You fucking dick! Attacking a teen again?"

"Julia. You're in danger. You don't know what these guys are up to."

"I know better than them. I did all the research. All the development."

"Julia?" Konrad asked.

"You wouldn't understand. You don't have what it takes to make a difference. You love your self-image and fame far too much. Don't see the suffering of the children. Let Gideon go, and I'll let you both leave. There's a secret exit."

Konrad eased his grip only a bit, and Gideon fought a way out. Julia grabbed the handgun from Gideon's grasp.

"It's mine. Give it back!"

"You don't need this anymore."

"Patrick said it's mine."

Julia took aim at Konrad's head and pulled the trigger.

Click.

"What the hell?" Konrad said, shielding his eye with his hand.

"Patrick takes no risks." Julia produced another weapon from behind her back. She switched the weapons in her hands swiftly a dozen times so that neither male knew which was functioning. "Patrick disabled your gun because he wanted to make sure you didn't blow your head off."

"He doesn't trust me?" Gideon said.

"He sees more in you than you know." Julia turned to Konrad. "Let's go meet the Judge."

"The one who plays executioner as well?" Konrad asked.

Julia pressed the cold metal to Konrad's forehead. "Among other roles."

53

THEO SHARED GLANCES with Patrick as Julia approached them with Konrad and Gideon.

Every soldier stopped in their tracks and drew their weapons, holding them low. Patrick signaled his men to stand down.

"They were trying to escape," Julia said.

Patrick ignored Julia. "This is my young soldier, Gideon. The agent of change who executed the first moral enhancement in history with style. And I could introduce you to the soldier as well: Konrad Loki."

"Back from the dead?" Theo said, eyeing Konrad up and down. "I don't know how it's still possible you're here with us, but you almost got me. I had my suspicions the minute you walked into my office."

"You had better use your intuition," Konrad said. "Might not see what's precisely right before your eyes."

Theo shook his finger. "You were lost. A good soldier would take any room in his control the second he steps in. But I saw potential in you. Your articulation and imagination were impressive."

"I barely see a compliment in that." Two seconds after Konrad opened his mouth, one of the agents smashed the back of his rifle against his face. His vision danced red on black. He gathered himself up from the ground, blood seeping from his lips. He blew an air kiss at the agent and braced himself for a second blow.

"Stop!" Theo said. "Surely he likes his head in place. Don't you now, Konrad? Are you listening?"

"Wrapping my brain around every word." Konrad revealed his bloodstained teeth.

"You should kill him," Julia declared and nudged the weapon at Konrad's neck. "Both."

"We are not monsters, Julia," said Patrick. "They're alive simply because of their potential."

"We don't need to study them anymore. You've already made sure their potential isn't fulfilled."

Theo face split into an enormous smile. "Julia. None of us would be standing here today if it weren't for you. I begin to believe there's a higher reason we have gathered here at this very moment. Looking at what's coming next for our world, we have replaced fear of the unknown with curiosity. That's why we are here. Curiosity. We are like new world alchemists."

Konrad applauded. "Bravo."

"You don't understand the power of unity," Patrick said. "We're going to reunite under one banner and universal language: morality."

"You waste your breath with him," Julia said. "He values only his own success."

Patrick was an inch away from Konrad's face. "I feel uniquely qualified to tell you that I'll leave this planet in better shape for the future generations than I found it. Can you say the same thing about yourself?"

Konrad paused, digesting the question.

Patrick continued. "Fear cloaks our children like a persistent fog. Adults have weakened them with ignorance and cowardice. Don't you want to reap vengeance on those who stood by and let innocent children die? Is there any more noble path than seeking revenge to bring harmony instead of misery and harm?"

"Am I talking to a wall?" Julia said. "He hates children and teens."

Patrick continued. "Nobody will steal the future of our children anymore. Nobody."

Konrad nodded involuntarily.

Patrick grew gentle. "By the way, I'm a big admirer of your work. During my missions, I listened to you and your views about humankind. You made me ponder the insanity of war and what else could be imagined instead. You were my inspiration."

"This is not quite what I was going for," Konrad commented.

Patrick glared at Konrad and Gideon in turn.

"We are the way forward. You know what needs to be done and how it'll end if you hesitate. Mankind—divided or redefined? Which is it going to be?"

At the same second two shadowy figures entered the main hall. Patrick and Theo seemed paralyzed as their gazes met. Konrad and Gideon spun around.

Nobody could believe their eyes.

54

VIKTOR VODYANOY STOOD just a few meters away with Iris, and still Konrad couldn't believe it.

"You all look like you're watching a movie," Viktor said. "I should have brought you popcorn."

"What is this?" Theo said. "You were on the plane to Moscow."

"A body double?" Patrick asked. "You were Ded Moroz?"

Viktor smiled. "It makes me wonder that with all your cutting-edge technology and intelligence agencies, you still can't see our counter-intelligence following your every move."

"Where's Eric?" Konrad asked. "Iris. What are you doing with him?"

"There isn't always gold at the end of a rainbow," Iris said and looked at Theo. "Sometimes there is a gay husband."

Everybody turned to Theo, who managed to keep his face deadpan. He drawled, "Did you kill Eric?"

Iris shrugged. "Hurts like hell, doesn't it?"

Konrad noted Theo's knuckles turn white in his fists.

"So! What a day of unlocked potential!" Viktor said. "I must thank you all for your creativity and pioneering spirit in interfering with global affairs. But time has come to a stop playing games and change the player. Since I happen to know all the players in the field better than anyone in this room, it is my pleasure to announce a new dawn of Russia." Viktor produced a ventriloquist doll from his pack bag, and everybody drew their weapons. "Tension. Tension. I like it. But gentle now. You may want to hear what I have to say."

Theo side-glanced at Patrick who was smiling.

"Son?" Theo asked. "Did you feed Intel to them?"

Patrick avoided eye contact.

"When your cyber spies hack into our systems," Viktor said, "they think they have gone through backdoors, but the holes have been deliberately created so that we can follow who searches and for what. Mostly you were in fake files. Only my personal timetables were real. Patrick has helped us a lot. A fine hacker, extremely gifted."

"Patrick. Tell me that's not true."

Patrick remained quiet.

"Tell me!" Theo demanded. "I know you better than you do. He's bluffing, isn't he?"

Patrick stood beside to Viktor and drew his weapon, taking steady aim at Theo's chest.

"Charming," Viktor said with a clumsy attempt to play ventriloquist with the doll. "It's not the General's luckiest day after all. Nothing hurts like losing one of the family, knowing you can blame only yourself."

"What are you up to?" Theo asked Patrick. "Why are you abandoning your own son, when we tried to build sustainable future for him?"

Then Julia changed sides and found her place by Patrick's side.

"You too? I provided you with unlimited resources!" Theo

said. "Do you want to cause a new clash of civilizations? What's the point?"

"Dad," Patrick said. "It doesn't matter which side we enhance morally."

"On whose authority? You think you're attacking your home country? We had clear objectives! You give up complete control for what?"

A few seconds of silence passed and Patrick said to his men, "Keep your guns trained on him. If he moves, make sure his blood coats these corridors. "

Konrad signaled Gideon to move with him to the neutral zone next to a wall. Theo was all alone.

Viktor said to Theo, "You are cornered and helpless because I know your move before you do. I know how you think. You think you're well connected and powerful, but you're merely a puppet. You tried to take justice into own hands. In Russia, we don't like people like that. They end up in early graves."

"Being so charmingly human isn't going to save you," Theo said. "The world knows your true face. You are no savior."

"I know how to shape public image better than anyone. Besides, anyone joining me voluntarily can avoid the global vortex of violence in the next crowded theater of war."

"The war doesn't end with you, Viktor."

"Don't take me for naive," Viktor said, "We both know there will always be skirmishes no matter what. It's a part of who we are. I will only end hegemony wars, the power struggles. Together with Julia and Patrick, we will wipe this world clean. First, we wipe out the poison called America. Your president will kneel to me. Then I make sure all of my fellow Russians living along our borders will be attacked. I'll make my neighbors Russiaphobic. With prejudices amplified, I can take justice into my own hands. Russia will rule. Every act is done in pursuance of that end and no other."

"Like many great men, you make up the rules as you go along," Theo accused. "But great men fall. Your pathetic human games will end with global sickness, minds twisted, brains mutated beyond anything medical record."

"Save your breath, old man," Viktor responded.

"Patrick," Theo said. "I trusted you. You are more of a thief and criminal than a soldier."

Patrick tilted his head. "You're right."

Patrick's stare made Konrad's blood run cold. Patrick locked his shoulder and aimed higher. Konrad thought he would witness Theo collapse on the floor—but abruptly, without moving his lips, Patrick's voice called out and filled the entire cave.

"I AM WHO I AM."

Yet Patrick pointed to his left at Viktor and pressed the trigger.

A spray of blood fountained in Viktor's hand, where the doll had smiled. Viktor fell to his knees, horrified, face whitened.

Julia shot Iris in the head in cold blood.

Konrad pulled Gideon behind him, and as they hit the floor every agent turned their weapons on Patrick and Julia. Nobody hesitated to shoot. The Cave echoed in explosions.

Then disbelief set in. Patrick and Julia stood unharmed.

"I-Impossible," Viktor said.

Patrick placed his gun to Viktor's forehead. "Smart bullets. Let's see what else they can do."

An altered, booming voice spoke again, the echo shooting off the walls. "ATTENTION!"

Theo and Konrad watched the agents snap to their erect position with heels clicking together. Then, "AT EASE!" In perfect accord, each agent stepped his left foot out shoulder's width and placed his hands behind his back.

Viktor snapped, "I'm your commanding officer! Stop it.

Now." Nothing happened. Viktor glared at Patrick from under the gun pressed to his forehead.

"I am the author of all pain," Patrick said. "I'll make the final call."

Viktor grit his teeth together and was about to growl, but something happened again.

"ATTENTION!" Heels clicked together. "ACTIVATE 101," the voice spoke again.

Every agent placed his weapon to his temple and pressed the trigger in perfect harmony of a ballet. And each fell to the ground like a domino of folding chairs.

"Who the hell are you?" Viktor demanded.

Konrad's ears rang as he guided Gideon toward a door leading to the last room of the Cave. The armory.

"I am the Veteran."

Patrick's eyes flashed fire as the president of Russia fell at his feet.

55

A MONG THE DEAD, Patrick and Julia kissed.

"Bravo, son," Theo said, his voice shaking. "I don't know what the hell just happened, but I knew our hearts belonged on the same side of history."

"It's our destiny to become the gods we once worshiped and feared," Patrick said. "But even the old gods have one above them."

"I guess I know what you're trying to say."

"No, Dad. You're stuck in the past. NATO and the US government take away hope and turn people into demons. You only have to look at the map of the world's military bases and see who is the most aggressive empire in the entire world history. You fear to take the last step of choosing the spiritual path that leads to unity. Our souls endure beyond earthly existence only if we fulfill our potential to the upmost. You couldn't put that purity to the ultimate test. You jeopardize the future by acting exactly the same as Viktor. Humans don't have any future left with leaders who want only control and more power."

"Son, don't assault me." Theo licked his lips. "Viktor was the one who wanted to be like the Messiah. I don't want power. I want the power struggles to end."

Gideon entered Patrick's personal space with his chin high to intimidate. "I recognized the voice. It was never my own father speaking when he was dying. It was you! You tried to brainwash me!"

"None of you understands what it takes to play this game." Julia stepped between Patrick and Gideon. "Patrick only tried to see if you can resurrect by touch. He improvised the words so that we could study you longer."

"All the now-dead agents," Patrick began explaining, "had their memories erased and identities altered. Their consciousnesses, however, didn't allow them to evolve like normal human beings. They lived a shadow life. The same happens eventually for the morally enhanced. But for the children and the young, it works. It works if the children are born enhanced."

"I don't understand," Theo said.

Konrad spoke. "Are you two planning to end the human race?"

"Always the anti-climactic, Konrad," Julia said. "We are going to show everybody the smile of a child. When people see the world as the first smile of the child, it will bind them together. Killing Viktor won't cause a war between the countries. His twin brother, who was satisfied in the background with women, drugs, gambling, and western entertainment, will become their new leader. And the new generation of babies will affect mothers now differently. Pregnancy won't make women forgetful or slow-witted. Motherhood won't be a lonely place. Hormone imbalance and mood swings will be less likely. The world doesn't need morally enhanced male leaders—the world needs morally enhanced new generations."

"A generation of Prophets," Patrick continued. "One generation during which the wounds are given time to heal. During this period, the world that was originally designed to discourage people will be turned into the Kingdom of Heaven. Spiritual greatness requires humility and humbling oneself to become children of God. Fear will cease to be the chief force governing human race. In the words of Jesus: *'Unless you change and become a child, you will never enter into the Kingdom of Heaven.'*"

"Child soldiers?" Gideon asked. "Is that it?"

"Teachers," Patrick crowed. "We are pushing for change while everybody else is busy making other plans that perpetuate the climate of uncertainty. The problems will soon blow up in their faces, but a new generation will come to save us. Every other option dooms us to be mocked up by history."

"Where are you planning to fulfill your plan?" Theo said.

"We have always been fans of Santa Claus. We are going to be his little helpers tonight," Patrick said. "I have reserved my calendar for this moment. But I haven't reserved spots for any of you. Father..." Patrick took aim. "You are my hero. You lived a long, honest and upright life, exhibited a good moral character. After you return to dust, your sacrifices will live on. That's the greatest reason why you were decorated and honored by men who have an infinite appetite for war. For too long too many people have weaved their way into doing something only for it to end up being nothing. Good news being few and far between, you always managed to convince your soldiers of the higher reason for fighting. But just as the First World War was literally stuck in the mud and the wars of this world have grown colder ever since, all great leaders have one fundamental flaw—your greed gets surpassed by your ego."

"I'm sorry to spoil all the euphoria," Konrad interrupted. "The future requires radical maneuvers, yes, but the world isn't run on instinct. I'm sure humans want to embrace the future on their own terms."

"Listen to him, son," Theo said. "You're playing with fire."

"Julia and I are giving the stolen power back to the people. Our success is inevitable."

"Why are you then still waving that gun?" Gideon asked.

"My dear troubled young soul rebel." Patrick shook his head. "The world has always been a stage to take full control. And one can only take complete control after going through the hell and torture of drifting in and out of consciousness and utter starvation. The stupidity of man becomes your arch nemesis in captivity. I fight for the future where nobody is allowed to control people. A future without fear. A future where our daughters don't end up raped or sex slaves. On Christmas Eve we will rise from our trenches and venture into no man's land to make peace like the war fed-up men in the First World War a hundred years ago. Only this time peace will be everlasting. No more high-ranking commanders to deny it."

"A saint in our midst," Konrad jibed.

"George Orwell once said, 'Saints should always be judged guilty until they are proved innocent,'" Patrick said. "Saints are always corrupted. You are doing the right thing by condemning me. But historians of the future will praise us. Every time you try to say I'm doing a wrong and horrible thing, you lack understanding of what morality is in the grand scheme of humanity. Morality is defined by time remaining before each apocalypse before the old world crumbles under the emerging new moral platform. Morality has its own evolution, progressing from revolution to revolution."

Konrad held his elbows wide from his body. "You're abusing Oona's teachings."

"Oona's teachings? She was the one who approved this mission all along!" Patrick's voice echoed in the room that suddenly became even colder. "Don't you understand? She volunteered to become the subject of study. She helped us break the bounds of science. She has been leading us all to overcome death. Isn't that your greatest wish as well, Konrad? That you don't have to die prematurely when there's so much potential left inside you? And think of all of the splendor she has brought upon us! She guided us all along to meet our loved ones in heaven! Not in the afterlife, but on heaven-like Earth, free from all bonds that make human love impossible. She taught us how to avoid pitfalls so our ever-advancing civilization didn't turn its technology against itself. We'll learn what is truly meant by *resurrection*—bringing humankind into Heaven and continuing to explore the Universe with Quantum Manipulation and Divine Source as ours to tap."

"So if we don't play Gods, no one does?" Konrad asked.

"Try to understand," Patrick said, "you and I aim for the same goal. We believe in the potential of men, but we don't *believe* in them. We want to alter the course of destiny, knowing exactly how fragile, weak, and self-destructive this human body is—an unfit costume for the future. With outdated biology of our species and democracy as the religion of death, ruins set in a matter of very limited time—when time could be unlimited and space manipulated."

Silence ensued.

Patrick spoke boisterously, mockery and murder in his eyes. "Being human is to stay human. Our destiny is to become the greatest version of ourselves."

"You are insane," Theo accused. "There's a beast intent on extinguishing all normal way of life, such darkness grew inside you in the battlefields. You are not my son. Come back to your senses and listen to yourself. You're going to surprise people with their pants down!"

"You know what," Patrick said, summoning a strained smile. A voice continued, a voice that didn't belong in that room. "That's isn't far from the TRUTH!"

A huge explosion followed. Everybody but Patrick ducked

and froze still. The truck that had been readied and loaded with equipment was in flames. Destroyed.

"Oh my God." Theo was hyperventilating. "Did you just blow..."

Patrick turned toward Konrad and Gideon, and without a hint of remorse in his eyes, he pointed his weapon at them: "Just a clean-up of loose ends... nothing personal."

A shadow fell across Konrad's peripheral view when the weapon in Patrick's hand roared.

Theo had jumped in between.

Patrick tilted his head. "Who's the dummy now?"

Konrad pulled Gideon through a door behind them, closed it, and broke the door handle. Through a bulletproof window, Gideon saw Theo on all fours on the floor with an exit bullet wound in his back. He found his feet, blood dripping from his fingers.

Patrick shot again.

Miraculously, Theo was able to maintain his balance. Even though Konrad couldn't see his face, he read the disappointment in the body of the father. Patrick gritted his teeth, this time aiming higher.

The last bullet knew its place, lodging inside Theo's head, sending a parabola of blood in the air.

Theo was dead.

Konrad and Gideon watched Julia and Patrick from behind the bulletproof window. The two shared a kiss and walked past the senseless massacre of elite soldiers and high leaders to the elevator. Once inside, they stared at Konrad and Gideon, hand in hand. Julia produced a remote control from her pocket. As the doors started closing, she pressed the red button. The Cave shook and rumbled. In a pit of fire and doom behind the mirror masses of stone began to crack and fall.

The laboratory was completely sealed and destroyed.

Somewhere above, water surged down through the cracks like a large fire hose let loose, and in a few seconds, the water surface was rising behind the window.

Above their heads, Konrad and Gideon watched the stone split in a slow motion of black lightning.

And then the window made its first popping noise.

56

K ONRAD WEIGHED C4 explosives in his hand. The cave would collapse at any second around them.

"We can't blast our way out." With a sour taste of defeat in his mouth, Konrad desired to be alone. "It's over."

"No! Give me that." Gideon took the explosives, walked around, fighting uncontrollable tears.

The water rising in the window was testing the peak endurance of the glass.

"I'm sorry, Gideon. It's solid rock above us at least fifty meters, and a pond on top of that..."

Lights flicked off.

In the darkness, Gideon repeated the word *No*. Konrad closed his eyes and expected the glass and water to finish them any second. He took a few deep breaths, knowing that relaxation would give him an extra stretch of time, meaning he would have to witness Gideon's gruesome death before his own.

Lights were flickering.

Gideon crouched next to the wall at the back of the room. His fingers touched a streak of water coursing down from the walls. The water turned lightning blue and sprang up into the chasms above. Inside the bedrock echoed the twisting sound of bent metal.

Impossible...

The bedrock shook. The exact same quality on cooling of antimony cracked through his skull.

"Gideon!" Konrad yelled.

The glass broke down, and the ocean of water moved in effortlessly. They both swam up with the torrent and hit their heads on the ceiling in the smallest of air pockets.

The sound of a majestic mountain breaking apart rolled into their ears.

"Take a breath!" Konrad spoke over the horrible rumble.

In a few heartbeats water filled the space and the ceiling tore open, letting them both want for fresh air and light.

Konrad pointed up with his finger, but Gideon had trouble keeping his eyes open. Konrad tried to guide him on the narrow path above, but he knew it would take too long to pull the teenager in the right direction.

Konrad swam behind, keeping his mind in a meditative state, while Gideon spent too much oxygen with kicking. Far in the distance, a faint source of light glowed that seemed like light years away and unattainable. After about ten seconds of swimming, Gideon grew restless and his knees scratched the walls of stone.

The last bubbles escaped Gideon's lungs. He stopped moving. Konrad swam past him and pulled him up to a place that seemed to be the bottom of the pond. Only ten meters separated them from fresh air, but now Konrad's body ached, his lungs about to explode.

It was a bright star in the cloudless sky that guided them this far, but Konrad had to make the hard decision and let Gideon go so that he could swim up.

Cursing inward after letting go, Konrad started his panicky

ascent. But just when he was about to gather air into his lungs he hit his head.

Ice sheet.

His world twisted. Konrad pressed his lips on the ice, his brain shrieking, overruling commands to stop the urge to breathe. His hand touched the ice, his life rushing in black-and-white images before him.

The alder tree...

Gideon's touch.

He turned and saw Gideon floating below him. Konrad pulled his hand and placed it against the ice...

It melted the ice open.

Konrad put his head out and gasped for air.

57

I N THE DARKNESS, wet and snowbound, Konrad gave CPR to Gideon.

Gideon coughed hard, sat bolt upright, vomiting the water out, gasping.

Konrad heaved a sigh of relief. "You're alright."

Gideon stare was shocked. "Where am I?"

"We got out of the Cave." Konrad pointed his finger at the hole in the ice. "I don't know what happened, but without your ability to affect forms of water we would be drowned."

Gideon's brow curled, trying to recall something. Or anything.

Konrad waited for a few seconds and then gave a clumsy punch at Gideon's shoulder. "Big man, you just bought more time for humanity."

"I did nothing," Gideon drawled. After a couple beats of silence, his eyes were more focused with a sudden burst of brilliance. "Patrick and Julia are thinking they're fulfilling a prophecy."

"Yes. But that's their weakness."

"What if their plan is just what the world needs? A world without wars."

Konrad scratched his forehead. He had lived long trying to understand why the world weaned off God felt empty and wrong. But Gideon was a miracle, a possible proof for an unidentifiable higher force. Like he was destined to do something extraordinary.

"There has to be another way."

"What should we do?" Gideon asked.

"Locate ourselves first. The attack will happen in Santa Village very soon. I'm sure of it."

"After that, they go to Israel."

"Following a symbolic path, it seems," Konrad said. "A ritual as good as any."

Color didn't return on Gideon's blue lips. "I'm feeling sleepy."

"Get up. You need to move to generate heat."

"My limbs are too frozen. I can't stand."

Konrad rubbed the back of his head. Turning and searching for firewood, Konrad saw somebody who looked about to succumb to death in a mental institution. All tired and weary, clothed in grab-what-you-can and get-a-move-on, this man was at the very end of his life.

Lennart Klemetti.

58

L ENNART MADE A fire with his cigar and shreds of birch bark.

"How did you find us?" Konrad asked.

"Don't look at me like I'm already dead." Lennart added more bark to the fire. "You expect you can just invite your pals and shoot around my house and get away with it?"

"Your anger led you here?"

Lennart cast a long glance at Konrad. "You are the most arrogant bastard ever. Beneath that cocky exterior is an even cockier asshole."

"I know. Sorry."

"My people have never been in or engaged in war, but you pulled me in," Lennart said. "I escaped the hospital when I heard odd drumming. My research and claims about the miracles in the Sámi homeland finally came into being. There was once an indescribable evil walking among us, raping us. The Germans caused the greatest havoc to our culture and spiritual legacy; they alienated us from nature, finishing the doom that the priests of Sweden, Norway, and Finland had practiced for centuries by burning the drums and desecrating sacred sites.

But the force of Nature has returned." Lennart pointed a steady finger at Gideon.

Gideon blinked. "What do you want from me?"

"You can command natural phenomena," Lennart said. "That's what the membrane was saying. You can be unbound by time and place, just like the best Noaidis. The Membrane is a *Remembrane*—a salute to the past knowledge and power. The evil is again among us, but you can prevent another tragedy."

"You came all the way here to ramble?" Gideon shook his head. "I thought I was weird..."

Lennart said, "The only toxic substance in this life is shame. Out of shame my people didn't stand up to their oppressors. Guilt still makes them fill the hollow in their hearts with alcohol. If you don't handle your internal conflicts, you'll pass it on to your children and generations to come."

"Gideon has suffered quite a lot, Lennart," Konrad said. "They tried to hide and keep his potential unfulfilled."

"The old man can waste his saliva if he wants," Gideon said.

"You found a hand mark, didn't you? A painted hand mark? Was it on a boulder or a tree? You discovered a sacred site, a spiritual focal point that the Noaidis used to paint with symbols. You touched it and saw into the other side of life."

A reluctant smile tugged at the corner of Gideon's mouth. "Look, oldie. I saw nothing."

"But you became someone. Someone important to the deities." Lennart raised his chin. "There are still stories where the Noaidis could communicate with the divine spirits through power symbols."

Gideon turned to Konrad.

"Could it be possible," Konrad said, "that he didn't see anything, but rather recharged the symbol? I touched the hand mark and saw some weird visions."

"An out-of-body experience. A Noaidi could charge gateways

to spiritual worlds. They got more powerful healing skills from these places, allowing transformation into an animal, for example. Gideon probably roamed in the woods disguised as a reindeer without knowing it."

Konrad thought of the black horse in the woods. Could it have been Oona, forcing him to solve the puzzle?

"I think, Konrad," Lennart said, "that you invoked a Dead Soul. Someone, perhaps, you knew. Contacting a Soul can go beyond our understanding and feel non-human. But it was a contact still."

Konrad and Gideon shared glances.

Lennart closed his eyes. "I can hear ancestral voices..." He tried to move and initiate a *yoik*, but he collapsed.

Konrad and Gideon watched Lennart lying down in front of the weakening fire. He spoke in his sleep, "The most vital forces of nature for Sámi people were the wind and the sun... the wind and the sun..."

Konrad reached to wake him up but withdrew his hand. Lennart didn't want to be woken up anymore.

The two walked away from where Lennart had arrived. As they moved through the trees, they both could hear peaceful snoring behind them.

Then the final, loud inhale and release.

The woods grew darker around them.

Konrad let a loose tear freeze on his cheek.

59

PATRICK PULLED JULIA closer to him and planted a kiss on her lips. A busload of Japanese tourists sprawled around them. A Japanese couple, as concentrated on each other as Patrick and Julia were, collided in Patrick's back. The rest of the visitors continued with their waterproof jackets rustling.

"I thought all Japanese were interested in the Christmas Land," Patrick said.

After a small hesitation and exchanging of blushes, the young couple cleared their throats.

"Our wishes have come true already," the man said, looking at his wife. "Christmas should be about family and love. All these decorations and lights, the money machine behind it, they make us sad. My father paid for our trip, so we don't complain. I might propose to her."

"We are glad you have found each other," Julia said.

The man and the woman stared into each other's eyes for ten heartbeats.

Another tourist bus with noisy brakes swerved into the parking lot. Patrick and Julia were delighted by the pool of multiple languages spoken among the flow of people: Chinese, Italian, Spanish, Russia, German, an Australian accent here, a word of Mexican there. Only an American arrogant accent was like a train screeching brakes in Patrick's ears.

Like you own the world...

The Japanese man pointed at the machine Patrick had just installed. A mixture of interest, hope, and anticipation grew on his face. "Is that what I think it is?"

"Yes."

"Delightful. People can forget all the troubles of the world, even just for a few seconds."

"I'm quite sure this little invention works as the opposite," Patrick said. "It will *remind* everyone what needs to be done. That we all must act as the ambassadors of good will, love, and peace."

The man nodded. He interpreted to his wife what the machine was and what Patrick had just said.

"Kawaii!" the woman enthused, and they both walked after the next wave of tourists.

Patrick grabbed Julia by the arm.

"Let's catapult civilization into new heights, shall we?"

60

KONRAD AND GIDEON dodged through the trees. Gideon slammed headfirst into a dark old warfare trench and knocked himself almost unconscious as all air was forced out of his lungs.

They had arrived at the road that connected Santa Park and Santa Claus Village. Konrad saw no emergency lights or vehicles parked at the entrance to the Cave. Hadn't anyone heard the blasts, or were those living adjacent used to bedrock explosions?

"Konrad," Gideon said. "The other day Patrick took me snowboarding with Viktor. Patrick replaced me with a skiing instructor. Just like that."

"What are you suggesting?"

"Santa Claus may be replaced. What if he's the one delivering the moral enhancement to children? Or to adults?"

"Delivering the presents to the world," Konrad concurred. "You are right."

Gideon shrugged. "Probably our best shot."

"But did you see anything on that day with the president?" Konrad said as they jogged toward the Santa Village. "Tell me everything."

Gideon recapped. He couldn't come up with anything new. "An invisible weapon. I felt they were bluffing about its existence."

"Damn, Julia," Konrad snapped. "What have you done..."

"Is she your wife?"

"Ex."

"How could she build something this big without you knowing?"

"She loves to work alone."

"You love her?"

Konrad leveled his gaze.

Gideon said, "What? We need all the leverage we can get."

"I have no idea what love is anymore," Konrad said.

"I think she loves you."

"Gideon, look. I messed up. She messed up even worse. End of story."

"But..."

"No." Konrad decreased speed, breaking their rhythm. "We have a two-kilometer hike ahead. Ten minutes. It might mean losing this war."

"Let's hope the party hasn't started yet."

"Come. The darker it gets, the darker it will be for the world. Santa will hold his welcome speech for the tourists and soon after that hop to his sleigh and depart with Rudolph."

"Their next target is Israel. I'm starting to doubt Patrick's replacing Santa. He hates animals. He wouldn't jump into Rudolph's sleigh."

"Santa is still our best bet. Besides, people change." Konrad held a pause. "Patrick may have Julia nearby in the woods so that she'll take the reins and guide them to the airport. It's their Symbolic Path. Eventually, they will fly, but with an airplane."

"Would they truly be that stupid? I mean going to all the

trouble? Why don't we just call or head to the airport or cause a scene that would ground all the planes? A bomb threat."

"We could. If anybody believed us and if it wouldn't jeopardize seizing them both."

"We had better behave well. We can only hope for a miracle."

"Have faith in me," Konrad said. "Hope is not our best weapon tonight."

"What is then?"

"I'm still working on it."

Gideon sighed.

"Don't worry," Konrad said. "The only truly frightening thing here is Patrick who thinks he's right. I don't believe Julia would ever match that."

"It's frightening that I don't have a clue what's right anymore."

"Chin up. Maybe we are here to find out what's right."

Gideon said nothing.

"I'm sorry," Konrad said. "I must have sounded just like your mother."

Gideon jogged for a few seconds in silence.

"It's okay."

61

AT THE GATES of Santa Claus Village, the artificial-snow-capped wooden buildings were bathed in all shades of pink, blue, and neon green. Pretty much the whole gigantic industrial complex was a decorated Christmas tree. Tourists flocked by the hundreds into the center where crossing the line of the Arctic Circle was an attraction. Darker and sinister back alleys branched like antlers, littered with dimmer lights.

"The people are waiting for Santa already," Gideon said. "What shall we do?"

Konrad remembered the vision of Gideon bombing the people.

"We'll spread out. Patrick and Julia might be anywhere, so be careful. Sneak. They're not expecting us to still be alive." Konrad snatched an elf hat from a tourist who left one unguarded. They separated, and Konrad gave the hat to Gideon. "Mask yourself. Do what it takes."

"What will happen?"

"I honestly don't know. Let's hope we still have time."

Gideon pulled the hat on. "I'll get up to the roof for a better view."

"Good." Konrad looked around him, searching for clues. "I'll go to meet Santa."

"Be careful."

Konrad drew in a breath. "Time to spoil the party."

"That's what you're good at."

"Really now?"

"At some point, it has to stop. Believers think their party will go on forever. Because their Big Boss says so."

"One day I'll tell you why it's problematic to use mental images as a hobby horse in one's favor. We must live our lives as if we deserved it. Many times, people believe that they're doing good, being morally enlightened, but their actions are born out of fear."

"How about us?" Gideon asked. "Aren't we scared? What if we aren't doing good?"

"We have lived thus far; we deserve this chance. I'm not going to lie to you—I have no idea how this day is going to turn out. Your mother believed in unity as one of the driving forces of humankind, but she also warned about the means to get there. I'm doing this for your mother. I'm only beginning to under-stand her strength in her Faith."

Gideon stared at Konrad, his face hardened with deter-mination.

"Let's do this."

"I'll sneak into Santa's chamber."

"Shall I try to call for backup?"

"No. We must avoid panic. More people will only be infected if they leave or run away."

"What if—"

"Gideon." Konrad placed his hand on the young man's shoulder. "It's only us now."

Gideon pulled in a deep breath.

"Okay."

They parted ways. Konrad walked through the tourists trying to get around the corner and behind the palace of Santa Claus. He passed one the biggest Christmas trees he ever saw and listened to all the languages around him. He glanced at the tree one more time and his heart gave an extra pump when he realized what the colorful hanging decorations were.

Country flags of the world.

GIDEON STOLE A mobile phone from a tourist's bag side pocket. Upon calling Ville, he was surprised he could remember the phone number. A familiar phone song sprang into life behind him.

Gideon hung up, turned around and saw Ville staring at his phone. Gideon tapped on the shoulder of the tourist and apologized to him in Finnish for stealing the phone from him.

"Merci!" the tourist said.

Ville spotted Gideon. "I'll be damned. The thief in action."

"I'm so glad to see you," Gideon said, "I need your help."

Ville shook his head and hid his phone. "Don't even try."

Gideon leaned forward and pressed his cheek against Ville's, whispering, "They killed my mother."

"Don't be ridiculous. You're trying to use me again."

"They. Killed. Ruut."

It took Ville's breath away.

"They are planning to attack this place any moment now."

"What?"

"My God!" Rebecca yelled close by. "Boys! Get yourself a room."

Now it was Ville who rushed to whisper the news into Rebecca's ear. She looked at Gideon, surrendered to a fog of confusion. "Tell me it's not true."

"I'll tell you both what's true," Gideon said, "and what will happen if we don't work together."

62

THE PITTER PATTER of eager tourists' feet in an outlet shop drummed while Konrad's stomach churned at the sight of the worldwide commercial holy day. The commercial orgy, spending in overdrive. Everybody barraged by the sights, sounds, and smells of Christmas.

Konrad sneaked into the Santa's Chamber through a cracked open window. Fire burned in a big hearth, and he saw a pair of Santa's boots in one corner, dark and heavy. Upon them, two jackets hung casually on a sofa, and in the warm light, the red appeared to be the deepest he ever saw. Two snow-white beards hung on a stand next to the door.

There's only one Santa Claus...

An intoxicating odor wafted to his nose, and it took only two seconds to realize who it belonged to.

Julia.

Her presence was haunting.

Something moved behind the door of the restroom.

Konrad jumped behind the door as quietly as he could but tripped and smashed his shoulder against the wall.

The door opened and for a second Konrad smelled the odor more precisely. He pushed the door hard against the man who seemed to threaten him.

The door hit the man in the head with a loud crack. Hands ready in fists, Konrad witnessed a lifeless body smack the floor. In a blur of adrenaline, Konrad gasped and held his head.

The man lying on the floor was his chubby doctor Olaf from the hospital.

A little side job?

Olaf was nearly all dressed for Christmas. Only his white beard was misplaced—hanging on his chest.

A knock sounded at the door, and a woman spoke in the clear voice of a rock musician manager. "Everything okay in there?"

Konrad mimicked the big man's voice by pulling his chin back, "Uno moment!"

Silence was tangible.

Konrad cleared his voice audibly as if preparing for a speech.

"Good," the woman said, "see you in five minutes."

"Where?" Konrad immediately regretted his words.

"What are you talking about? I'm coming in."

Konrad attacked the door with a panther's leap. He yelled in a low voice, "I just had to take a whole hectare of shit. Stomach problems. I'll change and come right up."

Again silence.

Nothing seemed to happen until a little white pill rolled under the door near the tip of his shoe.

"That'll help you over the worst," the woman said, "Hurry up now. The world awaits your speech and departure."

This time Konrad managed not to ask what the pill was. He picked it up and threw it into the fire. He planned to hide Olaf in the toilet and shove a sock in his mouth.

Then there were not many options left.

Konrad held up a sofa pillow against his stomach.

Father-fucking-Christmas...

63

GIDEON, VILLE, AND REBECCA spread out in the crowd. Looking for something they had absolutely no idea about felt hopelessly idiotic. Why didn't they just announce the danger, warn the people, and call the cops?

Gideon concentrated on the mass of individuals. Patrick and Julia could be anywhere. He did his best to figure out their plan, looked up, wished for miracle, but nothing gave him hope. Was their struggle in vain?

The bulletproof vest under his clothes kept rubbing, pinching and itching. Had someone told him a week ago about this situation he would have just shrugged. But the nightmare was real. Soon there would be no option but to act, threaten with a suicide vest if necessary. Nobody could escape.

Ville had climbed atop a snowy slope. He spread his hands at Gideon. Rebecca was gazing into the sky on the other side of the square. Something in her momentary calm spoke to Gideon, as if she was saying her goodbyes to Ruut's soul.

Gideon looked up, but quickly lowered his gaze to rooftop level. On one balcony was something familiar. A machine he had seen twice before.

In the snow hill.

In the Cave.

He made a three-sixty. Six more machines, barely visible behind searchlights.

The lights started turning slowly, automated toward the Santa Claus Office.

Two little elves, a girl and a boy, opened the entry doors. While they slowly walked down the stairs and the lights turned down on them, everybody grew quiet. The show was on.

In an eerily heavy silence, the elves placed their hands on their forehead and looked from side to side far away.

"Has anyone seen Santa Claus?" the girl elf asked, turning to the boy elf.

The boy wiped the back of his hand across his forehead. "Phew! We have wrapped the presents. Millions of presents. My hands are so tired and full of blisters. And we checked the weather and the route."

"Yes, but the primary mission still belongs to Santa Claus," the girl said. She added a big arm movement. "Every year he delivers gifts to children all over the world on Christmas Eve."

More time passed.

The elves looked at each other.

"Oh, no," the boy said and placed his hand near his mouth. "What if Santa is late? What will happen?"

The girl looked fearful. "Let's call his name."

After a few yells, the audience joined the chorus.

"Santa Claus—where are you?"

JULIA HEARD SANTA CLAUS' name being called a few hundred meters away in the woods. She gave a hug to Rudolph, the first in the line of reindeer.

"You always do all the hard work."

Rudolph didn't protest Julia's tighter hug.

"You are just like me. We work hard in the background so that everyone can lead their lives. So that Christmas can come every year. So that everybody around the world can forget war just for a moment."

Julia stared in the direction Rudolph was focusing on.

People celebrating,

Time to cross the Rubicon.

Julia kissed Rudolph's antlers, rose to her feet, and went to witness the miracle.

64

KONRAD EXITED THE ROOM, sweating inside the red clothes. The beard itched, but the combination of hotness and uncomfortable clothes didn't go near what bothered him the most. The overheated room had caused his body to protest. His body tingled all over, and every step hurt as if a thousand rusty needles were stuck in his thighs.

What the hell am I going to say?

There was no plan, no procedure. Probably everything the marketing bosses had expected was inside the head of the unconscious man lying on the floor of the toilet.

Hands and legs trembling, he took his balance from the walls. He feared falling on his face in front of the people. If his real identity were revealed, he would probably be killed by the angry mob.

Behind the front doors, he stopped to catch a breath. His back hurt as though he had been pulling a sled with the weight of an anvil.

His body was falling apart at the most critical moment.

The people were chanting the name of 'Santa' with increasing joy. Konrad opened the door.

Everyone cheered. Every pair of eyes followed his every move.

In the brightness, he felt reborn again just like in the hospital bed.

All the lights and cameras of the world were aimed at him.

65

KONRAD FOUND MANY children among the crowd taking pictures of him. There was a sea of mobile phones extended, selfie sticks moving back and forth, international reporters with big cameras and microphones.

"God Jul!" Konrad began, having no idea why he started with Swedish. "Merii Kurisumasu! Frohe Weihnachten! Joyeux Noël! Merry Christmas! Feliz Navidad! Hyvää joulua..."

The audience grew silent.

Konrad began, his chest bulged, "I can see in the eyes of the young and the old, the disbelief that has been with you all for as long as I can remember. You are wondering how I can circle the world it in one day and one night." Konrad paused. "I can break the spell for you and reveal a little secret." His hand cupped his mouth as though he whispered, "I can't do it."

Sharp inhalations whipped through the crowd.

"It's the elves who make Christmas possible! They are the scouts who report back to me about all the children who deserve presents. Their resilience makes it possible to answer all the mountains of letters sent to me. They are the mountain's echo, answering your every call."

"Don't forget the route plan and weather forecast," the girl elf stated.

"And the blisters on our fingers!" the boy elf said.

Konrad tipped back his head and bellowed a laugh, "Ho, ho!"

Good. The elves can improvise.

Konrad scanned the crowd and around during the silence that built more anticipation. Someone waved at him on the roof.

Gideon?

A Japanese man knelt down just a few meters before Konrad and plucked something from his pocket. The woman next to him blushed and placed both hands on her face. The people cheered at the sudden proposal.

"What do we have got here?" Konrad announced, delighted to gain valuable time.

What am I missing?

A mute film started rolling in front of his eyes. Everyone was cheering aloud, but Konrad couldn't hear them. Many parents quickly explained to their children what was happening. One child got Konrad's attention. The child didn't care about the happiness of the young couple, and somehow Konrad got a feeling he had been brought there involuntarily.

The child then looked up at caught a snowflake on his tongue. Their gazes met, and a smile visited the child's face.

Konrad saw a shadow on the roof and footprints in the snow.

"Can we have your blessing?" The Japanese man whispered to Konrad.

The woman's smile next to the man was tantalizing.

"Yes," Konrad said in a quiet voice.

Seriously? Do I look like a priest?

"May their love be eternal," Konrad announced. "And

remember, it's during the hardest times your love will be weighed."

The two bowed and stepped back into the audience while applause grew.

A gust of gentle wind played with the flags in the Christmas tree. Konrad felt in his guts once again that the weather was going to change, but the pain in his joints was just about the worsening of his symptoms. The final rays of sunlight touched the top of the Christmas tree and withdrew. He looked across to the pine trees that towered over the people, where light still won over darkness by a few degrees above the line where the branches were alive.

It started snowing.

People waited for his speech.

Konrad looked at the child who seemed to be the only happy human being in the crowd. The child smirked and showed his tongue. For one last time, Konrad gazed up, felt the light disappearing and losing the battle.

Then, only for the briefest of moments, there was a flash in the rain, the thing that bound every possible meaning together.

The past, the present, the future.

A rainbow.

It was like the last capstone had been placed in the moral arc. The solution was obvious.

The artificial snow. That's the plan.

"I have an announcement to make," Konrad said. "As we all know, at least as all children know, there is only one Santa Claus. And parents who are exactly as excited and expectant as you are, are ashamed to show it. They just don't want you to hear the secret that they feel like a child again. But I have a little moral dilemma. Perhaps you can help me out."

Konrad glanced at the elves and gave the nod meant to remind them of the chain of command.

"I deliver good will and presents. That's what I do best. Right before hopping in my reindeer-pulled sleigh, I always give this speech and send Christmas cheer to the people of the world. But every time I feel a little sad also. Why?"

Konrad paused.

"I give presents only if children behave well." Konrad tried to catch a glimpse of Gideon. More snow was falling. Unseen pandemonium was breaking loose. "What about the adults? Why aren't we judging them? I enjoy giving gifts. I believe Christmas is essential to human flourishing and family life. This year, however, something changed in me. The spirit of oblig-atory gift-giving has started to pain me, especially in my dreams. Christmas should not be an exercise in delayed gratification. A reward for a year of goodness can't be measured by the gifts one will get. A year of goodness is not January through November and then start building character. No. Each moment counts. Each thought counts. Each action has a meaning. I'm no pope to say this, but Christmas and happiness have become madden-ingly superficial, and I'm sure all you adults can understand what I mean."

Konrad sensed the two elves wondering what was going on.

"Deep in the original heart of Christmas is love," Konrad added. "And it has been such a pleasure and privilege to spread the word of love in this unique position. We are all one big family, uniting under the shadow of the tree of divine unity. My journey is about to begin, and I'm so glad to see you all here wishing me the best of luck with my adventures. Which is why we're going to have a little change of plans... if it's okay with the elves?"

The elves looked at each other, and the boy said, "If it's within the timetable."

"Marvelous." Konrad rubbed his hands together. "There's a little treasure hidden in the Snowman World for the children. X marks the spot. If my elves would be so kind and lead the children over there."

"Follow us," the girl elf said, and the boy walked next to Konrad, whispering, "I seriously hope you know what you're doing."

Konrad smiled back and said, "Excellent, excellent!" Konrad stopped to collect his wits and plan the next step. His heart pumped insanely as if a terrifying power was relentlessly counting down to oblivion.

The remaining adults started staring at the opposite sex with lingering interest.

"Sometimes, ladies and gentlemen, people look me all cross-eyed, when I speak about this…" Men's eyes were now set on the women as if glued.

Fear tightened around Konrad's heart. What could he do? Even a thinly veiled threat of violence or force might make Patrick and Julia suspicious. He had to act now before anybody managed to go over the fence of uninhibited flirting.

"Lapland is full of stories about shamans, spirits, and spells that stage supernatural sagas. But what you don't know is that especially the Sámi people had a way to turn on the flame of love. Step inside, and I show you one magical thing that compares to the secret food that can make even my reindeer fly!"

The adults stared at Konrad as if they had lost all reason, individually and collectively.

"This way. Trust me; you'll never forget this. Step into my vault. And I can almost promise you that you will no longer be a stranger to the Heaven within you."

66

KONRAD WAS ASHAMED at his choice of words, but at least it seemed to work. He was a preacher pouring poison into the deep waters of the psyche.

The first people were entering the building when Konrad saw Gideon on the edge of the crowd hustling a couple who tried to get away. Gideon had clearly made a threat, as he strode in behind them.

War was in the air.

Konrad smiled at the people, who barely looked at him. In the current, one man seemed to walk straight at Konrad, evaluating him. Konrad stretched for a broader smile and managed to keep it that way.

Patrick Praytor walked past him, silently, like a wolf, casting a momentary flat gaze at Konrad, who hoped he hadn't given any clues away in his speech. He was quite sure he hadn't. Patrick was observing his operation among the sheep. Where was Julia?

Konrad considered his options. What was he supposed to say or show inside? How could he make sure nobody would escape?

The man walking in front of Gideon had turned sheet white and his eyes beseeched Konrad for help. Gideon's fearsome glare turned Konrad's stomach inside out. He had flashed his bullet-proof vest.

A threat of violence.

The only possibility.

Everybody crept inside in slow motion, anticipation building with the silence. Konrad entered last and locked the door quickly. He turned back to the people, the pulse of panic pounding at his temples, focusing his gaze on...

A weapon.

Patrick held a gun to Konrad's forehead. The reek of gun oil buckled his knees.

The surrounding people saw what was happening, but before panic spread, and before Gideon could see Konrad was at gunpoint, Gideon screamed, "Everybody on the floor. Now, or I'll kill you!"

Patrick's pupils receded at the noise. Konrad jerked his head aside as Patrick pulled the trigger. The bullet went through his beard and the wooden door, and the pressure of the blast tore at Konrad's eardrums. Warm blood spilled onto his shoulder.

A quick shadow fell across Konrad's vision: somebody attacked Patrick and knocked him to the floor. Handcuffs clanging in the man's back pocket, he screamed, "Help! He tried to kill Santa Claus!"

Patrick's left hook landed on the man's jaw, which numbed him cold. Patrick shot him in the chest, people shrieked, many hit the floor, hands behind their heads. Patrick turned back to Konrad, took aim, but an old granny hit his face with a bag. Konrad dived at Patrick's legs and knocked him over. Konrad lost his beard as more people attacked Patrick.

Five men against one.

Gideon yelled, "Stay on the floor. Or we'll kill you." He moved quickly to the gun and picked it up.

He watched them wrestle, his palms sweating. Patrick knocked one man unconscious. Then another. Teeth and blood flew through the air.

Konrad found the handcuffs and signaled Gideon, finger spelling letter L, urged to pull the trigger. More people decided to go on assault against Patrick but one by one he managed to shake them off. Then Gideon fired at the roof.

Snow fell from the ceiling.

Everybody froze still.

Three bloody and bruised men let go of Patrick, raised their hands, and went down on the floor hands behind their heads.

Gideon aimed at Patrick's face.

No resistance.

"Get down," Konrad said and undressed. Patrick was on the floor on his knees as Konrad placed one of the steel rings around Patrick's wrists.

"Get up." Konrad roughed Patrick around and cuffed his hands around a steel pole.

"Where's Julia?"

"You're too late," Patrick said.

"I'm not asking again." Konrad pressed the barrel deep against Patrick's throat until he could feel his steady, calm pulse.

"Do it."

Gideon said, "Konrad. He's not going anywhere."

The people stared at Konrad. Many seemed to now realize who he was. He ran over to the wounded police officer.

"We need a doctor!" Konrad announced.

A hand lifted.

Gideon signaled the old lady could approach the policeman.

After a quick inspection, the old lady said, "We need to get this man to the hospital. Otherwise he'll die."

Goddamnit, Konrad thought.

They couldn't let that happen.

And despite all the chaos, they spotted a couple in the back of the room getting closer, their faces coming together.

67

"L ISTEN UP," KONRAD SAID. "I don't know how to put this, so I'll just state the cold facts. This man..." Konrad pointed at Patrick, "is responsible for the attack against you tonight. Gideon and I are here to undo what's happened. You are all infected. I don't have all the details yet how this particular kind of virus will affect you, but trust me, you'll all feel it soon enough."

"Are we going to die?" somebody shouted in the back.

"Spare us. We've got children!" a woman cried.

"Nobody is going to die," Konrad assured.

"T-tell that to your suicide bomber friend!" The wounded policeman groaned.

The woman doctor said, "He needs medical attention. Right now."

"Nobody is going anywhere." Konrad stood beside Patrick. "Tell them. Tell them all about your maniac plan!"

"Don't worry," Patrick announced peacefully. "Just do as your instincts tell you—and you will be freed from all the excruciating pain."

Konrad fired the gun at the roof next to Patrick's ear. "Listen to your ears ringing if you've nothing else to say."

"Oh, *tinnitus sanctus*. My ears have been ringing for ten years. I'm not only at the top of this game. I own it. I own you."

"Sorry, you're not my type," Konrad replied and glanced at the Japanese woman, who had just become engaged, on the floor. She eyed him back. Her eyes weren't flirtatious, but even a single slow blink of her eyes ignited a deep temptation inside Konrad's body.

It's happening to me, too.

Gideon seemed to realize the situation without exchanging words.

"Crap," Gideon said. "By the way, Julia isn't here."

"Maybe she had other plans," Konrad said. "Maybe she saw through me and went off to seal the victory."

"Is she going to strike somewhere else?"

"She has to. They don't take unnecessary risks." Konrad understood that even though they could contain everybody inside, sooner or later the police would storm in. Starting a massacre would send them in even faster.

"Jesus," Gideon said.

On the far side of the room on the left, a young couple started undressing each other like hyenas.

Konrad went over to them and asked them politely to stop. "People are watching you. Behave yourselves."

Behind a pillar, somebody broke a window. Cold wind blew snow inside.

"What now?" Konrad said, running to the corner.

Voices of struggle. Curses. A young boy screamed Gideon's name.

A young boy and a young girl had tamed a tourist who cradled his bloody nose on the floor. Ville and Rebecca came in through the window.

"Don't even think about pointing at us with that water pistol," Ville said, "We're on your side."

"I know them, Konrad," Gideon said.

Konrad nodded. "Did you happen to see if anybody left the crowd when I invited everybody in?"

"We're pretty sure you got them all," Rebecca said. "As long as you don't kill anybody, we can stay here to help. There's one police squad outside the building. They just called for back up."

"Soon the whole building will be surrounded," Gideon said. "And Julia will finish the plan elsewhere."

"Uh-mm," Rebecca muttered and noted the death struggle of the policeman. "Shouldn't we get this man to a doctor or something?"

"We can't," Gideon said. "He might spread the virus."

A man came into the room from the back room, holding his head.

"Olaf?" Gideon said. "Granddad? What happened to you?"

Konrad's heart skipped beats as he understood who he knocked out.

Ruut's father.

"Can you help the wounded policeman over there?" Gideon asked.

"What are you wearing?" Olaf evaluated Gideon. "Is that what I think it is?"

Konrad said, "Please help the man."

The policeman was crying in the gentle embrace of the other doctor, "Mother... mother..."

Olaf staggered through the people lying haphazardly under his feet. "You had better start explaining yourselves. Is your mother here, Gideon?"

Gideon tried to say something, but Konrad spoke before the shocking news might have crushed Olaf.

"Just for the patient's sake," Konrad said, "focus on him now."

"I see now why everybody was so interested in you in the hospital. You're a dangerous man. I knew it already years ago when Ruut was in your class. I should have placed dynamite between your ears when I had the chance."

"Do it next time," Konrad said. "I'll submit myself to you voluntarily." Konrad walked in front of Patrick to stare into his eyes. "Where's Julia?"

Nothing on Patrick's face gave any clues or emotions away.

"Where would Julia go if you ran into trouble?"

The two doctors managed to stabilize the police's condition. But they both agreed on the fact that he hadn't much time.

Olaf rose up and walked to a window to peek outside. "Rudolph is missing."

"That's it!" Gideon and Konrad said together.

"Your partner in crime decided to steal my reindeer?" Olaf asked.

"She's on a symbolic mission," Konrad said.

"Go after her," Gideon said. "We'll manage here."

"Don't let them touch each other," Konrad demanded.

"Easy. Teens always spoil the mood for love," Rebecca said.

Konrad threw a glance at the crowd, then said to the teenagers. "Let them hold hands if you think it's appropriate."

68

KONRAD ESCAPED THE chamber through a window. The dark sky flashed and howled with the arrival of police cars. A faint whirr suggested a chopper heading in their direction. Surely a medical helicopter, pretty much the only swift way to bring wounded and sick people to the hospital from all over Lapland.

His heart crunched at the realization that the shot police officer was going to die. The teens would have to watch it all.

Unbelievable bravery.

In the darkness of the woods, a reindeer attempted to acquire something to eat under the frozen ground. Next to it, the whitest of the herd had antlers only on one side. That branching sight reminded him of the painting in his home. The painting Julia held so dear.

The Antler Plan of Rovaniemi.

Julia was carrying out something sinister with Rudolph. It was the only explanation for her absence.

A memory shot through his eyes with husky dogs racing ahead of him, the sled's runners kicking up snow. The way Julia's father handled the dogs with confidence was unforgettable. He held Julia tight against his chest, feeling her warmth. But stiff-ness in her body revealed she didn't share the moment with him. Her mind was deeply distant with reindeer running toward the twilight far away, wrapping around an idea of fixing the world in a way no one would ever consider trying.

That was the time when they started to grow apart. It had to be.

A howl snapped him back.

A Siberian husky.

The memory of the sound of a husky choir's sonorous howling and how it had wakened him on so many mornings filled his heart with decisive energy.

One unmanned husky sleigh sat available.

Konrad aroused the dogs' attention and managed to silence them with the exact gestures of Julia's father. The dogs were eager to go on a run, their ears turned to the trail leading away from the place of sinister silence under the rising whine of the sirens. This ride was to be the mother of all brochure promises, not just a stroll around a small circle.

I know where you are going.

Konrad felt the power of the animals. The power came from the visible concord, months and years of training together as a team. He recapped the mushing sounds and anticipated to make the first kissing sound.

"Mush! Show me what you you're made of."

"HELP ME," the policeman begged and gasped.

The two doctors asked for mercy from Gideon, who refused to look. He loathed himself, the bitter tang in his mouth making him almost throw up. The more he tried to comprehend the situation and the repercussions, and the fact that his family was gone, the more compulsive his urge to flee. His mind didn't give up imagining and replaying the horrible last breath that would come any second.

"Back up," Gideon said to the doctors. He gestured to Ville and Rebecca to be on guard as he crouched next to the policeman, and took his hand into his. The pressure from the dying man's shake surprised him. He whispered in his ear.

"I know this is hard to accept. But you must understand that you're infected. Letting you out would cause worldwide problems. What's your name?"

"P-Peter. I-I have to take c-care... my children."

"You are. You are everything I wished my father to be."

"I don't want to die." Peter coughed blood on Gideon's face.

An instant tear formed in Gideon's eyes.

"It's all right; you are the hero of this day."

"Y-you think so?" Peter calmed down, something escaping him. "Tell my family I love them so much. Tell them I'll be waiting for them. Promise me."

A shudder passed through Gideon's body as Peter squeezed his hand. "I'll do everything that your name gets the reputation it deserves."

The people lying on the floor held their breaths as Peter's convulsions came to an end. The sound of his last breath was indescribably sad, yet soothing. A sharp pain stabbed Gideon's chest. The sadness for Peter and his family was intolerable. He closed his eyelids and whispered, "Thank you, Peter."

Eyes turned toward Gideon. By accepting the mantle of guilt, he hoped the message was clear and cold-blooded enough: he would spare no mercy to rescue a valuable life.

Ville's and Rebecca's eyes were shocked in the distorted wrecks of their faces.

Gideon's world teetered on the brink of total collapse. He turned to Patrick to launch a spear of sorrow-blinded rage...

"What in the name of..." Gideon rushed to the base of the stairs and screamed at Ville and Rebecca. "Where is he?"

The three of them came to witness the overwhelming reality of the situation. As though the earth had swallowed Patrick, only blood pooled on the floor.

And in that pool sat a gnawed-off thumb with shredded bone and skin.

69

ONLY TWO SLEIGH lengths ahead Konrad distinguished reindeer crap. The smell indicated it was fresh. Julia was here just minutes ago. He looked over the frozen river. A black dot was moving toward the city. Illuminated by two gigantic light sources, the Lumberjack's Candle Bridge dominated the nightscape while lighting up the riverbank as well. There was no way he could reach Julia undetected on the ice and no better way of moving, so he just had to hurry up.

The dogs' tongues dangled long as they mustered the strength.

"Be ready for the final ride." He commanded them to move. Julia was probably going to drop a present on her hometown, a city that had once wrapped its arms around them, and had been their own frozen cultural hub. Confronting the horror, scarcely imaginable, Konrad took the best out of the huskies.

Or was she a threat anymore? Until recently, she had always been the complete opposite of violence. How could she bear the burden of killing Iris?

The antlers had to mean something extraordinary for her.

His raw feeling was that they represented a non-ordinary aware-ness, a crown idea, bringing men and women closer to the sky and thus making them sacred. The symbolic nature of the antlers was the source of inspiration for her to get man's branching disagreements in check.

But what happened after the antlers growth had been completed? Didn't they just fall off?

Are you planning to do something to yourself?

70

GIDEON KNEW THAT Patrick was after Konrad and Julia. If Patrick was infected too, he could start spreading the thing on his own. Was it even reasonable to carry on detaining people inside?

"Look, uh, you've got to stop," Ville said to a couple drawing closer together.

"Make them stop," Gideon demanded.

"How?"

"Kick them in the head," Rebecca said.

Gideon did a quick analysis. "You're violating the rules. Move your hands away from each other!"

"I can't just kick them," Ville said. "See. It's no use to command. Whatever is inside them is taking hold."

"I have bad mojo about this," Rebecca said to Gideon.

"We'll tie your wrists together behind your backs if you don't obey," Gideon said. He waited for a few seconds before confirming the increasing activity everywhere. "Quickly now, Rebecca, how do we spoil their mood?"

She did a double take. "If privacy is not a problem I don't

think even bad music would do. Madonna would not get any attention."

"Think, think..." Gideon said to himself. "Ville, what the hell are you doing? Are you reading mood spoilers on your phone?"

"I got an idea how to buy us more time. YouTube..."

"Slowpoke, Madonna isn't helping."

"Chillax."

More than one couples started kissing. Gideon prepared to threaten the people with the bulletproof vest.

A baby started crying.

Ville raised the phone over his head victoriously while adding volume. "The medicine for baby fever!"

The people immediately reacted to the primitive voice, which turned their heads.

"Wicked!" Rebecca said. "A pacifier for adults' mouths!"

The solution lifted a chunk of bricks from Gideon's back but offered only a temporary relief. The burden of pain was there to stay.

His heart beat a strange rhythm. Like he was failing to defuse an emotional bomb exploding in his chest and dying all over again.

Ville's phone beeped once, and his already pale face turned ghost white.

Battery.

71

THE STRONG HEADWIND attacked Konrad's eyes with tiny frozen flakes. The sleigh moved on the ice track marked for snowmobiles much faster than Julia. His mind raced at its own pace. What would he say to her? Would she pull a gun and shoot him instantly?

Konrad looked over his shoulder, blinked the gathering ice out of his eyes. Then he concentrated on getting maximum output from the Huskies with kissing sounds.

The dogs gained speed, and in the darkness, they ran over a bump that hopped the sleigh airborne. What the hell did she think she got out of her symbolic path? The show was somehow too preposterous, too contrived to be like her. Even with her enthusiasm and devotion with celebrating Christmas something didn't either add up, or he simply didn't know her at all. But the ring tightening harder around his finger disallowed him to think they hadn't looked in the same direction. They had agreed that as long as Konrad's warnings were on an apocalyptic course, he was just fulfilling the promise of the Scripture. The world was heading headlong to destruction in either case, but crossing that line would be inevitable for better moral flourishing.

They had an agreement.

She had blessed his efforts.

Yet she turned her back on him.

Gritting his teeth, inside his head, a silent battle cry rang out. If he had crossed some too-holy line and she hadn't told him, he would not now feel responsible for her actions. The smile of Oona Louhi revisiting in his mind was now a distant ghost of memory that he felt sorry for no more. And that was not like him, either. Almost nothing added up anymore. He would reach her and force her to get to the bottom of it all.

The hair on the back of his neck sprang up.

A bestial sound of an engine reached behind him just as he turned around. But the metal beast knocked his feet out from under him and together they broke into the wooden frame of the sleigh and got stuck. In a flash, Konrad saw him again.

Patrick Praytor.

Konrad stretched his muscles and spun free from the rubble to the passenger side of the sleigh. Patrick hit the brakes, and the weight of the snowmobile yanked the sleigh to the left with a force that sent the dogs airborne and rolling like a lethal snowball. The animals squeaked in pain, but were chopped short as the sleigh exploded into pieces and the snowmobile overturned and cartwheeled over them. Metal and plastic parts shot in every direction in a cloud of gray smoke and snow.

Konrad lay pinched with an unconscious husky at his side, its tongue dangling and pierced by the animal's own teeth. It revived in a blink of an eye, brought its head upon Konrad's chest.

The dogs filled the silence with eerily sad crying.

Footsteps. He moved the dog aside as quickly and gently as possible and stood up from under the rubble. Patrick's elbow hit his chest, sending him down again. He sprang up with all the strength he could muster and managed to headbutt Patrick's jaw, the agony numbing them both for a second.

Both stood, wavering.

Rage and frustration galvanized Patrick. A dog attempted to lift its head but Patrick flung it down, the handcuffs clanging on his wrist. Konrad threw snow, targeting Patrick's eyes, but he moved like a steam train. The back of Konrad's head slammed against the ice with a crack.

"Now I'll make sure I hear your last breath." Patrick's blood spilled onto Konrad's face from his injured hand as he exerted remorseless pressure on Konrad's Adam's apple. Patrick's knees in Konrad's ribcage send a thousand electric spikes to his temple.

Konrad kicked and swung his arms inefficiently, attempting to dig fingernails into Patrick's face. But the dogs' reigns tangled his hands. He felt a hole being ripped in his throat. Time ticked away, his consciousness grew lighter and lighter moving into an eternal sleep. Something moved in the corner of his left eye.

A husky attacked Patrick without warning. Another. As Patrick cursed, Konrad rolled away on the ice, managing to untangle himself from the reigns. As he stumbled up, he freed another husky. The dog bared its teeth, growled, and attacked Patrick's thigh. The colossal man tried to hit back at the dogs, but the power behind his blows was weakening. The dogs bit and mutilated his face. A horrible scream rang in the night. Quickly, his vocal cords were chopped short as if under the blade of a guillotine.

The dogs continued finishing off Patrick while Konrad staggered over and tore the watch off Patrick's wrist.

Konrad turned toward the Candle Bridge. Standing on the bridge, Julia had seen everything. She made no move, her hands resting at her sides, looking down at him innocently but as shocked as a schoolgirl.

Konrad staggered up the river bank and tied the watch to his wrist. The pulse in his wrist raced against the strap as the watch sprang into life.

Tiny little white dots that Konrad first thought were flakes of snow filled the screen with a spinnable 3D world map.

It cannot be...

His world came crashing down.

72

"**T**HEY ARE SWEATING," Ville told Gideon.

Gideon had noted the growing restlessness. The baby was still crying for some time to come, but not long.

"Tell us, what's wrong with us?" a voice asked.

Gideon hesitated. "We are working that out. Keep your shit together."

The three of them gathered for a meeting.

"Hey," Ville said to a young girl. "No peeking."

Before they managed to hold a conversation, two pairs at opposite side of the rooms rushed to action.

"They have found something to stuff into their ears!" Rebecca yelled.

Chaos ensued.

Men and women rushed against each other and the walls, only searching for release.

"Stop!" Gideon screamed. "Or I will... I will..."

Rebecca and Ville both picked up a random couple and dove in to clear their ears. But getting only a few to calm down seemed only to add more speed to the profanity of the scene as clothes started flying all over.

Gideon touched one man's shoulder.

With coruscating light radiating for his fingertips, his mind visited a pregnant silence, a beautiful vision. The man lost consciousness and slumped like an abandoned marionette over the woman under him. The woman's eyes morseted her amazement at Gideon.

For a split second everybody stopped before continuing where they left.

The insight tore a blade through Gideon's guts. He had seen the potential baby boy of the couple. A morally advanced human being smiling in a wooden cradle. A mind so brilliant that as a grown-up it could revolutionize the moral code of mankind. But an ominous shadow appeared with a black tactical pistol placed on his forehead.

Gideon's heart faltered. Rebecca yelled something to him as he touched another couple. The light was like an explosion, repeating everything. As a hawk grabs its prey in its strong talons, his mind caught on another moment where an innocent child was again brutally executed.

He could stop the future from happening if he stopped everybody. If he wanted. But would the potentially good children ever get a chance to live?

Among the vicious hormonal attacks, in the middle of the room, a man stood still. His eyes locked with Gideon, jolting him back to the brutal reality.

An infiltrator.

Under the man's opened black jacket was a suicide vest. He took a succession of deep breaths. Then, like it was hate at first sight, he bolted toward Gideon, acting with deliberate indifference to the consequences.

"EVERYBODY GET DOWN!" Gideon screamed while instinctively running against the man.

A flash of unearthly white light.

Then heat.

Wooden structures came down from the ceiling onto their heads.

Smoke and blood and snow filled the hellish stage.

73

KONRAD STARED AT Julia from a few meters away. A woman so small, skinny and fragile, playing at the top among such deadly and powerful men, she seemed so...

Unaffected.

"Aren't you going ask me why I did it?" Julia said.

"You don't know what you're doing."

"Wrong." Julia folded her arms. She flashed her unique flirting smile that Konrad had always fallen for. Immediate twisted urge ignited inside his head. Konrad looked up at two large candles at the top in the pylons, then into the city over her.

"Antler Plan," he said. "How did you pull this off? The white dots on the world map... they are all live global covert operations. Aren't they?"

Julia acknowledged the plan by raising her chin. "You are so naive, Konrad. Risks are the price of progress. We have overpopulated the world. It would be just a matter of time before nature rebalanced things on its own catastrophic terms. With the new moral instinct, people will reach the right conclusions. It will transform everything. From sexuality to spirituality to moral intelligence. It's our right to gain power over our fates. Extending and expanding our reach beyond our limitations."

Konrad's couldn't look at her without twisted sexual urges. He took a step forward, avoided eye contact.

"Don't come any closer. Even though I don't wield a gun to commit suicide, I still have other means." Julia opened her mouth, and Konrad glimpsed something shaped like a false tooth.

A cyanide capsule.

"Is the US government behind this? Or Russians?"

"The Veterans."

"The Veterans?"

"The aftermath of war sends a human mind back to childhood—uprooted, orphaned, and spiritually injured. The nightmares of the veterans persist because of the fear that the war never ends."

"You just talked them over to comply?"

Her eyes were charged with outlaw energy and lit up with intense emotion. Konrad still tried to avert meeting her tantalizing gaze.

"Even you would have taken the cure if you were tormented by mental scars, hyper-vigilance, and nightmares in your everyday life. The Veterans," Julia nodded at the clock, "continued their war in their homes. Death followed them across their doorsteps. As if recovering isn't challenging enough, the insurance battles are even tougher. Nothing ever feels the same after the war, because the war brings the feelings of aliveness far above ordinary civilian life. Nothing brings them satisfaction after the comradeship and companionship tested in the extreme situations."

Konrad remained quiet.

She continued. "Imagine death tapping your shoulder, whispering, 'It's right to set your self free. Do it. Let it be your final mission.' Why is it that so many soldiers reach the point of completely withdrawing from their wife and children, away from the ones they loved and wanted to protect? Patrick and I came to their rescue. We offered them a solution. Something that would put an end to their blind search for something. War has been long who we are at our most primal level, as you've said. War has fused souls together throughout history and offered a perspective beyond any other human experience. But its momentum, unfortunately, was unstoppable."

Konrad experienced a breathtaking hormonal tsunami. He leaned over the metal rail. "Your work has blinded the sorrows of your heart. You think some things go too deep for healing, but that's not true. Nicholas died on a peacekeeping mission, doing what he wanted. We can't predict or prevent all accidents."

"Don't lecture me!" Julia snapped. "You put all the pressure on his shoulders! It was you who told him 'My father would have wanted you to go into the army.' Fuck you. I hate you."

"I hate myself for that," Konrad replied. "But we both failed in our mourning process. I turned against God; you tangled with His creation. But erasing negative experiences is not the way to build one's moral character."

"That's the way the world is hurting itself. Look at the city around you. It has risen from ashes. Risen from the seed of one architect's imagination and vision. Humans need a new moral author to prosper. Human potential shifted into higher gear. A broader sense of existence."

"People won't accept this."

"Of course they will. Three decades back in vitro fertilization was a total abomination, now its mainstream. Sexuality branches off into all areas of life, like how we educate our children and the moral structure they inherit and form. We need structures to keep this human story on course. Without morality, we can never grow rich people farsighted enough to support a system that demands sacrifices. It's not only material sacrifices and redesigning the distribution of wealth, but the elite would have to suppress unwelcome desires, turn off erotic sensibilities, and turn their heads to the world's hunger."

"But isn't sexuality our guiding spirit, its burning core? Everybody should have a right to control their own brain and body. Women should have the right to their womb. If you shut down the erotic sensibilities, what if we focus on something so hard that it leads human race to an entirely unintended environment?" Konrad spread his hands. "You can't possibly know or claim that this is fundamentally the best way forward."

"But the corruption of intimacy has already happened! We are already in the unintended environment. You don't give a shit about women's rights."

"Did you tweak my erotic sensibilities?"

"I did. Don't deny that it didn't help you to focus on your work. You were good in making people care, promoting science and reason. But then Nicholas died. You became anti-everything and got married to your new reputation. I couldn't take it. I assured your downfall."

"My affair with Oona was also part of your tests?"

"Yes. I needed access to greater power. Weapon industry had that power, and I needed to prove my competence. Oona's understanding about human potential was out of this world. She warned us about you. I tried to get rid of you. I was the one who put the bomb in your briefcase. I got help from Ruut who fixed your Parabellum. You were supposed to die."

"So, you kicked me out of bed, and used Patrick as well?"

"He fell in love with me before I did that to him."

"But why? I loved you, Julia."

"No. You depended on me. Acknowledge it. The brain is way too badly wired; you didn't really love me. You may think that the hijacking of the brain is not right, but that's the reality we have been living in for decades. People are misled all the time to desire whatever."

A sting of disappointment poked Konrad in the gut. He propped his hands on his hips and hung his head back.

"You are a good man, Konrad," Julia said. "But I don't feel sorry what you had to go through. I wish you'd died."

"I'll speak. I'll tell everybody."

"Why do you resist the inevitable? You are free to speak to anyone. But you'll achieve nothing. You'll be just another conspiracy theorist. Sex issues will still be taboos and kept private."

"The truth will come out sooner or later," Konrad said. He paused to follow the parade-long line of ambulances and fire engines rushing to the north. Emptiness, worry, and fear drew a chasm in his stomach. "I'll devote myself to destroy your plan."

"Good. The world needs a strong voice. Dissatisfaction is what fuels everyone to try harder."

"Listen to yourself!" Konrad screamed, his vocal cords sore. "We are not hardwired for evil and malevolent intent! There are good people in the army and weapons' industry on whose conscience the deaths of innocents weigh heavily. Ruut Stark was an example."

Julia shook her head. "But the circuits in the brain are just like a path in the forest; wider and more defined the more you use them. And the more inclined you are to use that shortcut. It takes too much time and patience to regrow the paths shut, especially our biggest and longest trotted missteps."

"You are neurologically enslaving people to purity."

"Deconstruction of the valorized notion of humanity wouldn't happen by any other means or within a reasonable timeline. Now we can build structures that keep warmongers and gun maniacs in check."

"Julia," Konrad begged. "Those who control war have no

power on the other side. Beyond our material world there is another dimension... spiritual... our limited vocabulary can't describe it. War maniacs will have no power at all if we just have..."

"Faith?"

THREE HUNDRED METERS away a man pulled a driver out of a car and hit his face forcefully against the frozen asphalt.

Quickly, the car's headlights turned toward the bridge and Konrad and Julia.

The car jerked aggressively.

The driver cut the lights.

"YOU LOSE, KONRAD," Julia said. "But it's not the end of the world. Go to the hospital. Heal your wounds. Come back stronger. Enjoy the new world."

"I won't let you steal your life."

"It's not for you to decide. I'm a girl who no one can fix."

"That's bullshit. I don't accept your methods, but you showed bedrock bravery in defying a whole system of moderators. It's a miracle you didn't get caught." Mental fatigue started taking its toll on Konrad. "What if God drew a line in the sands of time for this particular plan to never be crossed? Maybe the perimeters were set up so that we would evolve and be able to move on the next level."

"I'm sorry." Julia reached for Konrad, but pulled her hand away. "Cast away the watch and go away. Just surrender yourself to the reality."

Placing his forehead against the rail, Konrad gazed down at the waters.

"No."

Julia gritted her teeth. "Don't you ever know when to stop?"

"The watch proves your insidious crime," Konrad said. "I can still make things right."

"The cycle of revenge," Julia stated and made it sound like ancient history. She bit her lip, then edged forward and kissed Konrad.

A volcano erupted in Konrad's head, but he dropped to his knees before Julia managed to snatch the watch.

A sudden beam of lights blinded Konrad behind Julia, as a metallic beast rushed toward them.

Konrad bolted upright, grabbed Julia by her jacket, and managed to jump on the rail.

The car whipped Julia's legs out from under her; she slammed into the windshield, breaking it into a spider web.

The car stopped, Konrad ran after. But the car reversed, knocked him to the ground.

Konrad got stuck under the wheel, feeling his shinbone snapping in half. Electric fireworks on a black background. Intolerable pain.

The driver got out of the car.

Patrick Praytor's face was a bloody pulp from teeth and claw, down to the bone. He strolled to Julia.

"Patrick?" Julia moaned. "What are you doing?"

Patrick took Julia into his arms, lifted her over the rail.

"No! Let. Me. Go!"

Julia fell, screaming, her voice chopped by a splash.

The current swallowed her under the ice sheet.

Patrick kicked Konrad's leg out of the squeeze. The pain shut down his consciousness. Then, when his first cohesive thought registered, he was in the back seat of the car.

Patrick spun the car around, tires squeaking, the stench of rubber wafting. He aimed south against the broken rail and slammed the gas pedal.

The acceleration glued Konrad to the seat.

Metal twisted, exploding.

A few seconds of weightlessness.

The car smashed through the slush like a spoon through cream.

Water dashed in through broken windows. Patrick Praytor sat still, letting water shroud him. Konrad tried the backseat door. He got it open and tried to escape, but Patrick grabbed his leg and kicked.

The cold surrounding them was pure death, but it helped Konrad's body to function better. Like a shark, Patrick wouldn't let go of his prey until the resistance ceased. Every muscle pulled taut to bone, Konrad twisted his broken leg, hoped it to come off.

Pain seared through his body and skull—no use. After a dazed beat, Konrad surrendered to intuition and made his final effort. Using Patrick's strong pull to lower himself down, he planted a kiss on his ugly face while managing to wire the free loop of the handcuffs to the car's broken metal frame.

Patrick bit back, but Konrad had placed his feet on the passenger seat and pushed exactly when the car yanked Patrick at the opposite direction.

The car sank.

Konrad's sinking stopped.

Patrick stared at him, flabbergasted, cold water surging into his lungs.

The car sank into depths as Konrad swam up and struggled against the current. His body and brains begged for oxygen. He screamed his lungs out above the water and grabbed the ice, resisting the suction.

An emergency team had ladders over the rail. A man threw him a rope.

"Reach it!"

Konrad grabbed it and yelled. "A woman's under the ice... She might stand a chance. Cold reduces damage in the brain!"

The man barked orders above to the team operating on the bridge.

"If you find her," Konrad yelled, "get the cyanide capsule out of her mouth!"

"What?"

"Just do it!"

"Roger that. Come on. We'll take you to the hospital."

"The hell you will. You'll take me to Santa Claus."

"Sir, you'll die of bleeding."

"My call."

"No, sir." The rescuer overruled him. "We'll use force if you don't comply."

"No! I have to warn them all! Before hell breaks loose."

"What?"

"Do you want to three hundred people dead on your conscience? At least send a message. Tell Gideon to surrender. The Antler Plan has gone global!"

"That I can do. Let's go fix you up."

Konrad turned his gaze on the ice at the rescue team rushing with a snowmobile.

75

GIDEON LEAPED UPRIGHT. Death and gore and blood dominated the room. Tinnitus yelled in his ear canals; blood was everywhere.

I'm still alive?

Did Aslan want to create panic and make the police attack so that as many as possible could be saved to spread the madness? But why hadn't the police attacked?

"Are you okay, Gideon?" Rebecca asked, her face a blur.

"What the hell happened?"

"You have to see it yourself."

To his surprise, Gideon found his body functioning flawlessly. He was so surprised that only the detonator had died. Everybody else was okay, despite the bleeding from their ears. "We still have everybody inside?"

"Yes."

Did Ruut once again surprise everybody from beyond the grave? Had she managed to make a non-lethal explosive vest that only stunned people, but killed its carrier?

"They've voluntarily positioned themselves against the windows," Rebecca said, "so that no sharpshooters can take us."

"Yes," Ville confirmed. "They understood that we are on their side."

"How can they control themselves?" Gideon asked, taking the hint in somewhere from their faces. "The snow?"

"And they're fighting for the future." Rebecca beamed with pride. "I told them about the whole plot against humanity. Nobody is charging us if we let them all go."

Gideon let out a long breath.

A switch of relief went off in his chest.

KONRAD WOKE UP in the hospital bed. His vision was waving like a fun house mirror over the span of ten seconds before coming into focus.

He sighed and smiled at a beautiful nurse who had come into the room with a pair of crutches. She left them on the bed.

"May I be of service?"

Discarding his bruised ego, Konrad looked at her beauty without making it erotic.

"Can I take a cold shower?"

K

ONRAD AND GIDEON stood at Ruut's grave.

RUUT Stark
   23 October 1988 - 21 December 2017

A *MOTHER and a champion of light.*
   "Faith is God's plan lovingly accepted."

KONRAD HELD GIDEON CLOSE. His tear-swollen eyes were full of grief and disbelief, but carried no trace of hatred. The only thing that compounded Konrad's worry and anxiety to unsustainable levels was Ruut's harrowing promise which he couldn't share with Gideon if it were false hope:

Wait for my resurrection...

Julia was alive at the hospital. Bedbound. The oxygen deprivation had been devastating to her brain functions and made her vegetative state permanent. No way to discuss and dissect the plan or learn about her and Ruut's connection.

"Your mother always knew the best way forward," Konrad told Gideon. "She didn't want bullet-ridden corpses on her or anyone's conscience. She deserved a medal of honor."

Gideon tucked his hands behind his elbows. "She wasn't perfect."

A wandering reindeer stopped by, followed by a man who looked like he knew what to do. The reindeer stood next to Ruut's grave, its head hanging low.

"Is the Santa's reindeer he or she?" Konrad asked. "Reindeer cast their antlers after the fights of mating seasons, don't they?"

The man seemed like he had always known the answer to the question, but was now uncertain. Then light shone in his eyes. "He. Definitely he. Female reindeer are too small to pull a weighty sleigh. And it's likely that the early winter breeding season has made them pregnant."

"Still doesn't explain the antlers."

The man made a playful grin. "They simply don't fall off because castration stops the process of casting the antlers in the winter time. Once castrated, strong and peaceful they'll become. Lots of energy in store when having skipped the fights for love."

"So, they kind of focus on the essential," Konrad said.

"Wouldn't we all want to focus on that?" the man asked and prepared to leave with the reindeer. "Come on, Peter." Gideon studied the gravestone as though he was staring off at a nowhere point a million miles from here. Wind blew on snow, spawning snow devils on the frozen ground.

"I hope she has been uprooted somewhere else, somewhere better. A better garden. But I fear her end is only an end, nothing more."

Konrad fought off uncomfortable feelings of pessimism. "We

don't have to argue about what we believe in or not. Part of her spirit and ability to summon fresh energy has come to pass in me. And as she would have done, I'm not going to give in to cynical thinking anymore. The best example of her was that she didn't stop being good until her last breath became air."

Gideon inhaled, stared somewhere, deep inside of himself. He held his tears back and watched steam rising. "You think we can save the world?"

Konrad put a hand on Gideon's shoulder. "I can imagine quite a bit, and while at it, everything is possible. We have to understand your potential better. I'm not sure what the future holds, but I trust there will be people who want to take advantage of you."

Gideon gave an uncertain nod.

They were silent for a few minutes, sending the sweet memory of Ruut deep into their hearts. Konrad owned probably a fraction of her courage, which would never cease to remind him that unity was possible. It was the only thing worth fighting for. But in the grand scheme of global destiny, they would not only have to navigate through the unseen dangers of the future but help everybody in the process. The new generation of children—if Gideon were right—would stumble into the crosshairs of a new shadow war because those in power would fear and take them as threats. But could they break the pattern of persecution?

"Promise me one thing, Konrad," Gideon said, emotion choking his voice. "Don't ever pull a Houdini on me. Nothing hurts more than sudden disappearance. My dad did it to me once. I did it to my mother..."

Konrad placed his hands on Gideon's shoulders. "I promise."

The Adam's apple bobbed in Gideon's throat as he swallowed his relief. "Let's go. Ville and Rebecca are waiting for you to guide us."

Konrad nodded. Slowly, they turned to leave. As they walked further from the grave at Konrad's slow pace, sunshine lit their faces through the softly falling snow. Gideon broke into tears he didn't try to repress anymore.

Konrad guided him through an open gate.

ACKNOWLEDGMENTS

Thank you, dear reader, for spending time with my imagination. Whether to praise or otherwise, please review *Antler Plan* on Amazon and Goodreads.

This story wouldn't have seen daylight without the help of my beta readers, editor Lizzie Harwood, and my friends and parents.

A special thanks to my beloved wife, Marja who helps me to become a better human being every day. Your deep understanding of the realm of spirituality, arts, and education make life an amazing journey.

ABOUT THE AUTHOR

Joonas Huhta is an emerging author of supernatural thrillers that blend learning new things with psychology. Also known as "sci-fi thrillers with a technological twist." This is book one in the Konrad Loki series. He lives in Rovaniemi, Finland where he is a teacher, writer, igloo-hobo, and difference-maker (saving the world and trees hug by hug and one high five at a time).

For more information get in touch:
https://joonashuhta.com/